"IT'S A SETTING FOR LOVE, NOT SCIENCE."

Jake's eyes glinted in the moonlight as he spoke.

"Aren't they similar?" Denise replied, turning away from his gaze. "Scientists are lovers of the sea. They want to explore the hidden depths, the mystery of it, like— "

"Like a man discovering the hidden depths of a woman? Yes. But the sea remains cool, whatever discoveries a man makes, whereas a woman grows warm from his touch." Strong hands grasped her waist and moved slowly down her hips.

"Not all women!" she snapped, struggling to free herself.

"You'd have to prove that to me." He turned her to him, and his lips were on hers, the warm hardness of his chest pressing against the softness of her breasts. Wildfire sprang up between them, searing, melting the very core of her being—a core she'd thought was frozen.

AND NOW...

HARLEQUIN SUPERROMANCES

As the world's No. 1 publisher of best-selling romance fiction, we are proud to present a sensational new series of modern love stories—HARLEQUIN SUPERROMANCES.

Written by masters of the genre, these longer, sensual and dramatic novels are truly in keeping with today's changing life-styles. Full of intriguing conflicts, the heartaches and delights of true love, HARLEQUIN SUPERROMANCES are absorbing stories—satisfying and sophisticated reading that lovers of romance fiction have long been waiting for.

HARLEQUIN SUPERROMANCES
Contemporary love stories for the woman of today!

MAURA MACKENZIE

SWEET SEDUCTION

Harlequin Books

TORONTO • LONDON • LOS ANGELES • AMSTERDAM
SYDNEY • HAMBURG • PARIS • STOCKHOLM • ATHENS • TOKYO

Harlequin first edition, August 1981

First printing February 1981
Second printing March 1981

ISBN 0-373-70006-7

CHAPTER ONE

"WOULD YOU CARE FOR SOMETHING from the bar?"

Denise Jordan turned from her contemplation of cobalt-blue sea that had replaced the turquoise of Florida's coastline, already far behind them. The sun streaming through the small windows in the aircraft struck silver in her blond hair.

"Just some orange juice, if you have it," she told the trim flight attendant, whose attention went immediately to the man seated on Denise's left.

"Certainly. And you, sir?"

"Bourbon and water."

The man's voice was terse to the point of brusqueness; perhaps, Denise thought, from his last-minute rush onto the plane. Now she stole a closer look at her companion and registered the thick dark sweep of hair to one side, the well-tanned features marred slightly by deep grooves running from nose to firmly chiseled mouth. Early to middle thirties, she judged, suspecting that such a man must have been claimed long ago by a woman equally attractive.

The neatly sculptured lines of her short hair turned abruptly away from the cabin's interior, her eyes seeking again the swelling expanse of the blue beneath them.

The man beside her was around Sam's age—or the age her husband would have been if he were alive—and as dark as Sam had been fair. The two years since his death in a diving accident had done nothing to eradicate her deep-seated sense of guilt about the failure of their short-lived marriage. A failure that had, initially at least, been hers.

"Your juice, ma'am." The stewardess broke into her thoughts, and Denise reached automatically for the stubby glass of golden liquid, placing it on the armrest between her and the man who accepted his bourbon with a grunt of thanks.

Unlike her companion on the flight from San Diego, who had seemed not to notice her disinterest in his life's history, this man obviously had no intention of unburdening himself to a casual fellow traveler. Easing his long legs until they stretched far under the seat in front, he stared moodily at the cabin ceiling while sipping occasionally from the glass he held in his hand. A long, bronzed, well-shaped hand.

Her own long, slender fingers reached for her glass, gripping it so stiffly that she only then became aware of the tension filling her.

Jet or any other kind of travel was unfamiliar to her, a fact that had been forcibly brought to her attention when the flight attendant at San Diego had had to remind her to fasten her seat belt as the plane left the terminal. Perhaps if Sam had lived....

Honesty made her admit frankly, behind her closed and cool expression, that even had Sam lived there would have been no happy trips taken together, no strong male for her to hold on to as the girl across the aisle, obviously a bride, now held on to her new husband's hand. From the sparkling, half-seductive looks the dark girl slanted up into his face, Denise knew their wedding night would be one of blissful giving and receiving, loving and being loved.

A stab of bitter envy pulled Denise's head back to the window, where the fluff of white clouds had replaced glittering water.

Sam had had a normal man's expectations of a full and satisfying physical relationship with the woman he had married, and instead Denise had presented him with an incredibly naive bride who shrank from his ardently expressed passion on their wedding night. Why had the kisses she had enjoyed during their short engagement turned into a tightening of body and mind when Sam's hand went roughly, possessively, over her, kneading the breasts no man's hands had touched before, seeking the intimate parts of her that had lain in expectant dormancy, forcing the heavy weight of his body on hers until she had screamed out her terror and pain?

He had been contrite, apologetic, when the act was over, telling her that she would enjoy his lovemaking in future. But she never had. Not all the schooling in the world could relax the instant tightening of her reflexes when Sam reached for her in the wide marriage bed that had been her parents'. Something had frozen within her on that marriage night, and it hadn't been too hard to believe Sam's frequent assertions that she was frigid. She had been more relieved than saddened when he had turned to other women to assuage the amorous urgings of his nature.

Maybe it had been a mistake to make their home in the huge estate bordering the ocean in San Diego's most exclusive area. Maybe if their marriage had started in the normal surroundings of an apartment or a modest suburban house there might have been a chance for them.

But Sam had seemed to want the trappings of luxury, the ambience of an age gone by, in the home Denise's father had bequeathed to her on his death just before she had met Sam. The house servants she had taken for granted, having grown up with most of them, had seemed to give Sam a sense of importance he had never known before.

His upbringing in the Midwest had been as unlike her own as it was possible to be. Strict and highly religious parents had left him with an intense desire to savor all the pleasures in life that his parents had denied. Denise had been three when her young mother had left her much older husband, and through her growing-up years her father had jealously guarded Denise as she became more like her mother—a truly beautiful woman. Her mother had been killed not long after she'd left them, in the company of a man nearer her own age, but Philip Haymes had remained obsessive about his daughter, keeping her under his watchful eye when other girls her age were testing their wings in matters of life and love. He had permitted Denise to go to U.S.C. only because she could come home after classes to the imposing old house set on a hill overlooking the ocean.

The ocean that was so familiar to her, a result of her solitary forays along its shores, became her means of escaping the close confines of her father's narrow perimeters. Her graduation as a marine biologist had marked the beginning of freedom for her, and, more importantly, her father's death shortly after had released her from a lifelong guilt about her own femininity. That she had inherited considerable wealth from his banking interests scarcely entered her mind, for her own type of liberation had been far more important than financial independence. Freedoms most women took for granted were heady new experiences for Denise, and she was wide open to the advances of a Sam Jordan who had all the assets of the lover in her illicit dreams.

At the time it had seemed like a miracle when Sam had come into her life. Like a newly minted coin, dazzling and bright, he had exuded breezy self-confidence in the cloistered confines of her home. The house itself had lost some of its repressive air of formality under his eager and forceful personality.

But not long after their marriage, the loud, recriminatory voices, banged doors and blue shadows under the eyes of their young mistress had made the servants take a second look at Sam. None of them had any illusions about where he spent the long nights when he had left alone his bride of a few weeks, announcing his homecoming in the early morning hours with squealing tires on the graveled driveway—particularly Ellen, the elderly housekeeper. Ellen had acted as surrogate mother to Denise after she had been abandoned by her mother for a man rich enough to provide all the material comforts she herself could not.

Denise had known, too, and been ashamed of her relief that at least Sam had satisfied his physical appetite elsewhere. Guilt had added to confusion until she froze completely each time Sam joined her in the wide bed that had become theirs on their marriage.

If she had been able to respond to him, be the wife he needed, he wouldn't have died that day in the Pacific Ocean off San Diego—wouldn't have been drunk the night before a dive—wouldn't have been exhausted on the morning of the dive.

My fault. The words echoed like a litany for the millionth time in Denise's head as the plane tilted slightly and the scratchy voice of a crew member came suddenly over the intercom.

"We are now making our final descent into Nassau International Airport. We hope you have enjoyed flying with us, and that we will have the pleasure of your company again."

Would this new job in the Bahamas lift her out of the depression that had settled over her with Sam's death? She had continued to work at the Scripps Institution of Oceanography, not knowing what else to do. She had weathered the spoken and implied sympathy of her colleagues, few of whom knew that the marriage had been far from idyllic, but when this chance of joining a research team in the Bahamas came, she grasped the opportunity to escape the traumas that had surrounded her life until now. Perhaps in totally different surroundings she would find surcease from the gnawing pangs of guilt and inadequacy.

As the plane dipped lower, she could see the sudden change from marine blue to the incredible warmth of green water close to the island shores.

"Are you here on vacation?" the man beside her asked, making his first comment of the trip.

Her eyes, as green as the waters below them, swiveled around to meet the disconcerting gray of his. "No. I'm going to be working here for a while."

His gaze encompassed the well-cut pale green silk of her skirted suit, and his dark brows lifted inquiringly.

"Are you in the entertainment business?"

A small bubble of unexpected laughter escaped Denise's throat. "My work has never been described *that* way before. I'm a marine biologist."

The eyes, surrounded by a surface network of fine lines, narrowed speculatively. "You wouldn't by chance be on your way to the South Shore Project?" At Denise's astonished nod, he gave a tight smile and said, "That's where I'm heading, too."

Her eyes widening perceptibly, Denise asked, "You're on the research team?"

"You might say that. I'm taking over from Dr. Shepherd, who's been taken ill. I'm Jake Barstow."

Barstow? Jake Barstow? The name seemed familiar somehow—and then it hit her suddenly. Of course! Sam had mentioned the name several times, and she had read of his undersea exploits many times in scientific magazines. But her understanding had been that the Bahamas research effort was a comparatively minor one—certainly not of the kind to interest a big name like Jake Barstow.

As if divining her thoughts, he said with a touch of irony, "My appointment is purely a temporary one until they find someone to fill the gap on a permanent basis. Early next year I'm taking my own team to work off Sri Lanka in the Indian Ocean."

Sri Lanka, the old Ceylon, held a magical sound

for Denise. "That sounds fabulous!" she said, her overtone of envy only slightly sparked by his obvious enthusiasm for the project. What wouldn't she give to work with a research team in a locale like that? All her experience so far had come from the waters off California, collecting and assessing marine specimens that might have been damaged by pollutants being poured daily into the world's oceans.

Good experience, it was true, but now she was ready to widen her horizons. Maybe, she thought, casting a sideways glance at her companion, if she worked well on this project he would recommend her for a position on the Sri Lanka project he would be heading. Something about his remote coolness told her that a person would have to get by on her own efforts without help from him.

She caught just a glimpse of the flat scrubland surrounding the runways, and then they landed with a bump and a screech of engine reversal. As they taxied to the terminal building, she had a moment or two to assess Jake Barstow's profile as he unbuckled his seat belt and reached for the briefcase at his feet. The unexpected length of his dark lashes contrasted startlingly with the strong features of rugged masculinity that sent an odd kind of quiver through her. He must have been a devastatingly handsome man even before time and experience had stamped an added maturity around his eyes and mouth, a faint bitterness to his tightly held lips.

He looked around and unexpectedly met the curious green of her gaze, his gray eyes giving an illusive impression of darkening.

"You're being met?" One dark brow lifted in inquiry, and she nodded. "I imagine it's by the same person meeting me, so we'd better stay together."

It was only as she was following his broadly confident shoulders along the aisle that she realized his lack of curiosity about her own identity. The slight bruise to her ego was unassuaged when the stewardesses' eyes still held unabashed awareness of his male attractiveness as they wished Denise goodbye.

She hesitated briefly at the head of the aircraft steps, breathing in the unfamiliar headiness of a tropic air redolent with scents she could not put a name to but that conjured up visions of the tropic paradise depicted by many of the travel posters she had seen. The sultry air held the fragrance of exotic blooms, the spiciness of unfamiliar fruit. The landscape was flat, which came as little surprise to her after her reading up on the topography of the Bahamas, this island of New Providence in particular, where the highest point rose to a slight one hundred and twenty-three feet.

Jake Barstow's impatient glance from the ground initiated her descent to join him on the tarmac, her senses janglingly aware of his scrutiny of the slender turn of her long legs, the loose fit of her jacket that couldn't hide the well-formed curves of her breasts. In a partly unconscious gesture of defense, she raised her capacious handbag to her chest and stared coolly into the gray eyes when they reached up to her face.

With a slightly sardonic twist to his lips, he put light fingers on her elbow as they crossed the tarmac and entered the ramp leading to the immigration area. There they waited side by side in silence for their luggage, then impassive customs officers dealt painstakingly with the required formalities, and they were on their way to the front of the airport where hotel limousines and buses awaited the exodus of vacationing passengers.

A slim, brown-haired man of medium height detached himself from where he leaned on an open jeep and came toward them, a smile of greeting on his bronzed face for Jake Barstow.

"Hi, Jake, how are you?" He held out his hand, grinning broadly now as if genuinely pleased to see Denise's plane companion.

"Just fine, Paul, and you?"

"Couldn't be much better." Lightly humorous brown eyes turned on Denise appreciatively. "Don't tell me you've married again, Jake? If so, I greatly admire your choice."

Color swept in an embarrassed pink over Denise's face, but her new boss saved her the trouble of replying.

"No, I haven't married again, Paul. This is Paul Stein, and—" He turned with an air of an-

noyed surprise to Denise "—I'm afraid I don't
know your name."

"Denise Jordan. I'm—"

"Of course! How could I be such an idiot?"
Paul Stein slapped his head ruefully before looking apologetically at the research chief. "Sorry
about that, Jake. I just assumed, when you appeared together—"

"No problem." The other man brushed his
words aside brusquely, but there was a knitted
frown of abstraction on his lean face when he
glanced down at Denise.

"Well, it's great that you've already met each
other as you're going to be working together,"
said Paul. "Welcome to the Bahamas, Mrs. Jordan." He reached out a hand again and Denise
took it, liking the friendly openness of the man she
presumed was to be a colleague.

"Denise," she invited in similar fashion, smiling with a visible relaxation of the reserved manner she had extended to Jake Barstow.

"And I'm Paul. My wife, Marie, has really been
looking forward to having you at the unit. She says
I starve her of intelligent company." His laugh
belied the truth of that statement, and he turned to
beckon to a young black man leaning against the
jeep. "This is Perry Smith, who takes care of quite
a few things around the camp," he introduced
when the round-faced young man had reached
them, "and this is the new boss, Perry, Dr. Barstow, and our new team member, Mrs. Jordan."

Denise felt Jake Barstow's inquisitive gaze on her as she settled herself in one of the rear seats of the jeep, and was surprised when he elected to occupy the other seat at the back while Paul Stein sat beside the driver. His well-worn dark brown leather suitcases and her new dark green leather set had been stowed on a rack behind the vehicle and tied down by a suddenly active Perry.

"You're...*Sam* Jordan's wife?" Jake inquired sotto voce as Perry drew the jeep away from curbside with a jerk.

"I was, yes."

She heard his breath draw in sharply in self-recrimination. "I'm sorry. I knew about Sam's death, of course, but—"

"It's all right." Denise mustered coolness. "It happened two years ago, so I'm used to the idea by now."

"I'm sorry," he said again, and his light gray eyes warmed a little when he looked at her. "I knew Sam some years ago when we worked together on a project for two or three months." He paused, then added on a guarded note, "He's the last man I would have expected to die like that. He was good at his job."

"Yes."

"I just can't understand how it happened," he went on in a low voice. "He was a good diver, and from what I've heard—"

"I'd rather not talk about it, if you don't mind," Denise choked, on a sudden rise of hysteria. She really didn't want to talk about Sam; she had taken this appointment for the express purpose of forgetting him and their miserably unsuccessful marriage, and before she was ten minutes into her new life she was being quizzed by a man who had known him, had probably liked him as most of his colleagues had.

She was relieved when Paul Stein turned from the front, his short-sleeved arm stretched along the back of Perry's driving seat, to say, "The scenery isn't much to write home about from this angle, but wait till we get to the camp." Dividing his comments equally between them, he went on, "Did you know it used to be a resort complex? One that failed for some unknown reason. I'd have said it was the ideal tropical getaway setting, with a terrific stretch of white-sand beach and the cottages set apart for privacy in the belt of palms edging the beach. Maybe it had something to do with its relative isolation—you need motor transport to go anywhere at all." He shrugged. "But to my way of thinking it would be a paradise for families...and honeymoon couples, of course," he ended, grinning.

"Well, you and Marie fulfill the first part of those stipulations," Jake said dryly, adding with more than perfunctory interest, "how is Marie, and the kids, of course?"

"Just fine, Jake, although—" he laughed in Denise's direction "—Marie will likely tell you a tale of woe about how her   ind is stagnating in the softness of this climate." The laughter lines around his eyes easing out, he twisted farther around to address Jake directly. "David's at school in New York State, but he comes back for vacations. Cindy's four now, and she's with us, of course. She keeps Marie hopping most of the time, but she won't hear of hiring somebody to take care of her." His tone changed to one of guarded inquiry. "Are you planning on having Meg here for the Christmas vacation? She'd really love it, I know."

"I don't know," Jake responded with a curtness that brought Denise's eyes around on him speculatively. "It depends on what her mother had planned for her."

"But I thought that you had vis— Oh, well," Paul tacked on lamely, "I just thought it might be a good idea if she and David traveled down here together. Is Meg still at school in New York State?"

"Yes. I wasn't aware of what accommodations were available here, so I made no arrangements."

"You have a two-bedroom cottage to yourself," Paul said eagerly, as if to expiate himself. "Tom Shepherd lived there with his wife and teenage daughter. There's lots of room for Meg."

"We'll see," was the noncommittal answer, and silence fell on the jeep's occupants.

Denise looked out at the uninspiring landscape on either side of the road Perry careered along. Scrubby pines and undergrowth gave way now and then to what were obviously cultivated fields, although how anything could be grown in the stark white lumpy soil was beyond her understanding. Sharp disappointment flooded over her. She had expected so much more of this tropic paradise than stunted growth and barren-looking fields. If there had been glimpses of turquoise ocean she had missed them; she'd been too absorbed in Paul Stein's disclosure of Jake Barstow's personal affairs.

He had been married, as she had suspected, and divorced, as she had not expected. Somehow he seemed to her the kind of man who would need a woman in his life, a woman of poise and beauty to match his own male attractiveness. And he had a child, a daughter named Meg, a child born of a passion she visualized in embarrassing detail. She knew he would be a passionate lover. His long thigh brushed and pressed hers as Perry drove his erratic course, and she knew this man was a wholly sexual being under the cool facade he presented to the world. With the impartial certainty of experience, she felt he exuded the same sensuality as Sam had, only his was a harder, more tempered and deliberate acceptance of the man-woman relationship.

Shaken by her own thoughts, she was relieved when Paul said with his own measure of relief, "Here it is. The South Shore Project."

Perry had turned into a driveway of crushed white coral that curved in a dazzling downward arc in the direction of a long, low white building nestled under the moving fronds of high-topped palms and spreading casuarina trees. Parking with a flourish in front of the building, he jumped smartly from behind the wheel and came to hold Denise's door open with a courtliness that spoke of another age.

"I'll take your cases to your cottage, Mrs. Jordan," he said, beaming her a dazzling smile.

"Thanks, Perry." She stepped from the jeep and inhaled a deep breath of the thick air that was tempered by a breeze from the far side of the building. "I think I'm going to like it here."

"Wait till you see the other side." He nodded toward the white building. "You'll like that even better."

She smiled, partly because of his obvious enthusiasm for his native shores, but mostly because his voice had a rhythmic sound, rising at the end of his sentences.

"I'm sure I will."

"And I'm sure you're ready for a cool drink," Paul interposed, coming around to take her arm and lead her to the low-linteled doorway into the building. "This way, Jake."

She was more conscious of the lean figure following them than of Paul's light grip on her elbow, but everything else was forgotten when a small, vivacious, dark-haired woman darted forward from the interior of the dim building as they entered it.

"Paul, what in the world kept you? I thought you must be waiting for the next plane in."

"It takes a little time for people to go through immigration, as you should well know," he returned dryly, then turned a smile on Denise. "Honey, this is Denise Jordan. My wife, Marie."

Denise found her hand enveloped by two eagerly pressing ones.

"You can't know how much I've been looking forward to your arrival," Marie Stein told her, alert bird-bright eyes going over her in sparkling appraisal. "I'm starved for—"

"Intelligent female conversation," her husband interjected before glancing over his shoulder at the silent team boss. "Meanwhile, if you can put your mind to a mere male, you might remember Jake Barstow?"

"Jake!" The effervescent Marie seemed to hop over the intervening distance to put up arms that were almost too short to reach around the tall neck. Planting a resounding kiss on a lean cheek, she drew back in the sinewy arms and looked critically up into his face. "You're much too thin and much too sad looking, Jake."

"I'm about the same weight I was last time I saw you, Marie," he returned with a good humor Denise hadn't seen in him before, "and if I look sad it's because I'm badly in need of a drink, so why don't you offer me one?"

Marie looked searchingly into his face for another moment, then broke away from him and took Denise's arm. "Come on," she said with a gaiety that seemed slightly forced. "Drinks are this way."

The long building seemed to be divided by partitions into two separate areas: the one on their left obviously for dining, with about twenty individual tables scattered around it, and the other laid out as a lounge area with armchairs and deep-cushioned couches arranged into small groupings complemented by low coffee tables. It was to one of the latter that Marie led them, still chattering volubly.

"Did Paul tell you this place used to be a resort? The American government bought it for a song because the owners were desperate to unload it, and it couldn't be more ideal for our purposes."

Denise, wandering over to the sea-facing windows that looked directly onto a wide, screened veranda, agreed with her. Beyond the veranda and the sloping trunks of palms lay a scene directly from a travel poster. A curve of dazzling coral sands bordered an ocean of myriad colors, from the translucent green close to shore to the dark cobalt of the deeper waters farther out. At the far end of a concrete pier thrusting smoothly across the water lay a large ship that dominated the half dozen smaller vessels. The research ship.

A tingle of excitement shivered down Denise's spine. However many trips she made in a research vessel, her job always held an almost obsessive fascination for her. Perhaps because in the cool silent depths on a dive she seemed to lose all the ties and constrictions that held her on shore. She was free down there to be—

She started when Marie touched her arm lightly.

"Come on, dreamer," the dark woman laughed, pulling her over to where the others had settled on chairs and sofa. "Believe it or not, you *will* get used to that view and hardly notice it after a month or two."

"I can't believe that," Denise protested, allowing herself to be seated beside a sprawled Jake on the settee. "It's like something you dream about, but suspect doesn't really exist."

"Oh, it exists all right." Marie's voice held a dry note, like a world traveler jaded by too-familiar contact with the world's wonders. "Anyway, what will you have to drink?"

"Oh—" Denise shrugged vaguely "—sherry, or something like that."

"No way." Paul grinned, getting to his feet. "Perry makes the best Goombay Special in the Bahamas. Perry?" he called across the room to the white-jacketed driver, now evidently fulfilling one of his other roles about the station. "Make Mrs. Jordan one of your most special Specials, will you?"

Perry's face split in a brilliant white smile. "One Special coming up."

"What's in it?" Denise asked apprehensively as Paul reseated himself opposite. From her upbringing by an abstemious father and the ugly effects of too much liquor on Sam's personality, she was more than a little suspicious of unknown concoctions.

"Nothing too dangerous," Paul soothed. "A little rum and a few nontoxic mixes. It's very refreshing on a warm afternoon."

And so it proved to be, with its fruit slices split around the tall glass edges and ice cubes tinkling gently when she lifted it to her lips for the first taste.

"Mmm—yes, it *is* good."

"It's hard to believe you were married to Sam Jordan," Jake put in with a laconic drawl. "As I recall, he liked his liquor."

The words dropped an embarrassed pall over the group, then Marie said, overbrightly, "I love your suit, Denise, but this might be the last time you wear it until you leave here. We live in as little and as casual as possible."

Denise pulled her eyes away from the piercing, almost brutal, gray of Jake Barstow's. "That suits me just fine," she said with more breathlessness than she had intended. "I was brought up on the seashore."

"In...?"

"San Diego. We had a house—right on the ocean. I guess that's why I chose marine biology as my specialty."

Her words came out in jerky spasms, and she colored in embarrassment. No one else, not even Sam, had ever had the power to make her lose her cool. Yet Jake Barstow had reduced her to a stammering schoolgirl within minutes.

"You're lucky," Marie commented without rancor, yet her eyes went to Jake in brooding puzzlement. "The nearest I ever got to the sea when I was a child in Milwaukee was a school-band trip to San Francisco."

Paul's chuckle brought all eyes on him as he looked with teasing affection at his wife. "Tell them what instrument you played."

Marie grimaced at him before turning back to Denise and Jake. "Basically I played piano, but there wasn't much of a demand for piano players in the school band, so I took up the instrument there was a vacancy for."

"And that was?" Jake prompted, an indulgent smile that Denise thought must be a rarity, playing around his firm but mobile mouth.

"The trombone," Marie said defiantly, her dark eyes flashing around their faces in a search for derisive laughter. "And I played it well, too."

"I'm sure you did," Jake said with no trace of humor. "I seem to remember that you do most things well."

"But I'm glad you stuck to piano after that," Paul said, reaching over to the adjoining chair arm to take her hand in his sensitive, long fingers. "What would we do without you on our social evenings here?" To Denise he explained, "Once in a while we all get together and have a party. We have the stereo system for dancing, but what most of us seem to enjoy more than anything is standing around the piano singing the old songs Marie plays."

"Sounds like fun," Jake said, rising to his feet and clearly conveying his impression that such simple pleasures were far from his idea of fun. "If you'll direct me to my quarters, Paul, I'll get settled in before I look around."

"Oh, sure." Paul drained his glass and rose, too, looking down at Marie as he said, "You might as well come and show Denise her cottage at the same time, honey. We're having a little welcome party here tonight for you two," he told Jake as they went toward the door. "Carl Madsen and Toby Winters should be back by then."

"Back from where?"

"They're diving off the reef. We've been doing that on a regular basis, checking that...."

Paul's voice trailed off as Denise and Marie followed the two men, and Marie grimaced.

"Men," she said disdainfully. "Their sole topic of conversation is their work."

"Scientists do seem to be that way," Denise agreed diplomatically, feeling the sudden blast of heavy heat when they stepped from the breeze-cooled building. Her head felt thick, too, perhaps from the supposedly innocuous drink Perry had concocted for her. She was tired from the endless hours of travel and could think of nothing more inviting than to be completely alone to rest on a comfortable bed.

"You must be tired," Marie commiserated, as

if reading her thoughts. She picked her way with surefooted ease along a sandy path between the palms and shrub growth. "You'll have lots of time to rest before dinner at seven-thirty. What do you think of the cottages?"

Denise, who had been eyeing the ground as she struggled through the sand in heeled shoes, lifted her head and saw the first of several pretty palm-thatched buildings scattered randomly through the treed area. Some were bigger than others, but each one had a minuscule porch fronting it and vigorous plants twining on every available surface.

"They're very...picturesque," she answered Marie's question after more of the small buildings came into view.

"They're not as primitive as they look," Marie chuckled. "The people who owned the resort didn't skimp on home comforts. They're all fitted with bathrooms, and the larger ones, like ours, are even complete with kitchens. Can you imagine me taking my four-year-old brat to the clubhouse for breakfast? That's ours there." She pointed to a more substantial white-walled structure to their right, which fronted on the beach and had the added distinction of a fenced rear yard where play equipment could be discerned through the tropical foliage.

"The four-year-old being...Cindy?" Denise hazarded, and Marie threw her a quick smile.

"I see Paul's already been indoctrinating you. Yes, her name is Cindy, and we have a boy away at school, David." Marie's voice softened when she mentioned her son. "I wish we could all be together, but Paul thinks it's more important for David to have a settled education. Look, there's your cottage," she ended on a relieved note, as if glad to leave the subject of her absent son.

The small cottage Marie pointed to now was, like hers and Paul's, situated at beach edge and almost hidden by the lush foliage surrounding it.

"I hope you won't feel lonely," she continued, leading the way to the front of the cottage and up the three wooden steps to the tiny porch, halting there to laugh and point to either side. "If you do, you don't have far to go to find company. Carl Madsen and Toby Winters are to your right, and Jake's in that pink-washed place to your left through the trees. Toby at least will be more than happy to keep you company, I know."

About to ask more about the people she would no doubt come to know extremely well in the months to come, Denise refrained from doing so when Marie threw open the door to her cottage and beckoned her inside.

"The living room." She made a comprehensive gesture with her arm around the small, comfortable-looking room with its deeply padded chairs and settee in white velour, occasional and coffee tables in a dark polished wood, cinnamon-colored broadloom covering the floor wall-to-wall. "Through here is your bedroom, and the bathroom opens off this hall."

When Denise had completed her inspection of the tiny bedroom with its double bed filling most of the space, and the small and scrupulously clean bathroom with its tiled shower, she felt a deep glow of happiness in the promise this small abode held for her. Surely here, with its exotic exterior and peaceful interior, she would be able to forget, and find a new direction in her life.

"There's a hot plate here—" Marie indicated a recess opposite the bathroom "—but it's not much use for making anything but coffee. I'm afraid you'll have to take all your meals in the clubhouse."

"That's all right." Denise's eyes glowed as they went again around the sitting room. "I think I'm going to love it here."

"You won't mind being alone?" Marie asked with an anxious air, rushing on in embarrassment. "I mean, you've been— Well, I have to admit that the thought of solitude seems an unreachable dream to me sometimes, but—"

"Sam died two years ago, Marie," Denise said gently. "And before my marriage I spent a lot of time alone in a big house with my father and a few elderly servants. I'm used to being alone."

Marie regarded her curiously. "Coming from a background like that, what made you go into marine biology?"

Denise walked farther into the living room and shrugged. "Why does anyone take up a career? I wanted to do something, and the sea was always my main interest. I used to spend hours down on our beach," she went on with a dreamily nostalgic look in her green eyes, "making my own primitive experiments with plant life and collecting shells and driftwood." Coming back to reality with an embarrassed smile, she said wryly, "I think I must have a direct link to our earliest ancestors, who came from the sea."

"Well, you certainly seem to have chosen the right profession. You sound remarkably like Paul and Jake and any number of marine scientists I've met." Marie's tone held that dry note again, and Denise looked speculatively at her.

"What did you do before you married Paul?"

"I taught high-school history," the dark woman said with a resigned shrug. "There's a world of difference between recounting Captain Cook's adventures and what Paul does."

"I don't think there's such a difference," Denise said thoughtfully, glorying abstractedly in the view of sand and sea from the window she walked toward. "They're both in the same class, experimenters in their separate ways."

"I knew I was going to enjoy having you here," Marie crowed triumphantly. "You can't know how much I've looked forward to some intelligent female companionship in this male world."

Denise swung around, surprised. "There are no other women here?"

"Just Christina Kell, who runs the office and

processes the data the boys collect. She's...man oriented, I guess you might say.''

Oriented to Paul, Denise wondered, but said instead, ''If she's the only available female in this male-dominated world, she should be supremely happy.''

''Oh, she is on the whole. But when she sets eyes on Jake she'll be elevated to seventh heaven. He's the answer to her dreams. Except that now—'' a small smile played around Marie's lips ''—she'll have some competition. You're far more beautiful than she is, and a lot more intelligent, which would count with Jake.''

''Me?'' Denise stared at her in amazement, then turned hastily back to the window. ''I'm not in the market for romance.''

Undeterred, Marie chuckled and went to the door. ''Wait till you've experienced a few nights under a romantic moon—it softens the coldest of hearts.'' Her hand on the door, she went on more seriously, ''As you said, Denise, it's two years since your husband died, and you're much too beautiful to spend the rest of your life regretting.''

''I've no intention of doing that,'' Denise said crisply, rousing herself from the soporific view to look coolly into Marie's darkly sparkling eyes. ''But Jake Barstow isn't the kind of man who appeals to me.''

''Then you're alone among women,'' Marie retorted, rolling her eyes exaggeratedly. ''If I didn't love Paul so much, I could go for Jake in a big way."

"Right now I'm not interested in men, paragons or otherwise," Denise said tightly, and a compassionate expression immediately clouded Marie's eyes.

"I'm sorry," she said softly. "I guess you're still very much in love with your husband." She opened the door. "Would you like us to call for you around seven-fifteen?"

"Thank you," Denise said jerkily. "What... kind of thing do you wear for these parties?"

"Anything that's long and cool."

For a long time after Marie had gone, Denise stared out at the exotically satisfying view, her tiredness forgotten momentarily.

The dark woman's linking of herself with Jake Barstow in a romantic sense had come as an unpleasant shock to her. But why? It wasn't as if she herself had begun to harbor pairing thoughts with him in mind—was it? The very thought was ludicrous, but there was more pain than humor in Denise's eyes as they stared without seeing at the spreading view before her.

He was a virile, attractive male who obviously had no problems with his sex life; women, as Marie had indicated, would flock to him and be more than happy to fill his physical needs. Women who weren't cold, frozen... frigid.

CHAPTER TWO

PUTTING THE FINISHING TOUCHES to her makeup, Denise stroked translucent green shadow lightly on her lids before darkening her lashes with mascara and pencilling her brows to disguise their fairness. The art of makeup had been forcibly taught by her fellow seniors at the private school her father had insisted upon, and even they had been amazed at the new Denise who emerged from their ministrations. No doubt her father had been right in telling her to scrub the heavily layered cosmetics from her face before the graduation dance that night; the humiliation she had felt then no longer had the power to hurt her, but her father's punitive scorn was still with her each time she creamed and powdered her skin and applied light-colored lipstick across her lips.

The effort was worth it, she decided as she stepped in front of the full-length mirror, even if only for the confidence it gave her. The simple lines of her white cotton dress, scrolled with bright splashes of emerald green, fitted the curves of her figure without particularly emphasizing them. Her shoulders were bare apart from two slim straps crossing her tanned skin at the back to meet the bodice line just below her shoulder blades. Yes, she had confidence in plenty to meet Jake Barstow's cool gray eyes.

She gave an irritated exclamation and turned back to the small dressing table to pick up the white earrings laid ready. Clipping them onto her delicate lobes, she wondered in self-disgust why her every sense seemed to be aware of the research chief, an awareness that had disturbed the rest she had desperately needed after Marie had left the cottage. He was a man like any other—well, no, perhaps not just like any other. There was more force and personality in one flicker of his gray eyes than she had ever known in any man, yet it wasn't attraction she felt toward him. Quite the opposite, in fact. Something about him inspired a morbid kind of fascination, a sense that was almost...fear.

A quick tattoo of raps on the outer screen door sent her scurrying for her white sandals, her eyes flying to the slim gold watch on her wrist as she hurried to the door. Marie and Paul were surprisingly punctual, a quality she wouldn't have expected in Marie, at least.

The breathlessly welcoming smile froze on her face when she opened the inner door and stared through the screen at a man she had never seen before. Young, handsome in a whimsically lopsided way, wide and friendly smile—all these things registered in her fleeting inspection.

"Oh. I . . . I thought you were—"

"The Steins," he supplied when she broke off. "Marie's having problems with her offspring, so she asked me to come and collect you." His eyes showed appreciation as they went slowly over her and came back to her face. "I have a feeling I'm going to be grateful to Marie for the rest of my life," he said with an impudent grin designed to forestall any possible objections to his familiarity. "I'm Toby Winters, and I work with the team, so you don't have to be afraid of letting me in."

"Oh. I'm sorry." Denise belatedly pushed on the door catch and a moment later the young man was beside her, his slightly overaverage height tempered by the stockiness of his body. The soft brown hair that flopped over his forehead contributed to his boyish look, and Denise felt herself smiling indulgently as she looked into his mostly hazel eyes.

"I just have to get my purse," she murmured, and heard him follow her as she stepped back into the living room. "I'm afraid I can't even offer you a drink," she apologized from the entrance to the middle hall.

"That's okay," he said easily, his eyes going approvingly around the cozy living arrangement. "Contrary to general belief, I get by on very little liquor each day." His dancing eyes came back to Denise. "It's nice that you have your own place. If I want to do any entertaining, I have to do it under Carl's jaundiced eye."

"Carl?"

"Carl Madsen, our second-in-command with reluctance," he explained lightly. The tie encircling the neck of his short-sleeved pale green shirt sat awkwardly on him, as if unaccustomed to being there.

"Is he reluctant to be here at all, or only at being second-in-command?"

The hazel eyes went over her face speculatively. "I think I'll leave you to find out the answer to that."

Shrugging, Denise turned away and retrieved her pencil-slim evening bag from the bedroom. Whatever else the youthful Toby Winters might be, he obviously had no intention of letting her in on the personality quirks of her coworkers.

"What do you do at the station?" she asked conversationally as she came back into the room and crossed to the door, then turning to wait pointedly while he reluctantly came from the depths of one deep armchair to join her.

"Me? Oh, I'm kind of a general dogsbody, but mainly I pilot the sub."

"Really?" He seemed young to have the necessary experience to manipulate the controls of the submersible. But then, she reflected wryly as they stepped onto the soft sand beyond the porch, he must only be a couple of years younger than her own twenty-six.

"Really," he affirmed gravely, putting a hand under her elbow when she stumbled in the powdery sand at the bottom of the steps. "I don't have the qualifications to take one of the more glamorous scientific jobs."

Denise felt the fine sandy particles infiltrating the open spaces of her sandals, and shook one foot after the other as they walked around the cottage to reach the communal path connecting the residences. The gentle swish of ocean on beach followed them as they plowed through the sand and gained the winding path.

"Glamour is in the eye of the beholder," she panted, feeling a strong urge to take off her sandals and let the undergrowth do what it would to her panty hose. She stumbled again, and a strong arm came to circle her waist. Then, before she had time to gasp out a protest, muscular arms scooped her up and held her close to a male chest that crushed one of her breasts painfully to its solid surface. Visions of her ignominious arrival at the clubhouse in that position sent power to her struggling limbs. "Put me down," she gasped, steadying herself with one hand on his green-clad shoulder. She could imagine Jake Barstow's sardonically raised brows when she arrived at the clubhouse clutched in the arms of a laughing young man who ignored her indignant protests.

Her worst fears were realized when Toby Winters strode up the wooden steps to the main building and deposited her laughingly, albeit reluctantly, on solid flooring. She faced the party members, whose expressions reflected a gamut of emotions from Marie's sparkling approval to Jake Barstow's frowning disapproval.

"One guest of honor delivered safe and sound," Toby intoned, retaining one arm around Denise's slender waist as his triumphant look around the assembled company conveyed his pride of first possession on the newest member of the team.

Marie, her small, rounded figure encased in an off-the-shoulder white dress that contrasted dazzlingly with her darkly tanned skin, stepped forward to draw Denise away from Toby's hold.

"We were wondering what had happened to you," she said, smiling in a way that made Denise sharpen her glance suspiciously. It was almost as if the older woman had realized the satisfactory outcome of a devious plan.

Obviously acting as hostess of the occasion, Marie ushered the group into the lounge area and organized Paul into taking orders for drinks while at the same time cajoling everyone into a bonhomie they were far from feeling.

"Jake, you've already met Carl, but you haven't got to know Toby yet. Toby Winters—Jake Barstow." Jake's eyes were narrowly appraising as he stretched out a bronzed hand to meet Toby's, but Denise turned her attention to the tall and thin man whose light blue eyes assessed her dispassionately when Marie introduced them.

"I am delighted to meet you," Carl Madsen

said with a faint, undiscernible accent. "Your expertise is sadly needed on the team. None of us has the necessary knowledge to evaluate the effects of pollution on the waters that surround the Bahamas. It would indeed be a pity if the oceans of the world fell prey to undisciplined discharge."

His pedantic speech, emitted through narrow lips, sent a chill through Denise, but she summoned a smile as she said lightly, "The waters surrounding the Bahamas are the clearest in the world, I believe. That is," she amended hastily, "they were until the recent outpouring of pollutants from oil and chemical plants south of the American border." Her eyes took in the precise cut of his blond hair. "That's why I'm here—to measure the effects of pollutants on the natural flora and fauna of undersea life."

"Of course. We have a small laboratory where you will be able to ply your arts, and you might be interested to know—"

"What will you have to drink?" Paul interrupted them lightly, the sparkle in his brown eyes denoting that he had already indulged himself from the bar captained by a busy Perry. "Another Goombay Special? Or would you like a glass of the vintage champagne purchased specially in honor of the occasion?"

"The champagne, thanks," Denise smiled, thankful for Paul's downright hominess that was in sharp contrast to Carl Madsen's European-style formality. "I think I'll save Perry's Specials for...special occasions."

"Good thinking," Paul approved with a grin before turning to Carl, the smile narrowing on his mouth. "How about you, Carl?"

"I will have the same, thank you."

After Paul had brought their drinks, Carl steered Denise to a settee grouping away from the others, seating himself a circumspect distance from her on the comfortable sofa.

"You are more fortunate than I," he said with a wry shrug of his shoulders. "When I arrived here there was no fanfare to mark the occasion."

"The fanfare isn't for me particularly," Denise told him dryly, her eyes reaching to where Jake Barstow listened with attentive politeness to the red-haired girl who bent her slim but voluptuous body toward him. "It's mainly for the new head of the team."

"Jake Barstow, yes," Carl nodded, his pale eyes narrowing on the other man. "He was chosen as chief when Dr. Shepherd left here."

The bitter tone of his voice made Denise, surprising even to herself, defend the new head of the South Shore Project. "He's very good at what he does. Famous, in fact."

"Yes, famous. So why does such a man condescend to fill a vacancy on a minor project?"

Denise jerked her head away from the somehow disturbing scene involving Jake Barstow and Christina. "Is it so minor? Pollution control here could make a tremendous difference to the countries touched by the drift of the Gulf Stream.''

She flinched at the familiarity of a male touch as an arm slid across her shoulders. Toby Winters, perched on the sofa arm, interrupted the conversation with a breezy, ''No shoptalk allowed on social occasions! Anyway, we're just about to hear the welcoming speeches, and—'' his arm tightened around Denise as he smiled down into her face ''—the acceptances from the new arrivals.''

Forgetting her instinctive wish to move away from his impudent hold, she stared back at him in an excess of shyness. ''I won't have to make a speech, will I?''

''But of course.'' His eyes glinted wickedly. ''Everybody wants to hear your voice to see if it matches up with the rest of you. You're a lot more beautiful than our esteemed new chief.''

Without conscious volition her eyes sought the tall, spare figure of Jake Barstow and felt an electric shock run through her when her gaze met the sardonic gray of his. Significantly, his eyes dropped to Toby's possessive hold on her, and she jerked away from the younger man with a violence that took him by surprise and spilled the remainder of his champagne down his shirtfront.

''What the—?'' He looked at her in wide-eyed amazement, an embarrassed tinge creeping under his skin.

''I...I'm sorry, I—''

"Perhaps the lady does not care to be pawed on such short acquaintance," came Carl's accented voice, coolly amused.

"I wasn't *pawing*, dammit! And what would a cold fish like you know about it if I was?" Toby's nostrils flared, all traces of his good humor gone.

"Please—" Denise put a trembling hand between the two men, as if expecting a fistfight to erupt at any moment, knowing that if one did the fault would be hers. "I'm sorry. I just got cold feet at the thought of making a speech. I don't do that kind of thing very well, and—"

Mercifully, Paul interrupted, his eyes going from one face to another in question. "I thought this might be a good time to say a few words of welcome to the newcomers. Do you want to do the honors, Carl?"

"No. I'll leave it in your hands, as Dr. Barstow is a friend of yours." The snide tone left little doubt in the minds of his listeners that Carl had small regard for the new boss, and as if to emphasize the point he laid his glass down on the table behind him and with a cool nod in Denise's direction he stalked to the door. She stared after his slicked-back blond hair with a sense of despair. She had certainly made a mess of her introductory evening in the camp. Two men at each other's throats within minutes of them being together with her, one of them already stirring fondness in her. She blinked and focused her attention on what Paul was saying.

"...worry about Carl; he's a moody cuss at the best of times. I guess it's up to me to do the honors, then." His eyes went to the glass Toby still clutched in his hand. "Here, let me get you a refill."

"I'll get it," Toby said, his voice clipped.

"Oh, dear," Denise sighed as his stocky shoulders disappeared in the direction of the bar. "I'm afraid I've upset Toby, and I didn't mean to."

Paul smiled wryly. "I doubt if it's you he's up-tight about. Carl has that effect on him—in fact, Carl has that effect on just about everybody."

"That must make it difficult to work together."

"It has its moments. But Carl's pretty much a loner and most of us are glad he is." Making a rather obvious change of subject, he asked, "Have you met the others?"

"Only Toby and Carl." She put an appealing hand on Paul's wrist. "Do I really have to make a speech? The thought of it just terrifies me."

He eyes her searchingly. "Not if you don't want to. I'll get Jake to answer for both of you; he'll understand."

Would he? As Toby came back with his refilled glass and Paul left them, her gaze homed in to where Jake now stood with Marie, bending his head to listen to whatever she was telling him, her face animated. He seemed to regard Marie affec-tionately—the rigid lines at either side of his mouth relaxed indulgently whenever he was with her. Had he always been like that, before the bitterness of his divorce? Who had divorced whom? Was he still in love with his former wife?

She turned with a start when Toby spoke to her in a low, intense tone. "Look, Denise, I'm sorry if I offended you a while ago, but there was no offense intended. I guess I'm just a physical person, but if you'd rather not be touched—"

"You didn't offend me, Toby," she said in quick empathy, even though the statement wasn't quite truthful. She wanted no intimate contact with any man, even one as innocuous as Toby. Before she had time to say more, Paul was calling attention to where he stood just outside the group.

"I think I speak for all of us when I say we'd like to welcome our new chief, Jake Barstow, and a much needed addition to the team, Denise Jordan, who'll be making proper use of our biology lab at last.

"Jake, as most of us know, needs no introduction as a leader in the field...."

Whether or not Jake needed an introduction, Paul went on for some time, enumerating in scientific detail his achievements in the world of oceanography. Denise let her eyes wander to where Jake stood, his head bent attentively, the inevitably bourbon and water in his leanly shaped hand. His hair, she noted with a faint sense of surprise, showed under the ceiling lights to be dark brown rather than black, and the carved lines of his profile more hawkish than she had thought.

And then it was Jake's turn to speak to the small group he would be directing for the next few months. Denise let his words flow over her consciousness without actually hearing them, her senses seeming alert only to vibrations emanating from him. Concise, authoritative, a man who would brook no slipshod work in the field of marine research, yet there was an underlying stream of camaraderie that, she noticed from the faces turned in his direction, was evidently a quality his subordinates appreciated. She felt the same electric shock when his eyes, sparking a faint light of mockery, found her.

"I'm sure I speak for... Denise, as well, when I say that your hospitality tonight is appreciated." So Paul had spoken to him, and he had agreed to speak for both of them. Her body grew rigid with his next words. "I'm not personally acquainted with Denise, but I did know and work with her husband, Sam, a few years ago. His death from a diving accident two years ago robbed marine science of a brilliant man. However, I'm sure that Denise has her own brand of expertise to bring to our teamwork here."

Denise didn't hear his final wrap-up, so absorbed was she in her own jumbled emotional state. At Scripps everyone had known Sam been aware of his death, so there had been no need for announcements such as Jake Barstow had just made. She felt curious, sympathetic eyes on her, as there had been in the days following the accident, and it was like reliving the worst scene of her life. Now, as then, overwhelming guilt rose to choke her. She hadn't loved Sam, so he had died.

"Come and meet Captain Mike." Marie materialized beside her. "He's a real character—straight out of a book. He's sailed the seven seas, and he'll give you a blow-by-blow account if you let him. I think he feels captaining a research vessel is beneath his dignity, but it's that or skippering a tour boat over the undersea gardens off Nassau."

The old man Marie led her to was indeed the traditional seadog, with bristling white brows over a weathered brown face and, despite the piercing look he gave her from bright blue eyes, Denise liked him. He had lived too many years to let the worries that troubled the young bother him anymore. He left a battered black pipe in his mouth while he talked to her.

"You're still a widow?" he said forthrightly in a voice roughened over the years by tobacco and alcohol. His sharp eyes had already made a thorough inspection of her from shining bright hair to sandaled feet.

"Yes. It's just been two years since—"

"Two years is a long time for a pretty woman to be without a man. What's the matter with the young fellas nowadays? Forty years ago I'd have put some sparkle in your eyes. You wouldn't be mooning over a man long since in his grave."

"My sentiments exactly," a laconic drawl came

over Denise's shoulder, and fiery color ran up under her skin. Jake!

"Oh?" the old man looked at him suspiciously. "Then why aren't you doing something about it?"

"Maybe I will," Jake told him, laughing in a low, amused voice that set Denise's teeth on edge, "once I've found my way through the surrounding prickles."

A young black girl appeared in the doorway and nodded meaningfully to Marie, who immediately clapped her hands and said with a general swivel of her dark head, "Come on, everybody, time for dinner. Philly's made a special effort tonight, so let's not spoil it for her."

There was a general movement toward the dining room, and Denise found her arm held lightly at the elbow by Jake's hard, warm fingers. The touch was like flame on her skin, and she was glad to pull away from it at the entrance to the communal dining room and exclaim in genuine wonder at the beautifully laid long table that was obviously put together from three of normal size. Gleaming silver place settings were arranged at each side and one at either end of the snowy white linen cloth, and bowls of scarlet flower heads were arranged down its center in vivid splashes of color to contrast with the white cloth. Sparkling water glasses and wineglasses complemented the silver settings, and Denise was pleasantly surprised to know that life at the station wasn't to be as primitive as she had half expected.

"All this is just to make a good first impression," Toby, his good humor evidently restored, whispered at her ear. "Usually we have bare boards and metal dishes."

"That I don't believe!" Denise smiled at him, relieved that the sunny gleam was back in his eyes, the awkwardness between them forgotten. Maybe that was because of Carl Madsen's absence, but whatever the reason, she was glad of it. Instinct told her that Toby could provide a friendship that would act as a buffer between her and the more disturbing personality elements at the research unit.

And of course she could rely on the friendliness of Paul and Marie Stein; they were a nice, normal couple, and obviously the station's social life revolved around their family unit.

As guests of honor, Jake and Denise were seated at either end of the long table, and it was inevitably that green eyes met gray constantly as dinner progressed, Jake's narrowly assessing, hers glancing and sliding away. The creamy-skinned redhead, Christina Kell, just nodded coolly down the length of the table when Marie belatedly introduced them.

Denise's own awareness of Jake irritated her, but she seemed helpless against her interest that noted the turn of his well-shaped head to listen to what either Christina on one side or Marie on the other were saying; the way the harsh lines at either side of his mouth lifted when he smiled; the economical movements of his hands as he ate the Bahamian meal.

The station cook, whom Marie had referred to as Philly, had really exerted herself on the delicious food. The thick red peppery conch chowder was followed by red snapper bathed in a tangy cream sauce, sweet potatoes, baby peas, colorful diced carrots, and a refreshingly light dessert of mixed tropical fruits topped with whipped coconut cream. Sparkling rosé accompanied the meal, and a variety of liqueurs, which Denise refused, were served with American-style coffee to round off the dinner.

"Now let's dance it off," Marie suggested gaily, her slightly sallow skin lighted by a wine-induced glow, and there was a general groan of protest.

"Why don't you play something on the piano?" Captain Mike countered gruffly.

"Not tonight," Marie giggled. "I doubt if I could find the keys. Come on, Paul, let's start the ball rolling."

In the general exodus from the dining room, only Denise looked back at the table to the accusingly unused place setting. Where had Carl Madsen eaten his dinner? He seemed to be a loner, somewhat of an outcast of the group, and Denise felt the stirrings of sympathy.

A few moments later she was in Toby's arms, moving to a slow, popular tune. Her body responded to the music but her mind was far away, back in time....

Dancing had been a learned ritual to Denise before she met Sam Jordan, but in his arms, moving slowly around a dance floor, she had felt the excitement of her body pressed close to the hardness of his. She had wanted him then, wanted the fulfillment of her young romantic fantasies, wanted—needed—the obliteration of the slow ache that spread from her thighs to every part of her, the pain only he could transform into pleasure with the fullness of his possession.

"Oh, God, I didn't know," he had groaned on the night of their marriage, when she lay under him, numb even to the pain in her savaged breasts, her lacerated mouth. "Why didn't you tell me you'd never been with a man before?"

Because I wanted my wedding night to be something special that I would remember the rest of my life, she had wanted to scream at him, but her voice lay numb in her throat, as numb as the once-bright flickering of desire she had felt during their whirlwind courtship.

"Hey, remember me?"

She blinked away the mists of memory and stared blankly for a moment into Toby's faintly concerned eyes, coming back gradually to the atmosphere of the comfortable lounge where she moved automatically in the young pilot's arms.

"I'm...sorry," she apologized, stumbling on his feet as reality flowed back to her. "I was thinking of...something else."

"Or someone else?" he countered shrewdly, his

face unusually serious as they danced nearer
to Jake and Christina, who were dancing close,
and Paul and Marie, dancing even closer.
"You were thinking about your husband, weren't
you?"

"Yes," she admitted with an unconscious sigh,
and his hand tightened on the smooth indentation
of her waist.

"He must have been one hell of a guy." Toby
was silent for the space of a few moments, then he
said, his voice strangely constricted, "But you
can't go on living with memories of a dead man
forever, Denise. I know that sounds hard, maybe
even cruel, but you're a beautiful woman, and you
could be happy with somebody else if you'd let it
happen."

"Maybe one day," she said noncommittally,
but Toby, to her dismay, seemed to accept that as
a half promise of being open to his advances in the
future.

"I have a lot of patience, surprising as it may
seem to you," he said huskily, drawing her nearer
to the warm firmness of his young body, seeming
not to notice Denise's recoil as the record ended,
and she pushed out of his arms.

The tiny hammer blows of a beginning headache were her excuse to say good-night to the
small group before the next dance tune was put on
the turntable.

"No, I'll be all right." She smiled wanly to the
anxious Marie. "I'm just beginning to feel the

effects of a long day's traveling. Please—don't
break up the party because of me."

"I'll see you back to your cottage," Toby offered, frowning his displeasure when Jake interposed.

"I can drop Denise off on my way back. I'm
suffering from the same kind of fatigue, so an early night won't come amiss."

"No!" The vehemence of Denise's response
overrode the regretful murmurs of the others,
and she felt a warm flush bathe her cheeks
when they turned to look curiously at her.
"I mean, I don't want you to leave the party
because of me." She forced a laugh. "I'm quite
capable of seeing myself across a few hundred
yards."

"As I've said," Jake reiterated evenly, "I'm on
my way to bed. We might as well go together."

"That would put the sparkle back in her eyes,"
chortled Captain Mike, now nursing a large
brandy and soda, ignoring Marie's irritated glance
in his direction. "Nothing like a good man to keep
a woman happy."

"You're drunk—again," Marie said disgusted-
ly, turning back to say to Denise, "come and have
coffee with me in the morning after you've looked
around. Paul's planned a diving trip for the men,
so we'll have time to get acquainted."

For the men. Denise winced inwardly in recognition of Marie's assumption that she would be
more interested in womanly chitchat than in the

plying of her profession. However, she managed a nod of acquiescence.

A big white moon bathed the area in a brilliance almost like daylight when she stepped out of the clubhouse. Jake fell into step beside her as she turned in the direction of the cottages. The powdery softness of the sand filled her sandals after the first few steps, and she bent impatiently to slip them from her feet and loop her fingers through them.

"It might be easier going on the beach," Jake suggested, fastening the warm strength of his fingers around her upper arm and veering off to their right.

Saying nothing, but agonizingly conscious of his warm flesh upon the cool smoothness of her arm, she allowed him to lead her across the coarse sea grasses to where the sand was firm and damp under her nylon-clad feet. A yard or two away the moon-gilded waters swished gently up the shore before withdrawing silently to mingle with a new wave making its advance to the acquiescent beach.

"It's more a place for lovers than scientists." Jake's voice broke the stillness. His hand, still firmly lodged against Denise's arm, provoked a momentary closing of her throat muscles.

"I don't know," she managed at last, glad of the sharp pressure of a fan-shaped shell that pressed painfully against the arch of her stock-inged foot and gave her an excuse to pull away from his confining fingers. "Aren't the two terms synonymous? Lovers of the sea want to explore the...the hidden depths of it, the mystery. Rather like—'' She broke off, confused, and looked back to where their two distinct sets of footprints traced a path across the damp sand.

"Like a man discovering the hidden depths of a woman?" he continued for her, his detached tone bringing her eyes around and up to the moon-shadowed leanness of his high-boned cheeks, the straight thrust of his nose, the firm outline of his sensually shaped lips. "Yes, it's essentially the same thing. The only difference is that the sea remains cool whatever discoveries a man makes about its mysteries, whereas a woman has the capacity to change, to grow warm from his touch." There was a brief flash of white teeth as he smiled and shrugged. "Maybe that's why we scientists can never be completely satisfied with what the ocean has to offer."

He turned away, resuming their seafront walk, and Denise had no choice but to follow, her long footprints still outsized by his.

"I imagine you've never had a problem getting that kind of satisfaction," she said, without knowing where the words came from, and was instantly appalled by the realization of what he must think of them.

His head swiveled toward her, and his voice sounded lightly amused when he said, "I can't say that I have. How about you?"

"Me?"

"You've been married," he said shortly without breaking pace. "And with your looks I doubt if you've been without male attention since your husband's death."

Her face revealed none of the rage that swept through her at his assumption that Sam's death had made her easy prey for any man who cared to cast licentious eyes over her. "I haven't needed male attention since Sam died," she said, ice chilling her voice.

"No?"

They had stopped again, and Denise faced him with the confidence of anger. "No," she repeated cuttingly. "Does that come as a shock to your male ego, Dr. Barstow?" she mocked. "That a woman can live quite contentedly without a man in her life?"

"You'd have to prove it to me," he said in a level voice that gave no warning of the swift reach of his arm, the jerking of her body to the ungiving hardness of his, the swooping descent of his mouth as it claimed her lips.

Shock, rather than the viselike hold of his muscular arms, held her still as his mouth pressed her lips, his tongue forceful in its efforts to penetrate the barrier her teeth represented.

Her hands came up in an automatic gesture to press against the warm hardness of his chest, feeling and discounting the deep thrum of his heartbeat against her palms. One of his hands lifted to her head and brushed roughly through the short strands of her hair, anchoring her head with his hard fingertips, forcing her to accept the warm thrust of his tongue into the sensitive recesses of her mouth. His hand dipped down to the rounded line of her hips and pressed there, raising them to mold her against his hard masculinity.

It was like a nightmare that went on and on with no end in view. Struggling against his overwhelming strength became an exercise in futility, and she capitulated with a suddenness that evidently surprised him, because his mouth gentled to her yielding, softening as it touched the shallow hollow at her throat, the sensitive cord of her neck. Heat sprang like wildfire from his body to hers, searing, melting the frozen core of her, lifting her hips to the insistent pressure of his and fusing their swaying bodies together....

"You see?" his voice murmured at her ear, warming her skin while cooling her brain, then she felt his lips against her temple, at her hair.... "Your needs are like anyone else's, aren't they?"

"Let me go," she said dully, coldly, and felt his surprise as his arms fell away from her. "Don't ever touch me like that again or I'll report you for attempted rape."

"*Rape*? Good God, because of a kiss?" His nostrils flared for another reason now. "What's the matter with you? Are you still stuck on a dead man? Look at me." His fingers jerked her chin in an upward angle, and he said deliberately, "It's too bad that Sam died, but you can't bury yourself along with him. I've watched you tonight, and I've seen how you react when even a kid like Toby Winters comes near you. Do you think that's how Sam would have wanted it, seeing you shut off in an icehouse of your own making?''

"Let me *go*!" she panted, jerking her chin away from his confining fingers but taking only one step backward on the sand before facing up to him aggressively. "What do *you* know about Sam or what he would have wanted? You think you're so smart, don't you?" Her voice grew bitter. "Drawing your conclusions after observing me for a whole three hours! You've missed your calling, doctor; you should be in instant psychotherapy!"

"I'm sorry," he apologized stiffly. "I thought I might be able to help you, but it seems I was mistaken." Tight-lipped he turned and struck off in the direction of the pink-washed cottage he had been assigned, clearly visible through the trees from where they were standing, as white sand sprayed up behind his heels as he went.

Denise, stomach churning, stood and watched him go, unable to move until at last she bent to pick up the sandals that had fallen from her fingers when he had pulled her into his arms. Slowly she made her way to her own cottage, her feet sinking into the cool depths of the sand.

Never in her life had she spoken to anyone as she had to Jake Barstow tonight. What had got into her? God knew she was used to men playing the part of savior to what they imagined was her deprived sexual state—she had even experimented with one or two of the do-gooders, but the results had always been the same. She had been able to take—even enjoy—the preliminaries to love, but when the breathing became heavier and a deeper commitment was called for, she had always become rigid and withdrawn.

The classic symptoms of frigidity, she reflected dryly as she went up the steps to the cottage and let herself in, automatically locked the door behind her, then leaned back against it after switching on the light and stared sightlessly ahead.

Why had she let Jake rile her so much? Subduing her temper had never been a problem for her before. Her long lonely childhood days, which had never seemed lonely to her because she had no standards to compare them with, had provoked no childish flares of passion, no fighting against the stricture her father placed on her. Docility and passivity had been built into her from an early age. Even in the tangled mess of her marriage to Sam, the loudest voice in their quarrels had always been his. But now Jake Barstow had demonstrated that she was not as immune to basic human passions as she had thought.

She pushed away from the door and walked to the bedroom, thoughts still churning endlessly in her mind. Dropping her sandals on the closet floor, she reached behind her for the zipper of her dress, then dropped her clothes around her as she went to the shower.

There, under the warm, comfortable element
that was most familiar to her, she mulled over
what had prompted her outburst of anger. Jake's
assumption that, because of her looks, men had
fallen over themselves to satisfy her physical appetites was, she realized now, a gambit to draw her
out about her sex life. He had already passed judg-
ment on her, thinking she still cherished Sam's
memory. Toby had thought the same thing.

Well, why not? She stepped reluctantly from
under the warm spray. Let them think that her
marriage to Sam was so ideal that the thought of
another man's touch was abhorrent to her. Wasn't
that better than them knowing the truth?

But later, as she lay waiting for the blessed
oblivion of sleep, she still felt the imprint of Jake's
mouth on hers, the pressing urgency of his male
strength against the softness of her yielding body.

CHAPTER THREE

MORNING BROUGHT the surprising realization that she had slept better than she had in a long time. Although the hands of her watch pointed to just after six, Denise felt the charge of energy that told her she had slept enough.

After padding into the living room, she drew aside the floor-length draperies and looked out, enchanted, at the glittering movement of the ocean, the wide swath of dazzling sand bordering it. The water beckoned like a siren, and she reminded herself to get coffee supplies as she skipped back to the bedroom and threw off the light nylon of her nightdress. Nude, she searched for one of the brief bikinis she had unpacked the day before. A swim before breakfast had always been one of her special delights, one she had been fortunate to indulge most of her adult life on her private beach near San Diego.

Minutes later she was wading into waters of dazzling clarity, touching her fingertips to its velvet smoothness as it lapped around her knees. Early morning silence still lay over the cottages behind her, and she gloried in the scene that was entirely and privately hers.

Tiny fish darted and veered around her alien presence, shy yet curious as they followed her into the shelving depths of the water where she swam at last with long lazy strokes that took her out to where the coral beds began and larger fish took over the vigil of their smaller cousins. As she submerged again and again, Denise delighted in the flashing brilliance of orange, red, iridescent blue, white, the pink of coral that would, she knew, build higher and higher until it formed an almost impenetrable barrier to deep-bottomed boats. But there must be a break in the reef, she reflected as she waded out reluctantly at last, allowing the research vessel free movement to the deeper waters of the Tongue of the Ocean, the deep channel bisecting the west and east islands of the Bahamas.

Her eyes went involuntarily to the pink-washed cottage set behind the trees and to the left of hers as she plowed through the fine sand that clung, sparkling like a million diamonds, to her wet feet. The porch door opened as she watched, and Jake Barstow appeared, long legs emerging from brief white shorts, and a dark-colored shirt flapping loosely around the cloudy growth on his chest. Over one sinewy arm he carried what was obviously his own personal diving equipment: vest, mask, fins.

Denise stood still, feeling an irrational panic

that made her want to become invisible, anchoring her feet in the sand. Her anxiety was misplaced, however, because Jake strode on toward the clubhouse without turning his head, and within seconds he was out of sight behind her cottage.

Having showered, and taking much longer than was strictly necessary to dress in cuffed chocolate-brown shorts and loose-fitting matching sun top, she sauntered along to the clubhouse, relieved when she saw the group of men gathered along the jetty beside one of the cabin cruisers. It was ridiculous to feel this way about a man she would inevitably be in close proximity with for the next few months, but at that moment there wasn't a thing she could do about the hollow feeling that hit the pit of her stomach even when viewing him from this distance.

The appetizing drift of coffee and other breakfast aromas quickened her steps into the clubhouse. Probably all she needed, she told herself dryly, was some solid food in her stomach.

She was helping herself to coffee from an urn in the empty dining room when a deep voice called out from the kitchen hatch, "Morning, Mrs. Jordan. What would you like for breakfast?"

Locating the substantial figure behind the counter, Denise went over, cup in hand, and was greeted with a beaming smile from an aging black woman.

"Are you the one I have to thank for the delicious meal last night? Is it Philly?"

"Well, that's what Mrs. Stein calls me, but my name is really Philomena."

Sensing the cook's dislike for the American penchant for shortening names, Denise said, "Then that's what I'll call you; it's a beautiful name. I can't remember when I've ever enjoyed a meal so much. Maybe while I'm here, I can pick up some of your Bahamian recipes. I know my...my friends would love to try them." Telling the gray-haired cook that she also had a cook at home would only start a stream of speculation as to why a woman comfortably situated should bother to work when she could live a life of idle luxury without lifting a finger. Several of the girls at school and college who might have become friends had been overawed by the feudallike system of loyal family servants Denise had taken for granted.

"I'd be glad to show you anytime, Mrs. Jordan," Philomena beamed. "Now, what will you have for breakfast? Pancakes, bacon, ham and eggs, sausages?"

"I'd been planning on fruit, but after my swim I'm a little more hungry than that," Denise confessed.

"Then I'll start you off with fruit and see what happens after that. I'll bring it to you."

Smiling her thanks, Denise wandered over to a table directly under one of the open windows and glanced through it to see the bluish vapor of the motorboat trailing behind the fast-moving vessel.

Relief mingled with an altogether different emotion as she watched the wake of the boat that carried Jake Barstow away from the camp. He would be gone for several hours, enough time for her to collect her senses and marshal them into some kind of order. It was, as she had thought before, a ridiculous situation.

HER INSPECTION of the research unit's perimeters was leisurely after the gargantuan breakfast Philomena had provided, but even so it was accomplished in less time than she had expected.

The small lab that she discovered at the far side of the clubhouse held few of the gleaming facilities she had become used to at Scripps. Nothing more than a basic analysis could be done here on these dusty benches holding the minimum of equipment; for any kind of detailed analysis, her specimens would have to be shipped to the mainland. How disappointing! It made her job, she reflected, no more interesting than that of the pearl divers in Japan whose only concern was the collecting of oysters, not the evaluation of their contents.

Out in the sun again, she crossed to the larger building closer to the base of the concrete pier and found a treasure trove of diving equipment: fins, masks, snorkels, pressure tanks, all neatly stacked on shelves or alongside the cool concrete walls. The very sight of it all sparked the longing she felt to explore the waters beyond the reef, to see with her own eyes the flora and fauna inhabiting the nether regions of an ocean unknown to her.

Walking farther around the bay to a slight promontory covered with long-legged palms, their tops swaying in the breeze, she looked out to the curve of the next shore and was surprised to see a collection of buildings there. Lines of colorful washing flapping in the sea breeze proclaimed inhabitation of the closely clustered cottages at beach edge, and Denise made a mental note to ask Marie about the settlement.

Reminded of their appointment for coffee that morning, she glanced at her watch and decided there would be time for a walk along the concrete pier before making her way back to the Stein bungalow. The research vessel, when she came to it, swayed rhythmically on the incoming tide, her masts and cranes creaking with a lonely sound that suggested no one was aboard.

Denise lightly swung up the shortened gangplank and called as she stepped on the bleached boards of the deck, "Anybody there?"

Encouraged by the silence that greeted her words, she ventured farther into the ship to the bridge room, where a bewildering array of gauges and dials confronted her, then to the spacious saloon with its dining table stretched at its center. As well as providing dining space, the saloon boasted lounging areas of faded linen-covered couches and armchairs at either side of the table.

Beyond the saloon a narrow passage lined with

brown-varnished doors led to an exit companion-way to the aft deck. Enjoying her sole occupation of the ship, Denise opened each of the doors in turn and found that they enclosed sleeping cabins of differing size, but with a uniform absence of luxury. Four were double-bunked, three single, and the last was marginally larger with a set of double bunks against either wall. Shower and toilet facilities were arranged at either side of the companionway leading to the upper deck.

She would have liked to explore further, but a glance at her watch as she came up into the sun-shine again made her retreat along the narrower deck past the small, round portholes set high in the cabins below.

Crossing the sand toward Marie's cottage, Denise approached a small girl with curly brown hair, who looked up and pointed immediately to the yellow-checked gingham sundress she wore.

"I got this dress," she said without preamble, looking down at its frilled hem as if doubting its value as play apparel.

"It's a lovely dress," Denise assured her grave-ly, then looked around searchingly. "Where's your mommy?"

The question was answered by Marie's anxious call as she hurried from the porch of their cottage. "Cindy? Cindy, where are you? Come back here this minute." She caught sight of Denise and her errant daughter and rushed barefoot across the sand, a child's sunbonnet twirling on her fingers.

Jamming the hat on her daughter's head and fastening the narrow straps under her chin, she said to Denise, "Nothing's guaranteed to shorten a woman's life like having a four-year-old who disappears the second she turns her back."

"Give lady some cookies now?" Cindy wheedled with an all-too-feminine upward tilt of her eyes, which were Paul's in shape and color.

"Your generosity is exceeded only by your extreme greed," Marie commented dryly, taking the child's hand in hers and giving Denise a wry smile. "I'm afraid she's more interested in filling her own stomach than yours with cookies, but come along into the house. The coffee's ready."

Denise put a hand down and a chubby warm paw immediately reached up to it and allowed the adult fingers to encompass hers. A pang that was half pain, half longing shot through Denise. Had he lived, would she and Sam ever have had a child like this one? Perhaps with a child—

"I saw you on the ship," Marie cut into her futile thoughts. "What do you think of it?"

"It seems very well set up for what it's intended to do."

Marie grimaced, then held the screen door open for Denise to pass in front of her. "It's no luxury liner. I was sick as a dog when I went out on her once, but maybe you have a stronger stomach than I have." She laughed, dark eyes sparkling as she leaned around Denise to hold open the inner door. "But then that's your job, isn't it? Go ahead, and welcome to our humble home."

It wasn't exactly humble, Denise reflected as she stepped into a living room that was almost a replica of her own except for its larger size. One end of it was occupied by a good-sized dining table and built-in china cabinet, an added refinement, and the rear hall was considerably larger than hers with a wide passage leading off to the bedroom area. The main difference was in the surprisingly well-equipped kitchen overlooking the enclosed garden at the rear.

Following Marie and the tantalizing smell of coffee, she found herself in the spacious kitchen with its tiers of cupboards and square central table covered in a floral print and decorated with the same low scarlet blossoms as had been used in the clubhouse the night before.

Marie took cups and saucers from one of the cupboards and set them on the table, waving Denise to one of the straight-backed chairs. "Hope you don't mind the kitchen, but Cindy makes such a mess with crumbs, and Esther's already cleaned up this morning."

"Esther?" Denise put down a hand to help the diminutive Cindy into a chair before seating herself.

"Oh, I guess you haven't met her yet. She housekeeps all the cottages and babysits Cindy when I go out. Her husband, Henry, works on the research vessel, and they have no children of their own. They're saving up to buy a house, so the extra money is welcome."

Denise laughed. "My place is hardly big enough to warrant a housekeeper!"

"Don't make waves about it, or they could decide that all of us can get along without her," Marie said with a grimace, handing a cookie to the clamoring Cindy and coffee to Denise. "Here, pest, you can have this and some milk and then a nap."

"Isn't it lonely for her here?" asked Denise, eyeing the curly head and chubby body that still seemed active although seated. "Or are there other children around?"

Marie put a plastic cup before Cindy and sank into a chair. "Unfortunately, no. That's one of the drawbacks about this place. We're completely split up as a family, and I miss David so. But—" she sighed "—Paul sets a lot of store by a steady education, and I do, too, but it's harder for me. Paul has his work to occupy him."

Again there was that note of discontent Denise had noticed before. "I imagine Paul misses his son, too," she said softly.

"Yes, he does, but it's different for a man somehow." Marie deftly rescued her daughter's almost empty cup and rose to scoop her protesting form into her arms. "Come on, poppet, time for a rest."

"Want to see lady some more," Cindy protested, wriggling energetically.

"You'll see Denise some more tonight." Marie looked over her shoulder at Denise in a wry manner. "I'd meant to ask you in a more civilized fashion, but would you like to have dinner with us tonight?"

"I'd love it."

She sipped thoughtfully on her coffee while Marie was away, reflecting that the Steins, who seemed the epitome of marital bliss, could have a rat in their woodpile. Marie's discontent with a situation Paul had no control over could deepen to a corrosive bitterness that would be hard to blot out even when the family was united again. And that would be a shame. Their closeness while dancing last night had made it obvious that they couldn't wait to be alone together to make love in a way that was excitingly familiar to them. Her fingers tightened on the cup handle. Didn't they know how lucky they were?

"Phew! Now we can have a chat in peace." Marie came back into the kitchen and seemed more relaxed as she dropped into her chair again. "Never marry an oceanographer," she advised ruefully, then clapped a hand to her forehead as embarrassed color swept under her skin. "What an idiot I am. Forgive me, Denise, I'd forgotten that—"

"It's all right," Denise inserted quickly, looking down into her coffee cup. "It's been two years since Sam died, so I'm used to the idea now."

"Are you?" Marie's gaze was shrewdly penetrating. "You can't have been married for very long when it happened."

"Just over a year."

Quick sympathy registered in the older woman's eyes. "In some ways that must be worse than when you've been together for a long time. You're so new to each other with all kinds of dreams that you'll never be sure would have come true. Very often they don't, you know."

"I'm not the kind to live on dreams of what might have been," Denise told her dryly. "I'm a scientist, remember?"

"But still a dreamer, I think, a romantic. Just tell me to get lost if you think I'm talking out of line. It's just that—well, you're very attractive, and I wouldn't like to think that you feel you have to wrap yourself in mothballs because your husband died so tragically. Believe it or not, there will be another man for you." As if embarrassed at her own emotional outburst, Marie leaped to her feet and went to the coffeepot. "Let me fill you up. Did I mention that Jake's coming tonight, as well? Let me hasten to reassure you that my motives in asking the two of you together are completely innocent. Jake's not the one I'd care to see you shed your widowhood for."

"Oh?" Denise schooled her hand to steadiness as she stirred cream into her cup. "Why is that?"

"Don't misunderstand me. Next to Paul, I'm fonder of Jake than any other man in the world, but he's poison as far as women are concerned."

A shiver ran across Denise's skin. What would Marie say if she knew that the imprint of Jake's hard body still held hers potently, that his questing mouth was still forcing its passionate warmth between her shocked lips?

"I...gather so," she managed in a light disinterested tone, "or his wife wouldn't have divorced him, would she?"

Marie seemed to have noticed no change in her expression. "I'm not sure who divorced who in that marriage," she said darkly, "but it wouldn't surprise me to know that Jake initiated the proceedings. Barbara's a complete bitch, the classic queen bee—rich, beautiful, spoiled and amoral to a staggering degree. The surprise to me was that it lasted as long as it did. Meg might have had something to do with that, of course."

"Jake's daughter?"

"Yes. She's a strange little thing," Marie mused thoughtfully. "Very quiet, self-contained, old beyond her years. Of course, that isn't surprising with a mother like Barbara."

"Does she live with her mother?" Her own curiosity about Jake Barstow and his marital situation was unforgivable, but Marie evidently had no such qualms.

"In a way." Marie burst out with sudden anger, "Can you believe a woman who would send her ten-year-old daughter away to boarding school in Long Island when she lives in New York, only a few miles away? Of course, Meg would present a problem when her mother's entertaining her men friends.''

Marie's motherly instincts were protectively aroused, but a different sort of feeling flitted through Denise, one she wasn't prepared to analyze at that moment.

"It's surprising that," Denise hesitated, "a man like Jake would allow his daughter to be exposed to...that kind of thing, if it's true.'' Marie's fondness for Jake could well lead her to exaggeration of his ex-wife's faults; after all, she was hardly in a position to know the truth of another couple's affairs. "His wife must have been awarded custody of the little girl, so she can't be all that bad.''

"She got Meg because they decided Jake couldn't provide a stable home for her," Marie scorned, her eyes fiery, "and Barbara didn't fight the custody suit because she wanted the child with her. It was just a way to score off poor Jake. Another twist of her knife was that she married again almost before the divorce dust had settled.''

Denise shrugged. "Wasn't that the best thing to happen? If the marriage was over anyway—"

"That's the problem." Marie frowned, speaking slowly as she went on, "I don't think it *is* over for Jake. Oh, he's been around with other women, but none of them's ever lasted longer than a few months. Incredible as it seems, I think he's still in love with Barbara. They were young when they married, and—"

Denise, her breath suddenly caught suffocatingly in her throat, tuned out the rest of Marie's revelations about Jake and his disastrous marriage. Because it wasn't her business, she told herself; and she had enough marriage-related traumas herself without getting involved in someone else's, particularly Jake Barstow's. But Marie's words stirred up an all too vivid memory of last night's deliberate assault, supposedly made to force her into realization of her sexual needs. Had Jake simply been staking an early claim to sole rights in an affair that would, as Marie said, last only a few months? The thought of his using her as a sex object would be funny if it hadn't been so insulting. For a moment a spark of humor gleamed in her eyes. It might be a salutary lesson for him to learn that not all women were vulnerable to his prowess in that direction. Surprised at her own levity about a subject that had appeared to have no lighter side before now, she struggled back to attend to what Marie was saying.

"Where are you? I don't believe you've heard a word of what I've been saying." The older woman seemed not to be offended by that fact, though. "Paul's always telling me I talk too much, but in the year we've been here, apart from a couple of trips home, I've had very little female companionship."

Denise roused herself. "What about Christina Kell?"

"You saw her for yourself last night," Marie

grimaced. "There's no way she and I could talk like this. Did you notice the way she hung closer than a limpet to Jake?" She chuckled. "I have an idea she'd come out the loser, though, in a battle of the sexes with him." Her eyes assumed a thoughtful look as they went over Denise's face and smoothly tanned shoulders. "Actually, he seemed more interested in you."

"Me?" Denise forced a laugh and got to her feet. "If he was, it would only be in a professional way, wondering if I'd rock the boat when I'm out with an all-male crew. Most chiefs have that kind of hangup."

"Mmm, I guess they do, the world being what it is," Marie returned, but absently, as if she was thinking of something completely different.

"I've really enjoyed having coffee with you, and meeting Cindy, but I really should go."

"Why don't you stay for lunch? The men won't be back till later this afternoon, so Jake's obviously not expecting you to buckle down to work for today, anyway."

"Thanks, but—I'm expecting some stuff to be delivered—my stereo and records particularly— and I'd like to be there."

"Okay." Marie followed her to the door. "It was good thinking to bring your record player. TV here doesn't have very good reception. There's one in the lounge, but it's such a hit-and-miss affair that hardly anybody watches it." She called after Denise, who lifted a hand to shield her head when the hot sun struck it, "I'll lend you a sun hat when you come tonight. Is seven-thirty all right?"

Nodding and waving, Denise continued on the beach route to her own cottage, her eyes turning constantly to the turquoise water lapping gently at the shore. She was going to love it here in this place that held all the elements important to her—the sun, the ocean, the warmth of another woman's friendship, which Marie, voluble and temperamental as she seemed, would provide. She had been right to come here; already she felt the lightening of the emotional load she had carried for so long. The guilt of failure softened in the brilliance of life-giving sun as it glinted off sand so white that the reflection hurt her eyes. That she might have assumed a burden of a different kind was far from her mind as she went with a pleasant sense of ownership into her cottage.

LATE THAT AFTERNOON, as she stepped from the shower, Perry delivered her crated stereo system and carefully packaged records. Calling to him through a crack in the bathroom door, she told him to bring the packages in.

"And could you unpack the record player for me, Perry?"

"I'll hook it up for you if you'll let me play a couple of your records," he called back in his laughing, singsong voice.

"You're welcome to, if you can find something there you like."

Which she doubted, she smiled secretly as she dried herself and wrapped a short terry robe around her still damp body. Her musical tastes ranged from light classic to popular sentimental, and she guessed that Perry, in common with most young people, went for disco music, if not punk rock.

About to plug in her hair dryer, she heard him say something and called to ask him to repeat it.

"Ravel," he read off hesitantly, "*Bolero*. No, lady, that's not my kind of music."

Not mine, either, Denise retorted silently, her hand suspended in midair. Perry must have said something else. Ravel's *Bolero* was definitely something she wouldn't have packed, even if she possessed the recording. Shrugging, she connected the dryer and drowned out the sounds of Perry's departure. When she emerged from the bathroom minutes later the living-room area was empty.

Perry had set up the turntable on the low table at the window, the speakers spaced at the two adjoining corners. The record he had casually discarded lay on top of a compartmented packing box on the floor, and she picked it up, the smile fading from her mouth when she read the title: *Bolero*—Ravel—New York Symphony Orchestra.

The record definitely was not hers. Plunging her hand into one compartment after the other she came up with Wagner, Stravinsky, Mahler, Beethoven, all indicating a taste far heavier than her own. Bending, she read the stapled tag at the side of the box: Dr. J. Barstow, Tarbuck Cay, New Providence, Bahamas.

The records were Jake's! Her mind went back thoughtfully over the titles. Heavy classics were the last thing she would have associated with him; satirical pieces, yes, but not this overwhelming dedication to the solemn, the deeply significant aspects of music. On impulse, she placed the *Bolero* recording on the turntable and set it into motion. The volume was tuned to a low pitch, but the wild, insistent music filled the room, out of place with the peaceful setting of tropical sea and sand outside the window. Yet something in her blood responded to the strains that were insistent as life itself, and without consciously realizing it she was swaying and dancing in the confined space of the living room, carried away by an imagination that put silver bangles on her wrists, slender chains around her ankles—she was a Turkish slave girl, dancing for her master's pleasure—a master whose peculiarly light gray eyes spoke of that pleasure, approving, appreciative, sensual—

"Very nice," a male voice approved lazily from the door, and she whirled, arms freezing in midair, green eyes widening on Jake Barstow as he lounged against the inner door.

"What are you doing here?" her breath squeezed out in spasmodic gasps. Another part of her mind registered the lean maleness of his figure, the narrowed gray of his eyes, the softened line of his well-shaped lips.

"I came to deliver your records and reclaim mine," he said in a voice that was huskily amused. "Though I'm wondering now if it would be to my advantage to let you interpret the music for me; you do it so beautifully." He pushed away from the door and came farther into the room. "The only problem is that your Peggy Lee albums stir up more. . . nostalgia, shall we say, than a man can handle in the wee small hours when he's trying to get to sleep." The downward sweep of his eyes, encompassing the slackened opening of her robe, brought her hands up to clutch the white terry around her throat.

"I'd have thought she was a lot more soothing, under those circumstances, than Wagner," she mustered shakily, conscious of the rug's texture under her bare feet as she went to lift the stereo arm, plunging the room into a suffocating silence that strangely hurt her ears. "How—how did the dive go?"

His eyes took on a silver gleam. "Very well. You should have come with us."

"I might have if I'd been asked," she said with a touch of tartness she regretted immediately. Sulks for a scientist—particularly a female scientist—were definitely out.

"Madsen arranged the trip at my request. I took it for granted that you'd be coming along."

"Meaning that Carl's a believer in boys-only trips?"

He shrugged. "He's a little out of touch with

the progressive world, I think. But if you're anxious to get to work, I'll take you out in the morning. There's a lot you'd be interested in, if you haven't dived these waters before."

The statement was half question and Denise shook her head, her hand still on the closure of her robe as she walked back to stand before the couch. "I've been nowhere apart from the southern California coast. I—I've been looking forward to the differences here."

"It's a lot clearer, that's one thing. And it's really teeming with very colorful fish and plant life. You'll enjoy it." His eyes narrowed curiously on her golden-tanned skin. "What made you choose marine science for a career? It's not too usual for a woman."

"Because I love the sea and everything in it." Then, in case that sounded too sweetly sentimental, she added, "I grew up beside the ocean, and I—spent a lot of time when I was a child making my own primitive experiments." She laughed awkwardly. "You know, scooping a pan of water from the sea and leaving it on the rocks to evaporate. I used to feel like a magician when I'd come back and find salt crystals in the pan."

"Sounds as if you were alone a lot of the time," he commented, his interest polite but not probing. "Didn't you have a brother or sister?"

"No, my...mother died when I was young." She had never divulged to anyone, even Sam, that tempestuous saga that had shaken her parents' marriage. She hadn't lied; her mother *did* die when she was too young to know much about it.

"Well—" he looked at the broad-strapped watch circling his hair-sprinkled wrist "—I should get moving, I'm—"

"I know," she pushed in quickly, afraid that he might think she was angling to keep him here with her, "Marie's asked me to have dinner with them, too."

"Fine." He seemed neither glad nor sorry to know that they were to spend another evening in each other's company. "I'll pick you up just after seven; we might as well arrive together." He moved to the turntable and picked up the record she had been playing, then turned to say, holding it in the air, "Did you want to keep this to practice your dancing?"

Her eyes dropped away from the sardonic gleam in his. "No, I—no. I'm not in the habit of dancing by myself." She looked up then and her heart jerked and adjusted to a faster pace when she saw him put down the record without looking behind him and advance toward her, a strange light changing his eyes to opaque silver.

"Pity," he said softly, pausing just inches from her and lifting a hand to brush away a silk strand of hair from her temple. His fingers then trailed lightly down her cheek and his thumb traced the full contours of her mouth. "It's the first time I've seen you really relaxed. You act as if you've put yourself into voluntary cold storage since your husband died, and that's too bad, because a few minutes ago I saw that under that icy exterior there's a very. . . warm woman.''

Denise had frozen at his touch, but now she pulled violently away from it. "What I have or haven't done since Sam's death has nothing to do with you," she snapped, her voice like chipped ice. "You might as well know right now, Dr. Barstow, that I'm not in the market for a cheap kind of affair you men seem to think widowed women need. I'm perfectly happy the way I am."

"Are you? The message I got last night was that you'd made up your mind to freeze out a very important part of your life. My God, how old are you? Twenty-four, twenty-five? Are you planning to spend the rest of your life denying the needs of your body?''

"I'm twenty-six, and my needs are adequately cared for," she said, hating the ragged edges in her voice and hating him for his brash assumption that a suitably equipped male could solve all her problems—the physical ones, at least.

"Are they?''

She was unprepared for the deliberate outreach of his hand, its sliding descent from pulsing throat to perfumed valley where she still clutched at her robe. Her fingers fell nervelessly away as his hand nudged insistently against them, and then he was pushing beneath the thick terry to the globed softness of her breast, seeking and finding the nipple that hardened under his fingers.

Shocked, wondering, absorbed in the sensations his abrasive fingers were arousing in her sensitive skin, she was only half aware of his other hand tugging aside the tie of her robe, the exposure of her nakedness to the harsher texture of his clothes. Warmth swelled and rushed and cascaded through her veins and left her clutching convulsively to his hard shoulders as he lowered her to the cushioned softness of the couch.

"No, please—no," she moaned, twisting away from the looming descent of his head, the passionate curve of his lips. "Don't—"

The agonized echo of her plea lingered in the air around them as he bent, his body heavy against hers, to press the fiery warmth of his mouth to the honeyed sweep of her cheekbone, the fluttering pulse at the hollow of her throat.

"Don't?" His mouth brushed over the trembling parting of her lips. "Is it so hard for you to admit that you want it as much as I do?" he said huskily, shifting downward on her body until there was access to the swollen rise of her breasts that gleamed whitely where a bikini top had always covered. "That you want this—" His mouth traced the darkened pink surrounding an upthrusting nipple, then fastened over it in moist possession, the abrasion of his tongue evoking painful sensations that tautened the deep muscles in her thighs. "And this—" His lips moved up in an invisible line of deliberate sensuality to the shallow depression of her throat. "And this—"

His head lifted and paused so that she caught the gleam of silver in his eyes before he groaned and bent his lips to engulf hers.

Her body stiffened and then grew passive under his heavy weight as it pressed her into the cushions. In a dispassionate way she felt the deep, unsteady rhythm of his heart against her crushed breasts, the downward slide of his hands to cup her hips, the nudge of his knee at her thighs, and she knew that Jake was as capable of taking forcibly as any other man.

Then suddenly his head lifted, the tension easing from his body as he stared narrow eyed down at her. His nostrils flared as breath was snatched into them.

"I really don't turn you on, do I? It's like making love to a rag doll." The muscles of his arms tensed as he pressed down on the couch to raise himself. "And that," he said, standing over her and buttoning the steel gray of his shirt over the dark growth of chest hair, "is something that doesn't happen too often with me." The arrogance of his statement was lessened by the note of genuine curiosity in his voice. "Sam must have been one hell of a lover if you can't stand to have another man touch you two years after his death."

Denise said nothing. Instead, she pulled the edges of her robe around her and sat up, swinging her long legs to the floor and beginning to stand when a loud rap at the outer door froze her in a half-bent position, her eyes flying to Jake's. His head turned unhurriedly in the direction of the door, his lips tightening when Toby's voice came with the next knock.

"Denise? Are you home?"

Galvanized into action, she leaped to her feet, clutching the robe to her as she said wildly, "He can't come in! I—"

"I'll get rid of him," Jake said calmly, and smoothed back his thick, ruffled hair with both hands.

"But what will he think?" she whispered fierce-ly, oddly more panicked now than she had been under Jake's assault.

"Does it matter?" He shrugged. His lean figure moved to the record he had put down on the turn-table. "I came to collect my albums, remember?"

His concern was so minimal that Denise won-dered, as she fled into the bathroom, how many irate husbands had come home to find him mak-ing love to their wives.

Glad that she could hear only the murmur of voices from her hiding place, and soon after that silence, she turned on the shower and stepped under it after discarding her robe, forgetting that she had already bathed in preparation for the Steins' dinner. But that didn't matter, she shrugged, rubbing up a soapy lather all over her body, then rinsing it from her with the hottest water her skin would stand. She wanted to scrub the feel, the smell, of Jake Barstow from her.

The passion she had held in check while he

made love to her was released in a violent reaction
of hatred now. The pleasure she had initially felt
in being here was dissipated because of Jake. The
traumas of her marriage, which she had thought
might grow less in this beautiful place, had been
forcibly reborn in her memory because of Jake.
And because of him she would have to leave here;
to stay would invite other episodes like this afternoon's, and sooner or later Jake would know that
the reason for her coldness wasn't a continuing
passion for the husband who had died. And she
couldn't bear for him, of all people, to know
that truth about her. Sam had ground her pride
into the dust; she wasn't about to allow Jake
Barstow the same privilege.

But what finally brought the tears as the water
cascaded over the firm uptilt of her breasts was the
knowledge that for one fleeting moment, at the pit
of her stomach, Jake's lovemaking had provoked
a grinding need for fulfillment. The same fulfillment she had believed Sam would provide. It was,
she thought miserably, a cruel irony of fate.

CHAPTER FOUR

THE SUN WAS ALREADY EDGING ITS WAY down the sky when Denise stepped from her cottage and made her way along the beach to the Steins'. She was unforgivably early, but the thought of another solo encounter with the research chief was more than she could stand.

She had been of two minds whether to come at all, but the speculation her absence would have caused would amount to more trouble in the end.

A frazzled Marie came from the bedroom passage at the back of the house to let her in. To Denise's apology she waved a dismissing hand. "I'd still have been a mess if you'd come half an hour later," she said hurriedly. "Wouldn't you know, Cindy's acting up like crazy because she wanted to be around when you and Jake arrived. As you can see, I'm not even changed yet." She eyed Denise's tan shift dress that covered her shoulders and left her arms bare. "You look unbearably fresh and cool," she said without rancor.

"Is there anything I can do?" Denise offered, hoping that if Marie accepted it wouldn't be in the kitchen area. Her knowledge of cooking extended only as far as making a reasonable pot of coffee in an electric percolator.

"Well—" Marie hesitated. "Maybe if you could go in and see Cindy for a few minutes it would keep her happy. I'd like to be dressed when Jake comes."

Following her along the passage to the small bedroom at its far end, Denise wondered with a touch of wryness what the other woman's reaction would have been to know that Jake had lain on her own naked body not two hours before. But maybe that news wouldn't come as any surprise to Marie, who seemingly knew him well.

A small tousled head dived under the covers of a single bed as they went into the room, and Marie twitched them back with an impatient hand.

"Denise has come to see you, so don't act silly. Come on, up you get." With the expertise of long experience, she hauled the wriggling body into a sitting position and ran tidying hands over the rioting hair.

Denise felt helplessness wash over when she was left alone with the bright-eyed child. She had had even less contact with children than with cooking and suspected that Cindy saw shrewdly through her awkward efforts to appear at ease.

"Do you have a little girl?"

The suddenness of the question took Denise by surprise, but she answered with spontaneous regret, "No, I'm afraid not."

"A little boy?"

"Not one of those, either," she said lightly, then glanced around the prettily decorated
room with its white furniture and bookcase
stuffed with cuddly soft toys and haphazardly
piled books.

"Would you like me to read you a story?" It
would be one way of stemming the flow of intimate questions she could see forming behind the
dancing brown eyes.

Obviously deciding after a moment's hesitation
that her visitor would stay longer if she agreed to a
story, the curly head nodded vigorously and the
book with the longest story was selected from the
pile Denise fetched from the bookcase.

"You don't read like mommy," the scornful
voice piped after a scant half page.

"That's because mommies read stories best of
all," Denise told her with a firm calmness that surprised her and sent Cindy back against her pillow,
where she lay looking up at Denise speculatively as
she continued with the story.

Minutes later the heavy eyelids were drooping
despite their owner's efforts to force them open,
and Denise continued to sit beside her, a strangely
tender feeling forming a regretful ball in her chest
for the child she herself would never have. Her
hand stroked lightly across the tumbled hair on
Cindy's brow. Would a baby have made her marriage to Sam more bearable? She sighed. She
would never know.

A sixth sense made her look up, and she gasped

when she saw Jake leaning casually against the door frame. How long had he been there? She felt exposed, vulnerable, as he pushed away from the door and came softly across to the bed. His eyes held a special kind of tenderness as he looked down at the sleeping Cindy, and Denise remembered suddenly that he had a daughter of his own. Meg.

A shocking thrill ran through her when the gray eyes lifted and met hers, seeming to darken as they hardened.

"Marie sent me to get you," he said quietly. "She's about to serve the appetizer."

For several long-drawn-out moments his eyes seemed to hold her hypnotically while questions raced through her head. Did the pinpoint glitter at the back of the gray signify scorn? Anger? Or, worst of all, pity? Not knowing if it was any or all of those things, Denise dropped her eyes and got to her feet after a last glance at the sleeping Cindy.

"You're a born mother," Marie said exuberantly as she handed Denise and then Jake each a small plate and two-pronged fork in the living room, waving them to seats as Paul appeared with a serving dish piled high with long and tender asparagus spears. "Thanks, darling. Can you believe Denise had Cindy asleep within minutes of going in there?"

"The magic touch," Paul grinned, and held the dish low for Denise to help herself to the succulent spears. "We know where to come for a babysitter in future."

Denise laughed, embarrassed, as she made her selection. "I think it was the sheer monotony of my voice that made her blank out. She'd already made it clear that I didn't come anywhere near her mother's excellent reading ability."

"Let me get that, honey—" Marie took the dish from Paul's hand "—while you pour the martinis." Bent over Jake, she laughed wryly. "We're doing everything back to front tonight, but these should be eaten as soon as they're ready."

"They're delicious," Denise said, savoring the flavored spears with growing appreciation. "How in the world did you do them?"

"They're Paul's specialty, so I'll let him tell you."

"Nothing to it," he deprecated, coming back from the dining area buffet with two wide-mouthed glasses, handing one to Denise and the other to Marie. "A little butter, lemon, garlic and only enough cooking time to tenderize the asparagus."

"When are you planning to give up oceanography and open your first gourmet restaurant?" Jake put in, jokingly relaxed.

"As soon as I can persuade you guys to send all your exotic fish specimens to me for my discriminating clients."

"Considering your limited repertoire," scoffed Marie, "I doubt if you'd earn enough to keep your own body and soul together, let alone a family's.''

Denise felt the tension almost palpably disappear from her body as the lighthearted badinage continued through another cocktail and the American-style dinner, which Marie had cooked, that followed. She even found herself laughing across the table into Jake's eyes a few times, and it was as if the scene between them that afternoon had never taken place. As the sizable beef roast, accompanied by jacket potatoes, string beans and sweet corn gave way to cinnamon-apple pie, she could almost imagine that they were two married couples enjoying each other's company. The kind of compatibility with good friends she had always dreamed about in connection with a faceless husband when the sterile, gloomy atmosphere of her father's house had lain too heavily on her.

It was later, while the men smoked aromatic cigars over their coffee, that dissension crept into the group. Denise, her eyes straying to the unusual sight of gray eyes narrowing against grayer smoke, only belatedly realized that a silence had fallen over the group. Marie set her coffee cup down with a distinct clatter. Her voice was quiet by contrast.

"If you're thinking of asking Paul to go with you to Sri Lanka, Jake, please don't.''

"Now, honey—''

"That would be Paul's decision, wouldn't it?''

"Not entirely. He's been promised a job at Scripps when he's through here in a few months, and we've made up our minds to accept." Her eyes pointedly ignored Paul as she gazed steadily across the table at the other man. "We've waited a long time to be a complete family again, Jake, and I don't want you putting other ideas in Paul's head right now."

"Marie, you're embarrassing me," Paul said with unusual vehemence. "Jake hasn't even asked me to go, for Pete's sake!"

"But you were going to, weren't you, Jake?"

"I'd thought of it," he admitted, flicking the rounded ash from his cigar. He looked at Paul. "It would only have to be a six-month stint for you, but if Scripps won't delay your appointment there—"

Paul glared at his agitated wife. "I don't know what they'd agree to. If it was just a question of months—"

"No!" Marie was close to tears, and Denise intervened by getting to her feet and collecting the dishes from the table.

"Why don't you think about it while we clean up?" she suggested soothingly, and Marie, her lips pressed tightly together, nodded a mute assent.

"I wish Jake had never come here," she said in a tense half whisper, leaning over the sink and grasping its edges as if in pain. "He's like the Pied Piper where Paul's concerned."

"Paul loves you." Denise began to stack the

scattered dishes. "He won't do anything to jeopardize your happiness."

"Hmm. He loves his work, too, and a chance like this doesn't come too often." Marie's fine-boned hand squeezed liquid from a plastic bottle into the sink and turned on the tap. "I know it must seem to you—and Jake—as if I'm being plain bitchy, but David isn't happy at school, and we just have to get back together as a family." She brushed the free-falling tears from her cheeks and dumped cutlery and dishes into the sink. "I'm sorry, Denise. I'm spoiling what started out to be a lovely evening."

While Denise murmured words of comfort, an anger that wasn't entirely illogical filled her. Jake had spoiled this island for her, and now he was coming between this beautifully compatible couple.

But, as Marie had said, the lovely evening had been spoiled and not long after the dishes were put away she made her excuses and prepared to leave. Dismayed, she saw Jake unwind his long form from an armchair and come to join her at the door.

"I'd better turn in, too, if we want to make an early start in the morning."

"What?" She had completely forgotten his offer to take her diving the next day.

"I've arranged for Henry Thomas to take us out at seven," he said smoothly. "Is that too early for you?"

"No. No, that's fine." She forced a smile, but as soon as Jake fell in step with her on the powdery sand beach, she said in a low, furious tone, "You're out of your mind if you think I'm going diving with you tomorrow."

"Oh? I had the impression that you were...disappointed at being left out of this morning's trip."

"You know what I mean." She stumbled in the deep sand and flinched when his arm shot out to steady her. "After what happened this afternoon, I—"

"After what happened this afternoon," he said dryly, removing his arm from her waist, "I can assure you that you're safer with me than with any other member of the team. I got your message loud and clear. It's strictly business from now on."

The withering words fell like autumn leaves in another hemisphere, out of context with the soft play of moonlight on glass-smooth waters. She should have been glad—she *was* glad—that his statement released her from her earlier promise to herself that she would leave the island. And yet....

THE WATER WAS SILKY, warm, caressing to her skin after her backward dive from the boat. The irritation she had felt when Jake, with the fussiness of an old woman, she thought, had checked every item of her diving gear, dissipated in the wondrous new world that opened up to her with the flip of her finned foot.

They were just outside the coral reef that almost enclosed the bay. As her eyes greedily darted from sinuously waving sea grasses to exotically colored fish that wended their sporadic way through the spiny thrust of staghorn coral, she was only dimly aware of Jake on the periphery of her vision. A spiny lobster ambled warily past the deceptively inviting sea anemone and disappeared into a rocky crevice. A ray undulated across the sandy bottom, throwing up a mist of particles that obscured its passage to the covering of valleyed rocks and swaying vegetation.

It was a world of color, of symmetry, that she was reluctant to leave. Regretting her human need for life-giving air, she surfaced and submerged many more times before Jake touched her arm and indicated a rise with one upward pointing thumb.

"What's the rush?" she spluttered on the surface, still half lost in the underwater world and the reality of the low-sided boat where an impassive-faced Henry awaited them.

Jake, who had surfaced alongside her, detached the mouthpiece of his snorkel and trod water as he said, "Time for lunch and a rest."

Denise would have liked to spend another half hour investigating the shallow depths surrounding them, but she admitted to herself as she climbed the rope ladder into the boat that she was tiring.

Besides that, she was hungry; breakfast was only a dim memory in her mind as she slid off her flippers and mask and watched Jake do the same before he led the way to the foredeck where Henry was waiting with lunch: ice-cold orange juice and sandwiches made of fresh bread and ham, supplemented by crisp green lettuce. Perched on the narrow ledge surrounding the gunwales, Denise devoured the sandwiches with an appetite born of sea breezes and a morning of excitement in a world she loved.

"It's fabulous down there," she broke into the silence that had enveloped the three while they ate. She looked down into the incredible clarity of water where the undersea life went unconcernedly about its business. "I saw a ray, a spiny lobster, and—oh, a hundred different species I've never seen in their natural surroundings before."

Both men smiled tolerantly at her childlike enthusiasm, the lines around Jake's eyes deepening as he turned his head into the sun.

"Wait till we get out in deeper water," he said lazily. "I'm looking forward to it myself. Last time I dived in these waters we had no spheres or subs to get down to the bottom. Now we'll be able to spend the time below more profitably."

"Checking on contamination from the recent oil spills?"

He nodded. "That and the usual survey work—

currents, temperatures and so on. You'll mainly be involved with the pollution angle, of course."

Henry, sensing that the conversation was turning exclusively to shoptalk, unobtrusively took himself to the cabin area and disappeared quietly inside.

"I had a look at the lab yesterday," Denise said, her mouth firming as she recalled its less than professional state. "It's not exactly a biologist's dream!"

Jake looked at her appraisingly. "Most of the samples until now have been sent to the mainland for analysis."

"Which makes me an overqualified middleman," she retorted tartly, and saw his eyes drop to the curved swell of breasts barely concealed by her bikini top.

"I wouldn't have described you in those terms," he said, voice pitched to a sudden low huskiness that set off a warning bell in her head and sent her to her feet.

"I want to go down again," she said hurriedly, hating the quickened catch in her voice, knowing that he would interpret it in his own way.

"The only place you're going down is on the deck—with me." His hand reached up and clasped her wrist, his fingers widening as they stroked up her arm and tautened again above her elbow. "You must know that a rest is the order of the day after a meal."

"Then I'll sit here or use one of the cabin bunks."

A sardonic smile quirked the corners of his lips. "If Henry's the sensible man I think he is, he's already asleep down there. And while he might find no objection to a nearly naked female sleeping in the opposite bunk, his wife would likely look on it in a different light. As for staying here—" he squinted up at the midday sun beating forcefully down on them "—you'd be burned to a frazzle in no time. So you see, Mrs. Faithful, you have no choice but to join me under that crude but adequate sun shelter on the afterdeck."

Denise's eyes went to the crudely erected tarpaulin shelter, knowing the truth of what he said. Already her shoulders were burning, despite her tan, in the fierce noonday heat. Shrugging, she followed him to the small afterdeck and watched with cool eyes as he pulled two biscuit-thin mattresses from the storage locker beside the cabin entrance and arranged them side by side on the weathered boards of the deck. The shaded area was too confined to permit wider spacing, so she settled herself stiffly in a prone position, doing her best to ignore him as he lowered himself with a sigh beside her, long legs spread the width of the narrow mattress.

There was only the faint slap of water against the boat for noise, the gentle rise and fall for movement, and Denise let her body relax from its tautly held pose. He would hardly attack her within screaming sound of Henry Thomas.

It was warm, even out of the fierce rays of the sun, and her voice was drowsy when she said without knowing she was going to speak, "What does 'Mrs. Faithful' mean?"

She sensed his stirring from the stupor that was beginning to envelop both of them. She turned her head and saw that his eyes were closed. Without opening them, he smiled dryly and quoted sleepily, "A woman faithful unto death—and beyond, in your case."

"Is that wrong?"

"No. Just unusual."

His lips closed again over the strong white teeth and in the next second he was asleep. The arms he had crossed over his chest rose and fell with the deep regularity of his breathing, and Denise's eyes went with curious fascination over the hawklike strength of his profile, the thick hair that had dried after his dive and left strands falling across his forehead. That, and the relaxing of the deeply gouged lines beside his mouth, made it much easier to imagine him as the young man he once was, laughing, virile, handsome. The way he must have been when he had married...Barbara, that was his wife's name. According to Marie, a beautiful and bad Barbara who still held him in the thralls of love.

Her eyes went lower to the powerful lean line of his throat, the sweat-dampened hair between flat male nipples, the muscled flatness of his stomach, the masculinity revealed by the rust-colored swim shorts, the sinewy strength of his long legs.

His ex-wife must have been crazy not to hold on to him. The involuntary thought shocked her into turning her head back to where vapory clouds drifted lazily across the azure sky. How many people would have condemned her as being crazy if they had known how she had frozen at the first touch of Sam's heavy hands? Other women had found him attractive physically in a way she never could.

Jake's bronzed arm dropped to his side and clung to the sticky warmth of hers. Lethargic, she let it stay there.

IT TOOK EFFORT to lift a hand and brush away the insect tracing a path across her skin. Denise frowned irritably when it descended again immediately to pester her into full wakefulness.

Her eyes opened in a green haze to meet the silvered gleam in Jake's. "What are you doing?" she murmured, still sleepily immersed in a half-remembered dream of diving into waters deeper than she had ever known. It had been dark down there, her vision obscured by some swirling disturbance on the ocean floor. A man in an iridescent silver diving suit kept appearing through the curtain of sand particles to smile and beckon to her, disappearing tantalizingly before she had made up her mind to follow. In the way of dreams, she knew that he was responsible for the underwater chaos, yet he alone could lead her to the light and color waiting ahead.

"I'm waking you up before you push me completely off the mattress." His voice broke into her remembered fantasy and her eyes snapped open. "And I have no masochistic tendency to roast myself alive on the deck."

His head was so close to hers that his breath played warmly against her mouth. And not only that; her arm was wound so tightly around him that her body seemed glued to his from breast to thigh. Embarrassment swept through her in a sickly wave, and she pulled back, rolling onto her own mattress and turning her hot face away from him.

"I...I'm sorry," she whispered, drowning in her own misery. "I didn't know—" His fingers tightened like pincers around her chin and turned her back to the angry glitter in his eyes.

"For God's sake," he said roughly, "don't apologize for wanting human closeness, even if it's only in your sleep. All it signifies is that you can't live forever on memories of a dead man. Sooner or later you're going to have to admit that you have needs that can't be satisfied by stale memories of what went on in your life years ago. You're young and you're beautiful—too young and too beautiful to waste yourself on misguided loyalty."

"It isn't like that," she gasped, struggling vainly to free herself from his paralyzing grip. "You don't understand."

"Damn right I understand," he tossed back grimly. "Don't you think we all have to make adjustments when the partner we want isn't available to us?"

She blinked. He was referring to Barbara, the ex-wife he still loved. The one who had borne his child.

"It was different with Sam and me. We—"

"I don't want to hear about Sam," he cut in, adding with cruel precision, "he's dead, and he's going to stay dead. He's never going to hold you in his arms and make love to you again." Misinterpreting the shudder that ran through her body, he thrust his own against her so that she felt the surging maleness of him, the warm sticky heat of him. Hysteria bubbled up in her and threatened to destroy her dignity. If only he knew that Sam's death had been her release from the unmentionable horror of his lovemaking!

Then Jake's mouth was on her mouth, ravaging, forcing, biting in its pressure. His long-fingered hand, showing dark against her lighter tan, slid slickly over her moist skin and cupped her breast, searing its warmth through the flimsy nylon. Her hands pushed a soft protest against the springy dampness of his chest hair, but she was incapable of any real rejection. Waves of faintness came and went as the suffocating pressure of his mouth went on and on, but she was aware of a hardened nipple under the sensuous stroke of his fingertips, the sensations that spread from there to the female core of her and raised her hips to the hands molding them.

Her chest rose and fell rapidly as breath tore through her lungs when at last his head lifted. His face swam into her vision, blurred at the edges, so close that their breathing mingled. His eyes were a cool gray talisman that her own clung to in question and fear.

"I wasn't wrong, was I?" His husky tone betrayed his own arousal to passion, and she could feel his heart's deep beat in her own flesh, but she sensed, too, a controlled detachment as he bent deliberately to nudge against the thin covering over her breast and take the hard tip between his teeth. Her own teeth clamped down on her lip, and she moaned when the sensations he aroused flicked her into an explosive, wrenching response.

"Don't—don't, please—"

"You don't mean that." His mouth, moist from its laving of her breast, was at her ear now, his tongue darting sensuously into it so that she shuddered under him. "I could take you now, and you wouldn't do anything to stop me." His lips took on a languorous slowness as they kissed a shivering trail over her skin.

"We—we don't love each other," she gasped, lifting a nerveless hand to push against the dark blue shadow of his jaw. Her palm tingled and fell still.

"Love has nothing to do with it," he murmured at the jumping pulse in her throat. "You're a beautiful and desirable woman—too beautiful and desirable to sacrifice yourself on your husband's pyre."

A splash from the side of the boat brought his head into a watchful pose and reminded Denise shatteringly of Henry's presence on the boat. Giant waves of humiliation rolled over her and lent strength to the arms she now raised to push Jake up and away from her.

"Henry!" she gasped, struggling to sit upright, snatching at the lowered scrap of fabric under her bared breast. "He must have seen—" The crewman must have seen them, as there was only one way out from the cabin.

"Henry's a sensible man, and he seems a discreet type to me," Jake said unconcernedly. Propped lazily on one elbow, gray eyes amused under raised brows, he was a personification of all the sophisticated, arrogantly sure men she had ever read or heard of.

"Why don't you leave me alone?" she said fiercely, getting to her feet. Her eyes searched for Henry in the water and saw the brown limbs cleaving it some distance from the boat. "Can't you get it into your thick head that I'm not interested in your kind of animal coupling?"

"You were a minute ago," he pointed out with

maddening logic. He unwound his long form from the mattress, dwarfing her five-foot-six frame as he came to stand beside her. "Look, it's fine with me if you want to bury your light under a bushel. It just seemed to me that it was a shame to waste a good-looking woman. But if that's the way you want it—" he paused, the only sign of his anger a throbbing pulse at his temple. "—I won't waste my time."

"Who asked you to?" The words tore from her throat, words born partly of a basic female rejection of his male condescension, but mostly churned up from her own conflicting emotions. Not waiting for his answer, she ran to the low rail and mounted it, pausing for only a brief moment before diving into the clear green water without benefit of mask or fins. All she wanted to do was to put space between herself and the menacing figure of Jake Barstow.

She had handled the incident stupidly, like a teenager frightened out of her virginal mind by a date who came on too strong. But she wasn't a teenager. She was twenty-six and no innocent where men's sexual appetites were concerned. So why did Jake's lovemaking affect her the way it did? Was she flattered that a man as worldly-wise as he should find her attractive, desirable?

Surfacing, she wiped the velvet cling of water from her eyes and pushed back the sodden hair from her brow. Fifty yards away, Jake's figure was a blur as he moved about the deck. Henry's brown limbs ascended the ladder, pausing near the top rung as he listened to something Jake said. Then he was flipping over backward into the water, streaking in her direction with long, even strokes.

"Dr. Barstow wants to get back now," he gasped, coming up two yards away from her. "Are you all right?"

She nodded. "Yes, I—I'm on my way." She waited until he had completed a reverse flip that sent him streaking back in the direction of the boat before she struck out herself. There had been nothing to suggest it in his concerned query, but he must surely have his own ideas about what he must have seen on the deck before he had taken that dive from the side of the boat.

Drat Jake Barstow! It would be all over the station by nightfall that the new member of the team wasn't at all averse to amorous side play. And nothing could be further from the truth, she reminded herself silently as she clambered up the short ladder and accepted Henry's hand to help her aboard. Her body might respond—had responded—to Jake's arousal technique; it was another matter entirely to unblock the barriers Sam had discovered in her psyche.

THAT NIGHT CARL MADSEN JOINED HER at her solitary dinner table in the clubhouse. They were the only two dining there, it seemed, so it would have been churlishly antisocial to refuse his politely worded request to sit at her window-side table.

"You look very charming," he complimented in his faintly stilted accent. "I am surprised to find you here. Usually I am the only one who eats at the clubhouse on Sunday."

"That must account for the flurry in the kitchen when I arrived." She smiled. Her eyes had taken on a jade gleam from the sleeveless shirt dress she was wearing. "Where is everybody?"

He shrugged and adjusted the alignment of the cutlery hastily set by Philomena's daughter, Tess. "They go to the hotel close by to play golf, then they stay over for dinner."

"But you don't?" she quizzed, allowing her eyes to rove over his correctly brushed fair hair and Prussian blue eyes set in a tan as light as her own.

"Golfing was not one of the pursuits considered necessary for development in my country," he said with a deprecating smile.

"And your country is—?"

"Poland. We were encouraged to excel in the academic sphere, not the decadent Western pastimes of golf and tennis—unless, of course, we showed promise of ability to beat the West in those areas." His thin lips twisted in a sardonic smile.

"Oh." Denise leaned back when Tess arrived with the first course of thick conch chowder, a meal in itself. "How did you come to choose a career in marine sciences? Poland doesn't have direct access to the sea, does it?"

"No. But my specialty was mathematics, and when I came to the United States some years ago on an international congress, I decided to stay."

"You're a defector, then?" Denise asked, wide-eyed. She had never before met someone who had left the ties of home and country to start life anew in an alien land.

"I suppose so, yes."

"But what about your family? Don't you miss them?"

"The only family left to me are remote cousins who meant even less to me then than they do now," he said with chilling unconcern as he tackled the peppery chowder.

Denise plied her spoon more slowly. Her own life had been so devoid of relatives, even remote cousins, that she found it hard to believe that someone else could treat them so lightly.

"But marine science? What made you choose that?"

"Like most people brought up in an inland country, the sea fascinated me." He shrugged again. "When the choice was presented to me, I took the marine science."

"And now you've made it," Denise said admiringly, replacing her spoon in the emptied bowl. Carl's story fascinated her, partly because of his unusual background, but mostly because there were no sexual overtones to the conversation, as there would have been with Jake or Toby, the other two unmarried men on the project.

"Perhaps. Although judging by the appointment of Dr. Barstow to replace Dr. Shepherd, I have not progressed as far as I might have wished."

"I'm sure there was nothing derogatory meant to you by Jake's appointment," she said after a palpable pause. "He—Jake—is all set to head a team researching off Sri Lanka next spring."

"By which time they will have found a more permanent replacement among the hundreds of American-born scientists," Carl observed dryly, accepting unsmilingly the golden fried chicken surrounded by buttered corn niblets and sautéed potato slices that Tess set before him.

"I think you're wrong," Denise protested, disturbed that Carl should harbor suspicions regarding the American government's choice of key personnel for what was virtually an international distribution center of scientific information. "They probably didn't know what to do with a highly qualified man like Jake Barstow until he leaves for the Sri Lanka project."

"Maybe so," Carl conceded, changing the subject so rapidly that Denise was left blinking. "I heard that you had brought a stereo system—are you interested in music?"

From the reverential way he spoke the word,

Denise knew immediately that her choice of music would not be his. Jake's would probably be more in his line.

"I have my own favorites," she smiled deprecatingly. "Mood music, very light classics. Nothing a classical music lover would be interested in."

"Oh." Carl seemed disappointed. "I asked because I belong to a music society in Nassau. We meet once a week, and new members are very welcome."

"Dr. Barstow might be interested, then," she said, tongue in cheek, knowing instinctively that Jake wasn't the type to join any society, even one specializing in the deep classics he obviously cared for.

"Really?" Carl frowned, then added without enthusiasm, "I must ask if he would like to join us."

The simple dessert of tropical fruit was followed by coffee of the same delicious flavor of last night's. While Carl lighted a Turkish-smelling cigarette, Denise glanced over to the kitchen servery where Philomena's stout figure in garishly colored loose dress was still visible.

"Doesn't Philomena have days off? With so many people away, I'd have thought Sunday would be a good day for it."

"Officially it is her day off." Carl shrugged, narrowing his blue eyes against the spiral of pungent gray smoke. "But she lives here with her daughter at the other side of the kitchen area, and she seems content to stay around here most of the time. In any case, there is little for her to do when the team goes off in the research vessel. We are gone for one, sometimes two weeks.''

"I'm looking forward to my first trip." Denise shyly smiled her enthusiasm, a sparkle lighting the green of her eyes to a translucent glow as she looked at Carl across the table. His hand paused fractionally in its upward motion with his coffee cup, and he stared back at her intently, his eyes seeming to shade to a darker blue.

Denise dropped her lashes in a protective screen, an unaccountable shiver bringing out goose pimples on her arms. Why had she thought of him as a somehow sexless kind of man? Because of the coldly aloof front he had presented so far? But the picture she had fleetingly caught at the back of his eyes had been far from emotionless. Then he spoke in his normal, precise way and she mocked herself for being fanciful. Jake Barstow had done a thorough job of alerting her to danger where none existed!

"You must surely have dived before in a sub?"

"Yes, of course." She forced her gaze up to his again and found his eyes only politely inquiring. "But not very much. My work was mainly confined to the lab. That's one reason why I wanted to come here, to be more directly involved. Though," she added with a wry smile, "I seem to have gone from one extreme to the other. Lab facilities here seem to be nonexistent.''

He nodded. ''Yes. All I have been able to do was to forward the specimens to the mainland, and by the time the results filter back here, one's interest has waned more than a little.''

Denise's eyes widened in surprise. ''You? But I thought you were a—''

''I am interested in all branches of oceanography.'' He smiled slightly. ''Particularly in the biological sciences. For instance, I find the study of the larger mammals fascinating—particularly the habits of predatory creatures like the great white shark and killer whales. Do they really kill?'' He raised his brows in amused speculation.

''The great white shark certainly does, but,'' she mused, ''I'm not so sure about the killer whale. I have a sneaking suspicion that he may have been misnamed. There's a lot of folklore about him, of course, and I doubt if I'd want to put my theory to the test. We really don't know enough about him yet.''

''There are many things, are there not, that you know nothing about?'' he pursued, showing no sign that he was aware of the double-edged nature of his question. ''The tuna, for example. Does he or does he not sleep?''

Denise laughed. ''We don't know for sure if, when or how he sleeps. That's one of the problems that makes marine biology interesting. Strangely, we've been discovering lately that to find out more about the larger forms of marine life we're having to go back to where the chain of life starts, with the plankton.''

She was amazed at the extent of Carl's knowledge of biology as they chatted, smiling abstractedly at Tess when she sauntered across to fill their coffee cups twice more. The thought she had entertained the day before about leaving the project dissipated under the stimulus of Carl's knowledgeable interest in her own branch of oceanography, and the time flew past on gossamer wings until she glanced at her watch and saw that it was after nine.

"We really must go and let Philomena get cleared away,'' she said with a guilty glance in the direction of the kitchen, where the cook was clearing things away.

Carl rose politely. "I will see you back to your cottage.'' His brows rose when she felt the necessity to call her thanks to Philomena, who grinned and waved from the serving hatch.

Moonlight streaked the beach as they walked along to the cottage colony, and cicadas were well into their nightly unmusical serenade. For a moment or two Denise remembered the other figure who had walked with her along this beach, the tension between them with even the smallest exchange of conversation, and then she dismissed the remembrance from her mind. She was relaxed in Carl's company, finding the meeting of minds more to her taste than the physical entanglement

that seemed the inevitable outcome of her en-
counters with Jake. When Carl halted opposite the
cottage he shared with Toby and asked her in for a
nightcap and a sampling of his music, she hesitated for only a moment.

"I'd like to, thanks," she told him, the moon
reflecting silver strands in her eyes, "but not
for too long. I want to be ready for that first
trip."

Carl's hand reached out impersonally to help
her across the deeper, more powdery sand. "With
so many arrangements to be made, I doubt if a
survey could get under way much before Tuesday,
but certainly I will not keep you for long."

The cottage he ushered her into was larger than
hers, extending to a second bedroom and an effi-
ciency kitchen that had the pristine appearance of
disuse, yet the living-room area was of about the
same size with the same amount of furnishings.
Carl's stereo system was much more sophisticated
than her own and took up almost the entire space
under what had obviously been intended as a
breakfast bar between living room and kitchen.

"Please sit down." Carl indicated the seating
area with its well-worn, rust-colored upholstery.
Books and magazines were strewn haphazardly
across the sofa along one wall and overflowing
from the side tables and coffee tables. Denise
chose a separate armchair flanking the window
and noted the titles of some of the magazines
spread out on the small round table between the

two window-side armchairs. It needed only half an eye to see that this was strictly a bachelor apartment.

"The magazines are Toby's," Carl said, as if picking up on her thoughts, waving a derogatory arm that encompassed the girlie poses confronting her. "He tolerates my music, and I put up with his decadent taste in literature." Seeming relieved to change the subject, he asked, "What would you like to drink? Scotch, brandy, gin, vodka...."

Surprised by the extent of his bar, Denise opted for vodka and orange juice and looked speculatively at his trimly set figure as he busied himself at refrigerator and cupboard housing the wide array of spirits. At an age when most men would have been in the middle stages of marriage, he was unattached. Was he another casualty in the marriage stakes, like Jake? Had he decided to live a solitary life apart from the odd foray into the world of earthly sensuality? Somehow she thought not, as she accepted the tumbler glass of vodka-flavored orange juice. Carl had the air of a self-sufficient man who had no need for the softening influence of a woman.

"What would you like to hear?" he asked, turning to the elaborate stereo system.

"Whatever you'd like to play." Denise shrugged, feeling relaxed yet somewhat uncomfortable as plaintive piano notes filled the room. Carl's interest in music far surpassed her own, she reflected, conscious of his rapt air of attention as he settled into the chair opposite hers and gave every appearance of having forgotten her presence. Perhaps music was a substitute for friends in his life; judging from the comments of the others, he was far from popular with the team members.

She glanced at her watch and stood up as soon as the lingering notes had died away. "I really have to be going. Thanks for the drink and—" she hesitated "—I enjoyed our conversation earlier."

"But not the music, hmm?" He gave a stiff smile. "I have enjoyed the evening in your company. Perhaps we can do it again soon?"

Not wanting to commit herself, and having that uncomfortable feeling again, she gave him a perfunctory smile and moved to the door. "I mean to see as much as possible of the islands while I'm here, so I'll probably spend most of my free time wandering around."

As if being turned down was a well-known occurrence to him, he gave a little bow from the waist that looked quaintly European and leaned past her to open the door. "I will see you to your cottage."

"There's no need," Denise said quickly, and stepped past his lightly tanned arm. "It's only a couple of steps."

To her relief he didn't insist, and in fact had already gone back in when she glanced back from the beach. Had she offended him by leaving so soon and refusing his offer of walking her home? Shrugging in irritation, she slid off her sandals and plowed through the powdery sand to her own bungalow. She had enjoyed talking with him about her work, but that was no reason for the guilt complex she guessed he inspired very easily. Perhaps that was why the rest of the team shunned his company; people didn't like being made to feel guilty.

"Been socializing?"

Denise jumped and whirled around on the sand when Jake's voice accosted her from the rear. The moon's light gleamed across his carefully brushed hair, and he was more neatly turned out than she had yet seen him, in dark blazer, shirt and tie.

"You scared me," she accused, her heart beating like a trip-hammer in her breast.

"If you're so easily scared, you should have asked your—" his shadowed eyes flicked in the direction of Carl's cottage "—friend to walk home with you."

"Carl offered," she flared. "I hadn't expected predators to be prowling the beach at this time of night."

His cuff shot up as he consulted the luminous dial of his watch. "What is the time for predators? Is ten-thirty too early or too late?"

"Anytime is the wrong time for you as far as I'm concerned," she retorted sharply, pivoting to look at the ocean with as much dignity as she could muster in the fine, soft sand, then turning her head back to look calculatingly over his neatly turned appearance. "What brought you back from the ball so early?"

"Too many Cinderellas," he returned promptly, putting up one long-fingered hand to tug the knot of his tie, as if its unaccustomed presence irritated him. "A surfeit to choose from is almost as bad as no choice at all."

"Life is full of problems," she sympathized sarcastically, and turned to walk the few steps to the small cottage bathed in moonlight.

"None that can't be overcome." He had followed her, speaking at her shoulder. "But you don't go much for working through your problems, do you?"

"Do you?" she challenged, facing him again and wishing she hadn't. That afternoon, when he had deliberately set out to seduce her, was still too potently clear in her memory. "Do you call it working through your problems when you have meaningless affairs with different women when all the time you're still in love—" She broke off abruptly, knowing she had betrayed too much—far too much—interest in his personal life.

His head reared back and his eyes narrowed to silver slits. "I see Marie's been spouting off with her speculations again. Speculations, I might add, that could be way off base."

"Marie has nothing to do with it," Denise said in weak defense. "It's no more than a mathematical equation. One attractive divorced man, x number of equally attractive women who would no doubt be happy to become wife number two, but—how many years since your divorce?"

"Five," he said tersely.

"All right, five years after the divorce he is still single. Which adds up to the obvious conclusion that he is still hung up on wife number one."

"A very neat equation," he approved in a level tone that neither affirmed nor denied the deduction. "It doesn't take into account the variables, of course." He took off his jacket and hooked it on one finger over his shoulder. "You find me attractive, then?" he asked unexpectedly.

Surprised, Denise searched his face for signs of the male uncertainty his words implied, and found nothing but the arrogantly sure twist of his mouth. "In a physical sense, you'd be attractive to most women," she prevaricated coolly. "You don't interest me in a personal sense."

"Does any man, except the one who's planted six feet deep?" he put in with harsh cruelty, extending the cruel touch by saying mockingly, "Is that why you've spent the evening with a man who has ice instead of blood in his veins?" He took a forward step and fastened his fingers cruelly above her elbow. "That's it, isn't it? Madsen isn't the kind to make demands, physical or otherwise, is he? Because he's as dead as you are, in any meaningful sense.''

His short cut fingernails scratched across her skin as she jerked and pulled her arm away. "If you mean he doesn't force himself on me, you're right. In my eyes, that makes him a gentleman—a quality you obviously know nothing about.''

Jake's contemptuous ''Go to hell'' still rang resonantly in her ears as she leaned back on her closed cottage door. In any other circumstances she would have believed that Jake's ire was inspired by jealousy. Jealousy! A sob broke from her throat. That was an emotion she had read about, heard about, not one that had ever entered her life in any meaningful sense. The women Sam had turned to had never inspired more than a relieved gratitude in her.

Too restless to sleep, she took a shower and slid the diaphanous folds of a short, pale green nightdress over her head. Pausing at the bedroom dressing table on her way to bed, her eyes lowered reluctantly to where the dark tips of her breasts pressed against the filmy transparent fabric. Jake's long bronzed fingers had touched her there, had brought her breast's peak to stinging awareness of the femininity she had denied for so long. An awareness that had the power to hurt in its uselessness. . . .

CHAPTER FIVE

AFTER HER SWIM the next morning, a pleasure she had decided would be a daily occurrence whenever possible, Denise hesitated over what to wear for her first real day on the job. Still into the nine-to-five formality of San Diego, she decided that shorts were out and selected instead white cotton slacks and a lime-green sweater top.

Not that she expected the busyness that had filled her days at Scripps; her boss there had warned her that a small research unit would leave her plenty of time for relaxation and exploration of the islands. Dr. Seward, a kindly man past middle age, had kept a benevolent eye on her since Sam's death, and she suspected that he had played a large part in getting her this appointment. He had never quite believed that her solitary habits were not a form of morbid grieving for the husband she had lost so tragically, instead of the continuation of a life-style she had followed since childhood.

Going into the clubhouse, she was surprised to hear a burst of male laughter from the dining room. Pausing in the doorway, she saw the male members of the team gathered around a corner table, a map spread in front of Jake.

"Well, hi," Paul called as she crossed to help herself to coffee at the side buffet. "Come and join us."

Philomena smiled from behind the counter and said she would bring Denise's breakfast and was obviously reluctant to serve the simple meal of fruit and toast that Denise asked for.

She was embarrassed when Carl, stiffly polite, rose as she approached the table and pulled out a chair for her beside his. "Thanks, Carl, but please don't feel you have to do this for my sake. I'm a member of the team like everybody else, and as I've no intention of standing up when any of you come to the table, I don't see why you should do it for me."

"A feminist, hmm?" Paul twinkled across the table.

"Not altogether," Denise returned coolly, sensing Jake's level gaze on her. "I just think it's silly for any of you to make a distinction because of sex."

Paul chuckled. "Toby here was making quite a distinction last night at the hotel." He looked with amused affection at the younger man. "I don't know how you manage to remember all the vacation girls' names."

Toby scowled and got up to refill his coffee cup. "They all answer to 'honey' or 'sweetie,' so the problem doesn't arise," he said grumpily, and marched off.

"Too much of the grape," Paul explained to Denise, then turned to Jake. "Which reminds me—did you manage to get Christina tucked up safe and sound?"

The gray eyes met Denise's in a flicker before turning to Paul. "I deposited her in her cottage, but I didn't stay long enough for bed tucking."

So that was why he had left the hotel early, Denise thought. For some strange reason she didn't care to fathom at that moment, a small ball of warmth gathered in her chest.

Philomena arrived with Denise's breakfast at the same time Toby came back and slumped into his chair, black coffee before him.

"Why do you bother with those two-week girls?" she chided with motherly severity. "Why don't you find a nice woman like Mrs. Jordan and settle down?"

"Because there's safety in numbers," he said dourly, then shot a baleful look at Denise. "And the Mrs. Jordans of this world are interested in far bigger game than me."

Shaking her head in irritated bewilderment, the cook departed, muttering to herself, and Denise stared at him uncomprehendingly. What had he meant by that cryptic statement?

"I'm not after any game," she said quietly, "big or otherwise."

"Eat your toast before it goes cold." Jake spoke for the first time, and sudden understanding filled her eyes as they met his. What had he told Toby the other day when he had called at her cottage just after that traumatic love scene had taken place? Color flushed her skin, and she bent over the moist fruit slices to begin her breakfast. Surely Jake couldn't have told Toby the truth?

Talk drifted around her as she ate, but she made no attempt to listen until Jake said in his hard, clipped voice, stabbing his finger down on the marine chart in front of him, "We'll concentrate on this area for the next few days, then we'll gradually move out in this direction." His finger indicated an arc on the map, his lean face absorbed as he bent his dark head over it. "Our maximum depth with the sub is what? Two thousand feet?"

He looked up quickly at Carl, who shrugged and said, "About that, yes."

"You don't sound too sure," the brusque voice probed.

"I have myself taken the sub down to twenty-two hundred," Carl said stiffly.

"I'm more interested in safety than in overstraining the capacity of the vehicle," Jake snapped. "Did Dr. Shepherd approve dives to that depth?"

Carl shrugged again. "He was not well for the past six months. I was in charge of the survey trips for most of that time."

Jake's mouth tightened, and he seemed about to say more but then checked himself. Cold anger still burned in his eyes, though, when Denise spoke, and he turned them on her.

"When do we leave?"

"Wednesday. But I'm not sure it's necessary for you to come along on this trip. As you pointed out—" sarcasm edged his voice "—we're low on lab equipment. One of us can pick up specimens for you to send off to the mainland."

Anger sparkled in the green of her wide-set eyes, but disappointment made her voice quiver like a child denied a longed-for treat. "I didn't come here to operate a postal office, Dr. Barstow. My understanding was that I—"

"My understanding is that I was appointed to take full control of the research project," he broke in curtly, "and that, to me, includes the final say in who goes where."

The shocked silence around the table signified that the others were as stunned as Denise at this high-handed attitude on the part of the new chief. The scraping back of her chair sounded loud in the pool of silence.

"Yes, of course," she said tightly. "Excuse me."

Stumbling past the chairs circling the table, she heard Paul's, "What the *hell*, Jake!" as she half ran to the door. Blind anger blurred her vision, and she bumped into a female figure in the entrance. Christina turned to stare curiously after her, and then at the grim-faced man following her with determined strides.

Denise was at the foot of the clubhouse steps when Jake caught up with her and swung her around, one hand biting cruelly into her elbow. Green eyes flashed icily into gray as she faced him defiantly.

His mouth was a taut, thin line before he spoke. "Look, I'm sorry." He released her arm and ran his hand through his thick hair, ruffling its brushed neatness. "I was mad at...someone else, and I took it out on you." The someone else must obviously be Carl, she thought, her jaw softening as she unclenched her teeth. Apologies wouldn't come easily to Jake Barstow, but he had made one to her.

"I just don't see the point in my being here at all—" she kept her voice level, free of petty complaint "—if I'm not to be part of the team's work."

"It's never been my intention to exclude your specialty," he said just as evenly. "As a matter of fact, it was at my insistence that you were taken on in the first place. I want as much information as quickly as possible so that we know where we're at with this oil-spill business." He gave her a dry smile. "I should have been aware of the inadequate lab facilities here, but I wasn't. If you let me know what your needs are, I'll see that they're sent from Miami."

"That still leaves me with the status of a tourist when you leave on Wednesday," she pointed out tartly.

He looked at her thoughtfully for a moment, then grinned unexpectedly. "Make up a short list of your basic requirements, and we'll drive in to Nassau. I have a friend there who'll be able to tell us where to get the stuff if it's available at all.'' Not waiting for her agreement or otherwise, he was turning away when he looked back at her assessingly. "I'll meet you here in, say, an hour—and wear something female; then I'll take you to lunch.''

He went then with his rapid stride, leaving Denise staring reflectively after him. He was a strange, unpredictable man.

INTERESTING, TOO, SHE DECIDED while seated beside him as he drove one of the two slightly ancient cars from the station, he pointed out various landmarks with knowledgeable ease.

"Lyford Cay, where the rich live in pampered privacy—'' he indicated a guard-patrolled entrance to the tropical estates "—and the marina for their yachts.'' Masted schooners mingled with the latest of motor-powered yachts.

"Now those I do envy them,'' she exclaimed, craning her neck to look back at the soaring masts that conjured up visions of buccaneering days.

"Not the estates?'' He shot her a sideways glance, one dark brow raised.

Denise turned back into her seat again. "Not really. Apart from the more tropical setting here, it would be pretty much what I grew up with in San Diego.''

He looked at her again, more shrewdly this

time, and waited until his attention was back on the road before saying, "Mrs. Rich, hmm?"

"By some standards I guess you could say that," she agreed without arrogance. Her father's wealth had brought little joy into his austere life, his only concession to luxury being the number of servants required to run the oversize mansion. How often had she wished, at school and then university, that her background had been more in line with the other students? The ones who might have become closer friends had always seemed overawed by the things that she accepted as normal in her life. On the rare occasions when her father had permitted her to go to their homes, she had always felt faintly envious of the relaxed warmth generated between family members and somewhat shocked that the young people treated their parents more as equals than figures of authority. "I wanted to sell it after my father died, but...Sam liked it."

"I can believe it," Jake commented dryly, and she frowned as she looked at him. What was he implying? That Sam had been unduly impressed, as her friends had been, with the trappings of luxury she had inherited? True, he had enjoyed the ambience of the old house, but he had liked even more its proximity to the ocean where his main interest lay.

"How well did you know Sam?" she asked abruptly, and saw him shrug.

"As well as any person can know another on a

few months' acquaintance. Now look." He slowed the car and indicated a small stone ruin to their left. "That's where seven male slaves lived in the good old days."

"Seven?" she echoed disbelievingly as the tiny structure was left behind. Her imagination tried and failed to cope with a vision of seven husky men—weren't the slaves chosen for their able bodies—occupying a living space no larger than a single garage. "People were cruel then, weren't they?"

"They're still cruel today," he retorted cryptically, "although in other ways. Just ahead there are the caves where Blackbeard supposedly hid some of his loot, though I doubt if a man intelligent enough to plan looting raids on passing ships would have had so little foresight as to leave his spoils in such an easily discoverable spot."

He didn't stop as the caves, small black holes set some distance back from the road, flashed by. On their left a low wall enclosed a white-sand beach and the turquoise sea beyond.

"Whether it's true or not," Denise said softly, "it's still fascinating to think of the possibility that such a notorious character was actually here."

"I do believe you're a romantic, Mrs. Jordan," Jake said with an amused smile that faded when he glanced at her after negotiating a bend in the road. "And I wouldn't have suspected you of being that, somehow."

"Why not?"

His shoulders lifted and fell. "You're a scientist, and we scientists have supposedly dropped the rose-colored glasses in viewing the world."

"Not necessarily. Life would be very dull without our dreams and hopes, no matter how unrealistic we know them to be."

Sardonic amusement returned as he asked, "And what dreams fill your nights? What hopes churn in that very beautiful breast?"

Painful color ran swiftly up under her tanned skin, and she said stiffly, "Dreams and hopes are private. Would you tell me yours if I asked?"

He laughed outright. "I don't have any. I got over that a long time ago." They were passing resort hotels and exclusive homes set in tropical gardens that curved around a white-sand beach. "Cable Beach," he mentioned briefly, and seemed disinclined to talk as they approached the environs of Nassau.

Much of the excitement Denise would normally have felt in visiting the fabled tropical town was dampened by the speculations Jake's words had raised in her mind. He had had dreams once, some of which he had more than fulfilled as far as his career was concerned. Had the bitterness of divorce from a woman he loved soured him on dreams of personal fulfillment? Watching his long capable hands as he manipulated the car through a main street teeming with shoppers, she felt a tug of sympathy, an emotion she hadn't expected to feel for this man who had everything most men would have envied; a brilliant career, superb hard-bodied fitness and physical attraction that must make easy conquests of the women with whom, according to Marie, he had fleeting affairs.

Even she—her gaze hypnotically fixed on the brown hands flexed on the wheel, she recalled their expert touch on her skin and felt the involuntary tautening of her breasts against the close-fitting top of the white sundress she was wearing. How much more would he affect the women she categorized as normal, the ones uninhibited in their lovemaking?

"We'll park here," Jake said, and she blinked, realizing they had turned onto a side street that was far less crowded than the one they had come from. "Max's office is just back a little way on Bay Street."

"I can window-shop while you're with him," she volunteered, and felt his fingers at her elbow as if to keep her at his side.

"No way. Max is very happily married, but he's as susceptible to a beautiful woman as the next man. He'll do just about anything for me, but he'll do it twice as fast for you."

There was no time to argue his chauvinistic viewpoint at that moment, because they turned onto the main street and had to fight their way through the sauntering bodies on the sidewalk, mostly tourists with skins ranging from fiery pink of new sunburn to the teak of longer sojourners.

Denise would have been happier to join them in their casual shopping for souvenirs, but Jake directed her into a stairway between two stores and led the way to an upper floor where a set of offices opened off a central door marked Maxwell Pearson, Contractor & Developer. The secretary frowned when Jake asked for the principal.

"Have you an appointment?" she asked, glancing down at the blank time slot on her desk diary.

"No, but he'll see me if you'll just tell him I'm here."

Her finger had no sooner released the intercom button than a door behind her opened and a tall, fair, well-fleshed man erupted from it.

"My God, Jake, it is you! I thought Clarissa must have made a mistake in the name. How the hell are you?"

He pumped Jake's hand enthusiastically, beaming, then turned his sea-blue eyes on Denise approvingly. His next words must have been prompted by the fact that Jake's fingers were again encircling the smooth tan of her bare arm, his quick eyes taking in the slender wedding band on her third finger. "And you've married again! That's the best news I've had all year!"

As he spoke he ushered them into his unostentatious office, telling his secretary that he wasn't to be disturbed on any account.

Jake waited until the door was closed behind them before saying, sounding more amused than annoyed, "You're all wrong, Max. This is Denise

Jordan—Mrs. Jordan,'' he stressed, and Max looked ludicrously startled until his brain drew an obvious conclusion.

"Of course. I'm sorry," he smiled at Denise, "I've been married for so long that I automatically assume that—"

"Denise is a marine biologist working with me on the South Shore Project," Jake intervened smoothly, "and we need your help." He outlined Denise's requirements from her handwritten list, and Max Pearson lost his embarrassment as he listened to Jake's explanation of why they needed the supplies as soon as possible.

"Leave it to me," he said at last. "I can't think of anything worse for our economy than the effects of an oil spill on our shores." He looked seriously at Jake. "Do you think there's any real danger?"

"I'll be able to answer that better when Denise has had a chance to analyze samples from the Gulf Stream," Jake returned meaningfully, and Max Pearson hastened to assure him.

"I'll find the things she needs even if I have to rob every school lab on the island." Changing the conversation to a more personal level, he asked, "How is your daughter—Meg, isn't it?"

"She's fine," Jake replied levelly. "I'm hoping she'll join me here for her Christmas vacation. And how is your family?" he tacked on politely.

"Swelled by one member since you were here five years ago," Max told him, smiling despite the

nonchalance of his statement. "A hellion by name
of Max the Third. After two beautiful, docile
daughters," he explained, looking at Denise, "a
feisty three-year-old son comes as a traumatic experience for my wife."

"I can't imagine Madge being thrown by a male
of any age," Jake smiled, "let alone the heir to
your dominions."

"She says she is," Max shrugged, "so much so
that she's arranged for the kids to go to her
parents in Florida while we take a cruise in the
Caribbean this Christmas. Say—" his eyes glinted
as the thought struck him "—our house is going to
be empty till the middle of January; why don't
you bring Meg into Nassau for Junkanoo?"

"I'd planned on doing that," Jake admitted.
"In fact, I was thinking about making reserva-
tions at the hotel where I'm taking Denise to
lunch."

"Hotel? Man, that's the height of the season;
you won't get accommodation then. You're more
than welcome to bring Meg and stay awhile—
Denise, too." He smiled at her with friendly blue
eyes. "You must see our wildest celebrations of
the year—there's nothing quite like it anywhere
else."

"I'd love to," Denise smiled back reservedly,
interested to see the colorful parades she had read
about, but wary of committing herself to sharing a
private home with Jake and his daughter for the
occasion. Jake seemed to sense her hesitation.

"We'll take a raincheck on it for now, Max, thanks." He rose lithely from the barrel-backed chair he had used, the twin of Denise's at the other side of the cluttered desk. "We won't keep you any longer now. When can we pick up Denise's supplies?"

"Come back around three." The speculative look in his eyes as he ushered them out gave Denise an uncomfortable feeling that was intensified when he said that Madge would want them both to come to dinner at the house as soon as it could be fixed up. As if they were a pair.

The feeling lasted until they were seated at the harbor-view side of the hotel's restaurant and she found herself lost in the capacious depths of a Victorian fan-backed wicker chair. As if it had been planned for their entertainment, a four-masted schooner, sails furled, slid past the windows on its way to docking farther down.

"Looks like something Bluebeard might have used," Denise smiled, and Jake turned back to look at her, his eyes sobering strangely as they took in the sparkling translucent green of hers that matched the water outside the windows. "Would somebody own a boat like that these days?" she asked.

His gaze dropped to her mouth, touched lightly with coral lip gloss, and then to the smooth tan of her shoulders before he slowly turned his attention back to the graceful lines of the schooner. "I doubt it. It looks as if it might be a training vessel of some kind, with all those youngsters running around. Lucky devils. I'd have given anything to take a trip like that when I was their age." He sighed and picked up the red leather menu. "I guess we should decide what we want. I'm going to order just soup and a sandwich, but you have whatever you want. The seafood's very good here, steak not bad, or—"

"Soup and a sandwich is fine for me, too," she interrupted his flow of selections. "Conch chowder as the soup."

While Jake ordered their lunch, including a light beer for himself and an iced soft drink for her, Denise watched the busy scene outside the windows. But she only partially took in the sleek white yachts and their teak-colored owners, the graceful maneuvers of two young men skimming across the water on sailed surfboards. She was aware—far too aware—of the man opposite. Even though her eyes were directed away from him, she could still see the sinewed bronze of his arms, the rise of muscles where his white knit shirt molded closely to his chest. But her interest wasn't entirely physical. An insatiable curiosity filled her mind with questions. She knew next to nothing about his past, and she suddenly, achingly, wanted to know about his childhood, about the boy who would have given anything to sail on that schooner now safely tied up, about the hopes and dreams he had, by his own admission, once cherished.

What had he been like at eighteen, twenty, with his first love, his first experience of marriage, his first taste of fatherhood? Was he a good father? He would be a fair one, she decided, even if not openly affectionate.

"Is this a private party, or can anyone join in?" His clipped voice, amused, broke into her thoughts. Blinking, she brought her eyes briefly to his before dropping them to the drink that had arrived without her knowing.

"I'm sorry, I . . . guess I was miles away."

Jake stared hard at her for a moment then lifted his glass of sparkling light beer. "Or is it two years away?" he asked cryptically before taking a deep draft from his glass.

"I . . . I was wondering how you came to know Max Pearson," she prevaricated, feeling a surprisingly strong surge of resentment that he should put down her ever preoccupied moment to morbid dwelling on Sam's death.

"I've known him for years—since university. He was born here. His family goes away back in the Islands. English originally, but he was sent to an American university. He has a finger in a lot of Bahamian pies; that's why I knew he'd be able to help us with your stuff. We've always got on well, though we don't meet very often."

"This is your first meeting since your div—" She broke off, appalled by her own crassness in voicing the calculation her brain had automatically made from Max's conversation.

"No," Jake replied evenly. "I came here and stayed for a while with Max and his family just after my divorce. It was a kind of poetic justice, I guess. Max was best man at my wedding."

Not knowing what to say, Denise was relieved when the young waiter brought the thick red chowder, and there was an excuse for silence as they ate. As swiftly as her curiosity had arisen it faded away. She really didn't want to speculate anymore on Jake's past—particularly the past that involved his wife.

A SOFT BREEZE LIFTED HER HAIR and fanned her skin coolly as Denise leaned on the rail of the mother ship that dipped its way to the diving area. The cigar-shaped submersible was secured by cables and wires at the rear.

They were well into the Tongue of the Ocean now, the long thrust of water dividing the islands of New Providence and Andros. Excited anticipation sent adrenaline coursing through her blood and a sparkle into her eyes. Would she ever feel this alive in any other profession?

"So." Carl joined her at the rail, his right elbow touching her left. "You have prevailed on our chief to allow you to come on the survey. Such is the power of a woman's beauty."

Some of the glow faded from Denise's eyes as she turned to look at him, one hand holding back the wayward strands of hair from her forehead.

"Beauty or the lack of it had nothing to do with

my coming on the survey,'' she said coolly. "Jake managed to find some of the equipment I need to be useful to the project, that's all.''

"Yet I think that if it had been I, he would not have changed his mind so quickly. He is attracted to you, perhaps?''

Denise eyed him narrowly, her heart giving a nervous jump. Was it possible that Henry had, after all, reported the scene he had witnessed on the small boat? She had watched the others apprehensively, looking for signs of speculation about her relationship with Jake, and had found none. Not even in Esther, Henry's calmly competent wife, who took care of the cottages. She had assumed that Henry, for reasons of his own, had held his counsel. She chose a middle of the road answer.

"Jake isn't the kind of man to be influenced by attraction even if it existed, which I'm sure it doesn't,'' she said shortly. "And I don't like your implication that I have to rely on looks or sex to be able to do my job.''

His narrow, sallow-skinned face twisted in an expression she took to be embarrassment, and she turned to face into the breeze again, feeling its coolness fan her hot cheeks.

"Forgive me, Denise,'' she heard him apologize stiltedly. "It was not my intention to insult your professional capability. I merely wanted to—'' he paused "—warn you about a man of Barstow's type.''

"Warn me?" She swung around to stare at him in surprise.

"He has...a reputation, you understand? With women. I would not like to see you damaged in any way."

It was a curious choice of word—how could Jake "damage" her in any significant way? Yet there was something touching in Carl's wish to protect her.

"Don't concern yourself on that score," she said quietly. "I'm not vulnerable to Jake Barstow or any other man."

Carl shrugged. "A woman who has known love will sooner or later want to experience it again." He turned his head when Toby shouted irritably for him from the aft section of the vessel and excused himself with a polite bow of his head.

Denise turned back to stare pensively at the low dark lines of Andros, the largest of the Bahama Islands. What Carl had said was no doubt true, in normal cases. If she had loved Sam in the way a woman usually loves the man she marries, she might have been actively looking now for a replacement to fill the gap he had left in her life. The companionship she and Sam had never enjoyed, the closeness of a mutually satisfying physical relationship that had never taken place— what did she, a woman who responded to surface stimulation but froze when the moment of truth came, have to offer any man, let alone the worldly-wise Jake Barstow? Other men would react in the same way as Sam had, looking elsewhere for the uninhibited passion other women seemed capable of producing like water from a well.

She couldn't, she reflected with a macabre touch of humor, even fill in as an inadequate substitute for the wife Jake still cared for.

DENISE'S FIRST DIVE in the sub was in the shallower waters closer to home on their third day out. Jake, Paul and Carl had alternated as diver and observer in the deeper levels where they noted temperature and current figures. The more colorful shelves were her domain, and she felt a tingling of excitement as she followed Jake, who had elected to be her diving companion, through the conning tower of the sub, past the rows of dials and steering wheel under Toby's command, to the hatchway leading to the diving compartment she and Jake would occupy on their way to the bottom. Carl, in his observer role, would occupy the seat forward and on a lower level than Toby's. Portholes allowed both positions an unobstructed view of the underwater terrain.

A paralyzing sweep of claustrophobia turned her knees to jelly when Jake secured the hatchway between the two compartments. The subs she had dived in before off the California coast had been much larger, permitting freedom of movement impossible in the confined space of the diving chamber where she now sat with Jake's knees pressing with bony hardness against hers.

His eyes smiled at her through the eyepiece of his helmet, and the claustrophobic feeling fled to be replaced by an emotion equally disturbing.

For the three days of the survey he had been pure scientist, sexless in his attitude to Denise, the only woman on board the mother ship. Even in the soft lights of the saloon after a plenteous and well-cooked dinner, he had been content to nurse a single bourbon and water and talk shop until the team's early retirement to their cell-like cabins lining the aft passage. Several times she had caught herself watching too intently the long-fingered hand circling the glass, remembering the feel of it on her body, caressing, rousing. . . .

Stemming the unprofessional drift her thoughts had taken, she concentrated on the port beside her that reflected the green-hued underwater world the sub was penetrating in a slow, easy dive. Curious fish, exotically colored and striped, floated down with them, crossing back and forth as the metallic monster invaded their territory. She leaned forward when a hawksbill turtle, which would be ungainly on land, swam gracefully and uncaringly past.

Toby's landing of the sub was accomplished with only a faint bump on the sandy bottom, and she nodded when Jake touched her arm and indicated that he would go first through the lower hatch. As soon as his helmet disappeared, Denise poised herself over the narrow round opening and dropped feet first through it, landing on the soft ocean floor close to where Jake waited for her.

Taking the claw-shaped tool she used for breaking off hard samples, he gestured toward the front of the sub and swam off, trailing the air hose connecting him to the life-sustaining gas mixture from the sub. Denise followed, flutter kicking to where the powerful lamps of the submersible illuminated a vast wall of living coral and a seabed teeming with vibrantly colored life. Swaying green fronds housed shy gray angel fish; a deadly and deceptively attractive anemone beckoned alluringly to unwary passersby; spiny sea urchins clung like black pincushions at the foot of the coral reef and under the antlerlike staghorn coral dotted here and there across the ocean floor.

Joining Jake at the bright coral bastion, she indicated an outer projection and accepted the piece he broke off with the aid of the tool into the long plastic sample bag she carried. Other specimens followed as the two of them hugged the orange red reef; Denise added tiny silver-scaled fish to the comparatively giant-sized striped sergeant major.

Reluctantly indicating at last that she had enough specimens, she led the way back to the pressurized chamber to the rear of the sub. At this hundred-foot depth the samples would survive the climb to the mother vessel without the artificially produced mixture of helium, nitrogen and oxygen she and Jake would use in the decompression chamber.

Anxious to turn her new charges loose in the small, seawater tanks the mother vessel provided, Denise waited impatiently while the submersible surfaced. The process of decompression, which had once been a time-consuming bore, was now accomplished as the sub rose higher and higher.

"You look sexy even in a wet suit," Toby told her as she passed through the small control room, and she grimaced behind her eyepiece. Compared to his casual dress of peach-colored shirt and denim shorts, she felt vastly overdressed in a diving suit that covered her from head to toe. Gladly discarding it after stepping on deck, she was only vaguely aware of Jake's tall figure following her from the sub as she hurried to supervise the transfer of samples to tanks.

She was already slitting into the underbelly of a sergeant major when Jake came to stand silently beside her, clad sparsely in white swim shorts that clung to his hard-boned frame like a second skin. Several smaller fish in various stages of decomposition spilled from the stretched stomach.

"Greedy devil, wasn't he?" Jake said over her shoulder.

"She," Denise corrected crisply, indicating the symmetrical rows of female cells bared under her knife. "It's an awesome responsibility to wipe out that much potential life with a stroke of a knife." The bloodstained edges of the sharp knife nevertheless ruthlessly dissected the dead fish spread on the rough wooden board.

"I doubt if the ocean will miss one prolific mother," he observed dryly. His breath stirred her hair as he continued to look over her shoulder, making her too consciously aware of his volatile presence. "Will what you're doing now tell us what we want to know about the oil spills?"

"I hope so, yes," she returned absently, completing the dissection of the fish. "And from the contents of her stomach I can perhaps pinpoint just which foods have the highest concentrates of pollutants." She looked up and turned her head, then wished she hadn't as his warm breath fanned her face. "If...they're present, we have to find which direction they're coming from and—" Her voice gave out then, stifled in her body's awareness of his closeness as he pressed too intimately to the curves of her back.

"I see," he said huskily, his mind obviously far away from the potential hazards in the cleanly sectioned fish before them. The gray flash of his eyes tangled with the widened green of hers while the dimmed voices of the native crew manuevered the sub to its snug position at the rear of the mother ship. A strange, paralyzing weakness invaded Denise's limbs, and she had already begun to lean weakly back on the warm hard body when Toby, skirting the narrow deck area surrounding the cabin portholes, called out to them.

"Jake? Captain Mike wants to know if we can head for home now."

Like a slow-moving film, Denise felt Jake lift away from her.

"Sure, let's go."

She was still trembling uncontrollably moments later when the deep thrum of the engines vibrated under her feet and the ship rounded to New Providence. She was alone on the midships deck, but Jake's male imprint was still on her back....

CHAPTER SIX

TOBY'S INVITATION to tour the island with him two days later was offered so ingenuously that Denise hesitated for only a moment before accepting the offer. Her new surroundings held a magic for her, and she had intended exploring them to the fullest—why not with Toby, who was good, if irrepressible, company?

"I promise not to attack you," he said, the solemn note in his voice belied by the sparkle in his eyes. "At least," he qualified, "I won't unless my animal instincts get the better of me."

"Thanks for the warning," Denise retorted dryly. "I'll come prepared in that case."

"Not with a knife, I hope," he shuddered realistically. "Seems I was slain in one of my previous lives by a very sharp dagger, so I'm not anxious to repeat the experience."

"You're not serious?" She turned her head to look more fully into the hazel eyes, uncharacteristically clouded suddenly. "You don't believe all that stuff about other lives, do you?"

"Of course not. A couple of the guys in college did their final thesis on the theory of reincarnation, and I was one of their guinea pigs to prove their point. Strange though," he frowned thoughtfully, "I've always had a horror of knives, blades of any kind. Then these guys told me in living detail what my fate had been in a former life in the fifteenth century. Anyway—" he brightened "—all you need to bring along is your swimsuit. I know every secluded beach on the island."

So, early the next morning Denise presented herself in white cotton slacks and coffee-colored scoop-neck top, her blue, patterned bikini underneath. Toby, dressed in brief white shorts and eye-catching bright yellow T-shirt, greeted her from the jeep he had commandeered for the occasion.

"Won't anybody mind?" she asked, seating herself in the open vehicle, thankful for the shade her wide-brimmed white hat gave her.

"Mind? No." Toby flicked on the ignition and set the gears in motion. "The only objections to my taking you out for the day came from the male element—even Carl." He chuckled in amused remembrance as they traversed the crushed coral driveway to the south road. "He's a strange guy. He's never shown much interest in the fairer sex, but you seem to be an exception." He gave her a humorously significant sideways glance. "According to him, I'm Bluebeard and the Marquis de Sade all rolled into one, and he actually warned me very seriously not to impose my decadent ideas of morality on you. And Jake—" He paused briefly before turning out on the well-paved south road.

"Jake?" Denise reminded him tersely.

A smile parted Toby's generous mouth, revealing the white evenness of his teeth. "Jake," he stated with relish, "firmed up that jaw that is already formidable enough when he makes up his mind about something, and told me I'd have him to answer to if you weren't delivered back in one intact piece."

"*He* said that?"

"Words to that effect." He shrugged negligently, his expression sharpening as he drew the jeep into the side and cut the engine. "Here begins the first stage of our tour. We have to get out and walk, I'm afraid, but it's not far."

"To where?" Denise posed, as she swung her legs over the side of the jeep and stared at the tree-bordered track to their right.

"All in good time, my dear," his tone leered as he came around the vehicle to grasp her elbow and lead her toward the almost invisible path. Denise drew back involuntarily from the dense growth surrounding it. "It's okay," he assured, urging her gently but firmly on. "The only problem you'll ever encounter is the spider species peculiar to these parts, and they're a menace only when there's been a hard rainfall when they're forced out of their hiding places under rocks. We haven't had a recordable deluge in the past few days, so there's no problem."

Still Denise glanced apprehensively to either side as they went deeper into the thick bush edging the slight width of the rutted track. Even the twitter of birds, disturbed in their hidden homes, sent her head swiveling, her eyes neurotically searching for telltale black legs. Creatures of the deep, however oddly formed, she could face without qualm. Spiders were something else again.

Then suddenly, without warning, they came to an open vista of green grass, manicured to form undulating fairways, and Denise looked up at Toby in contrary accusation. "It's a golf course!"

"A little more than that," he responded cheerfully, pulling on her arm to urge her forward. "Just up here—yes, here it is." He drew her level with an innocent-looking pond surrounded by native growth. "Isn't that something?"

"It looks...very nice," she admitted cautiously, disappointed somehow.

"*Nice?*" he exploded, his eyes seeming to search the dark surface of the pond. "It's anything but nice! Do you know how deep this is? It goes down one whole mile! Not only that, it's connected to the ocean by a tunnel way down there. A while ago a diver went in from ocean side, trying to make some kind of record by coming up here in the pool, but something happened to his diving gear in the tunnel, and he didn't make it. At least, not alive. His body floated up here a few days later."

Denise shivered despite the heavy warmth of the

day around them. It was only too easy to imagine
a sharp rock or coral ripping the diver's suit, the
fight for survival as the ocean swell pressed him on
along the tunnel to this inland pool. A lost fight, if
Toby was to be believed. Shivering again, she
turned away from the now eerie surface of the
water.

"Where are all these beaches you've been telling
me about? I need a swim in warm water about
now."

"First one coming up." Toby fell into step
beside her, seemingly unaffected by the tragedy
that had taken place a mile beneath their feet.

The spot he took her to far along the hard-
topped road was idyllic. The white curve of beach
in a small cove bordered by native scrub and the
gentle sway of green-topped palms could have
been used as a location setting for a movie about
Robinson Crusoe. Like Crusoe, her slenderly
formed feet left indentations on the firm white
sand edging the ocean. Toby, preferring the
powder softness of the upper beach, kept pace
with her along the incurve of blue until suddenly
he stopped and lifted his T-shirt over his head,
dropping it to the sand beside him. The hazed
warmth of the sun lent a burnished copper to his
stockily constructed chest with its brown sprin-
kling of hair between neck and navel.

"Beat you in," he called, his hands already
busy with his shorts while Denise hesitated briefly
before pulling her top quickly off, revealing a long

stretch of tanned bare midriff. Catching Toby's involuntary male glance of appreciation over her scantily covered breasts, she colored slightly and turned away. Why hadn't she worn a one-piece suit? She trusted Toby completely, but for all that he was a man who made no bones about his normal impulses where women were concerned. Was he thinking her a tease, rejecting him one minute and the next appearing alone with him on a deserted beach wearing next to nothing?

But as if he sensed her embarrassment, Toby ran past her and waded rapidly into the water, and he was already splaying its sparkling iridescence behind powerfully stroking arms when she dropped her slacks beside her hat, top and sandals.

Cool at first, the water seemed to warm as she became accustomed to it. Determinedly, she struck out for where Toby rested from his preliminary labors, his voice seeming to echo around the empty beach when he called, "Come on, lazybones, I thought you were an expert at this."

"Who's saying I'm not?" she spluttered, coming up and treading water beside him, her hair turned to a metallic silver by the softly clinging water. The mock scowl between her brows melted into a smile as green eyes met hazel.

Then slowly the smile faded, too, and her breath caught huskily in her throat. The expression in Toby's eyes had changed to one she hadn't seen before in him. Serious, sober, it seemed to probe the innermost recesses of her mind. As before, she questioned the wisdom not only of wearing the briefest of her bikinis but in coming on this trip with him at all. What normal young male wouldn't be affected by the tropical beauty surrounding them, the palms, the powder white of the sand, the translucence of the water? The Bahamas were touted as the islands of romance, while their travel literature was designed partly to entice amorous inclinations.

"Your eyes are exactly the color of the water, did you know that?" Toby said with an intentness that shot panic through her veins and lifted her hand to fling a palmful of drops playfully against his chest.

"I'll prove to you how much of an expert I am," she called back in a slightly hysterical voice as she plunged away from him. "Race you to that point over there."

Not waiting to find out if he intended joining her, she struck out strongly for the jagged rocks curving along to a point at their right. The panic-roused adrenaline gave impetus to her strokes, and minutes later she was hauling herself from the water onto a semiflat surface to the rear of the farthermost point.

Toby had followed her, arriving mere seconds after she did, his impudent grin restored as he clambered, dripping, to throw himself down beside her.

"All right," he panted, hands raised in a gesture of surrender, "you win."

Too winded for conversation, they lay side by side on the narrow surface watching the sky, clear blue apart from an occasional wisp of white cloud drifting up from the far horizon. It was idyllic, Denise thought dreamily, reassured by Toby's return to his usual self. The day could be fun after all.

Later, when lethargy made movement difficult, she turned her head to glance at Toby's face and saw that he was asleep, the sandy brown of his lashes dropped firmly over the hazel eyes.

He was nice, she told herself drowsily; healthy, wholesome and attractive. Her gaze wandered down the length of him, the packed muscles of his stocky chest, the taut strength of his stomach and thighs, the powerful curve of his calves. A sigh escaped her salty lips. Apart from his physical attractions, his buoyant personality must make it easy for him to attract hordes of girls. So why did she feel nothing for him in that way? Although she was his elder by only two years, she felt like his mother or older sister.

Why had he asked her out today? Did it give him an edge with the older men at the research station? But why should they care? Paul was happily married, Carl wasn't the kind to reveal any male jealousy even if he felt it, and Jake...ah, Jake.

She was drifting, dreaming—a dream so real that she felt Jake's hard flesh, warm from the sun, pressed to her. His face hovered dimly above her, so close that she saw the tiny pores in his skin, the floating yellow specks mingled with the gray of his eyes, the firm outline of his mouth softened in passion. He was going to kiss her. Desperately, longingly, she wanted him to do so.

Warmth gilded her lower limbs and flowed upward, spreading until it built to explosive heat where flesh touched flesh. Her hands reached behind his head, drawing him down, down to where her lips parted to receive him. When their mouths finally touched and clung she groaned deep in her throat. She loved him—how could she have thought otherwise? Her hips moved, straining up to the male in him. How easy it was, she marveled—I love him, and I want him in the same way he wants me.

"Oh, God, Denise," a different voice muttered against her ear, "I knew I could make you forget him. You're so beautiful, so made for love. You want me to love you, don't you? I know you do...."

Horror surged and battered against her senses as Toby's hot mouth kissed feverishly over her skin and reached down to the exposed peak of her breast.

"Toby?" she gasped. "Toby, don't! I don't want *you*!" Disgust lent strength to her arms, and Toby was set back abruptly on the rock beside her. "How could you? Oh, my God, I feel sick."

Shocked contrition mingled with the bright flare

of passion in the hazel eyes. "Denise, I'm sorry. I thought you wanted me to. Really." He moved to sit heavily at her side again. His face was pale under the overlay of tan, and he ran a distracted hand through his mussed hair. "God! I don't know what to say! I thought I could make you forget your husband, but—"

"I was asleep," Denise accused wildly, jumping to her feet and pulling up the bikini top he had pulled away, "and you—you took advantage of that fact! Who appointed you as the savior of widowed women, anyway?" She turned back furiously to where he still sat on the light gray rock.

"Denise, I'm sorry. It was just that—"

She heard no more of his apologetic excuses, for she dived cleanly off their resting place at that point and struck out blindly for the beach.

Her anger had evaporated slightly as she approached the curving sand. It wasn't wholly Toby's fault. She had invited trouble when she had agreed to come out here with him. What else had she expected him to do? He was young, male, virile, and he had a savior complex. The same complex Jake had displayed on several occasions. Jake!

She reached down and found firm sand, then waded out before turning back to watch Toby's slower progress. She had thought it was Jake making love to her out there on the rock. Not Sam— never Sam. Had she mentioned Jake's name? But no, she couldn't have. Toby was still convinced it was Sam she hankered for, that she had imagined it was Sam making love to her.

There was lessened censure in her eyes when they met the abashed Toby's as he dragged himself slowly through the water.

"Denise, I'm sorry," he apologized again, but his square jaw firmed determinedly at the same time. "You looked so damn beautiful lying there beside me, and I'm as human as the next man. It seemed stupid to me that—well, that you should let all that's beautiful and loving in you go to waste because you've lost one man." His stubby fingers made tracks through his wet hair. "I thought I could be the man who'd make you forget, but I'm not, am I?"

She shook her head, unable to speak through the lump that had formed in her throat.

"It's all right," he filled in with a partial return to the impudent Toby she knew. "I've been turned down before—but now I can brag that I've been rejected by the best."

"Oh, Toby!" Denise smiled through the glint of tears gathering in her eyes. "You're an idiot—but a very dear one."

Strangely, he seemed more embarrassed by her genuine show of affection than by the rejection. "I guess you'd rather go back now then spend the rest of the day with a monster like me."

"You're no monster," she said softly. "I think I'd very much enjoy the rest of the day in your company." She moved off up the sand in the direction of their clothes. "And I'm getting to be very hungry. Where had you planned we'd have lunch?"

Toby bounded up the beach after her, like a puppy released from punishment. "It's a small place not far from here. It's not much, but it's quiet unless there's an island tour bus in."

Denise didn't care where they went. The awkwardness was behind them now, and she knew that as far as Toby was concerned there would be no more such scenes between them. It was as if that unspoken aspect of their relationship had had to be brought out, aired and banished. They could be real friends now.

At the back of her mind, too, was the knowledge that speculation would be aroused at the research station if they arrived back so early in the day. A speculation that would, she suspected, end in an educated—and correct—guess on Jake's part.

Damn Jake, she seethed quietly as she followed Toby to the jeep. Why couldn't he stay out of her thoughts, her heart, her life?

As Toby had predicted, the roadside café they stopped at was quiet and peaceful, bereft of tour buses.

"How do they make a living here?" she asked quietly when Toby held the screen door open for her.

"I hear it really jumps later on in the day with

the local folks," he replied as softly, and led her to a small table at the side, away from the spartan long bare-board tables in the center of the simple dining room. "It's a regular stop on the island tour route, too, so they get some business from the people out from Nassau."

Denise's eyes went interestedly around the room, noting the long counter bar with an array of bottles behind it, the inevitable yet surprising presence of a jukebox close to the entrance, the torn screen door that freely admitted the flies it was designed to keep out. Near the counter two local men, one short and fat, one thin and rangy, lounged aimlessly until the tall one moved languidly toward the jukebox and made a selection, leaving a trail of pounding rhythm in his wake as he sauntered back to join his companion.

From tranquil quietness, the room became filled with the sound of a pop record, and Denise looked despairingly at Toby when a plump, shy but smiling waitress came from behind the counter and recited the menu from memory.

Toby grinned, his more attuned ear having picked up the salient points. "It sounds like a lot," he raised his voice to explain, "but basically the menu boils down to chili or a kind of stew or sandwiches. You might like the club sandwich."

"Yes, I think I'll have that." Relieved, she nonetheless felt somewhat ashamed to order such a totally American selection in a café more truly Bahamian than she had eaten in before. Her misgivings were alleviated a little when Toby ordered the stew for himself.

"And I'll have a beer." He raised his brows across the table. "What would you like to drink, Denise?"

"Do you have white wine?" she asked the reticently smiling waitress, and at her confirming nod, Denise ordered a glass. "I wish I was a little more adventurous and had ordered something more exotic than a club sandwich," she confided wryly to Toby. "Even your stew sounds more authentic than a club sandwich."

"You're like the average tourist," he teased back. "We Americans spend millions of dollars every year on travel to exotic places to see how other people live, yet we come back discontented if unable to find a Howard Johnson's-type place, or a McDonald's with hamburgers and French fries."

"I've read that 'le hamburger' is very popular in France, and not just with the tourists," she defended hotly, then a penitent smile curved her mouth. "But you're right. I should have tried something different today." She glanced around the no-frills café while their drinks were set before them. "This feels more Bahamian than anywhere I've been so far."

Toby chuckled and lifted the long, cool glass of beer. "Don't feel too badly. For real Bahamian food you have to go over the hill in Nassau."

"This place has enough atmosphere for me

right now," she smiled, her head swiveling to the door as it was pushed forcefully open and a party of four entered, two elegantly pantsuited women and two hotly perspiring men.

The loud music ceased as abruptly as it had begun, and the taller of the two women, dark-haired and in her thirties, looked disparagingly around the simple café.

"For pity's sake, Harry," she complained in a loudly penetrating voice, "couldn't you have found something better than this? My God, the flies will have eaten half the food before it gets to us."

"It was you who wanted to stop," the portly Harry retorted, waving her to the long table closest to where Denise and Toby sat. His eyes landed longingly on the tall glass of beer Toby was lifting to his lips. "At least we can get a drink here. Jake'll find us something to eat when we get there."

The tall glass paused at Toby's mouth level as his head swung in unison with Denise's toward the party irritably settling themselves close by.

"Jake probably regards this as the local Ritz," the dark woman confided in a disgruntled voice to the room at large. "Who can blame Barbara for dumping a man who would drag her to places like this?"

"Come on, Sharon," the second man cajoled as he settled himself at the table and looked expectantly at the bottles ranged behind the counter.

"Most women would give anything they've got to be posted to a place like this."

"To Nassau, yes," she returned frostily, "or maybe to Freeport. But to stick somebody like Barbara in a godforsaken corner like this! Poor Barbara."

Denise's eyes met Toby's over the rim of his glass, and in silent accord they agreed to ignore the newcomers, who were obviously familiar with both Jake and his ex-wife. An agreement broken at once.

"It's a small world," Denise murmured softly.

Solemnly Toby agreed. "It is indeed." Ecstatically he slaked his thirst on the long beer, then his eyes went speculatively back to the foursome who were vainly trying to attract the waitress's attention as she stoically prepared Denise's sandwich. "I wonder if Jake knows they're coming? To misquote the woman in the purple pantsuit, it doesn't surprise me a bit that Jake dumped his wife if she's one of those beautiful people."

"That isn't something that really interests me," she lied, turning back quickly to the stemmed glass she held between her fingers.

"Isn't it?" he quizzed quietly. "I get the impression that he's mighty interested in you...and not as biologist for the team."

Regarding him over the rim of her glass, Denise said coolly, "Really? I can assure you that if that's so, it's purely a one-way thing. I'm not interested in him or his marital problems—or anyone else's."

"No, you made that pretty clear back there," he agreed with a wry smile that bore no trace of rancor. "Still, if any man could bring you back to the world of the living, that man would have to be Jake."

Her lids blinked rapidly and then she gave him a mocking smile. "What's this, Toby? You're handing me over like a neat package to Jake?"

"Not from choice," his agreement came soberly, "but I know when I'm beaten. I still think the right man could turn your life around. Let's just say it wouldn't surprise me if somebody like Jake will be that man."

"Let's just say we bury that subject once and for all," she retorted. "And either we agree to be good, polite friends, or you take me back to the station right now."

"All right, all right," he laughed, raising his hands in simulated fear. "You win. We'll forget everything that's happened today and start from here. Now—" he rested his elbows on the table and subjected her to the full battery of his sparkling eyes "—have you any idea what I have in store for you this afternoon?"

"No." She eyed him warily, setting aside her glass when the waitress brought their meal, then went unhurriedly to the clamoring foursome at the next table.

"Imagine, if you will," Toby began extravagantly, "these islands as they were in the early days of the buccaneers. Days when pirates, particularly Bluebeard, set up watching posts for cargo ships seeking shelter after weeks, months, of enduring the cruel sea on their crossing from the Old World. Their progress was tracked from the time they came into view on the horizon, and when they pulled into harbor, guess who was waiting for them to relieve them of that bothersome cargo they'd hauled all the way from Europe?''

"Not...Bluebeard?'' she widened her eyes in mock horror.

"The same.'' Toby glanced up suspiciously from the stew he was devouring hungrily. "Stop me if you've heard this story before.''

"Not this part of it,'' she consoled after swallowing a mouthful of the excellent sandwich before her. "Jake pointed out the caves where Bluebeard reputedly stashed the loot.''

"Oh, damn,'' he cursed, "that was to be the final stop on our tour of the island.''

"We didn't stop there. Jake just pointed out the caves as we drove into Nassau to see about my lab supplies.''

"Oh, well, you didn't really see anything.'' Toby launched enthusiastically into a richly embellished history of New Providence, and four pairs of eyes were drawn from the next table to theirs as laughter erupted frequently in Denise's throat. She was oblivious to their half-censorious, half-envious glances in their direction. Toby was good company, brimming with the good humor that marked his personality.

As chance had it, when she and Toby left the café half an hour later, the foursome followed them into the heat of the midday sun. The portly Harry called out to Toby as he led Denise, his fingers lightly guiding on her bare elbow, to the jeep.

"Say, do you know this place at all?"

Toby halted and looked back, his fingers tightening on Denise's elbow. "Pretty well."

"Have you any idea where the ocean research place is?"

Toby's brow wrinkled. "Ocean research? Can't say I have. What is it, some kind of secret naval installation?"

Harry looked nonplussed. "I don't think there's anything secret about it." He turned to his wife, who was poring irritatedly over a map of the island. "Jake's got nothing to do with the navy, has he?"

"Of course not," she snapped her scorn before flailing Toby with her eyes. "Obviously you don't know the island as well as you'd like to think. There is an oceanographical research station, an *American* research station," she stressed, as if doubting Toby's loyalty to his country, "somewhere around here."

"I don't think so."

"I know so," she raised her voice, then said impatiently to the hapless Harry, "Oh, come along, we'll find it ourselves. It can't be far now, that man in Nassau said—"

The strident voice faded mercifully away as the four got hurriedly into the air-conditioned car, and Denise looked at Toby with a puzzled smile.

"Why didn't you tell them where it was?"

"Why should I?" he countered, helping her into the jeep. "I reckon I've done Jake a favor, throwing that old bat off his trail."

"He may not think so."

He shrugged, climbing in beside her and flicking the ignition to roaring life. "Can you imagine any man in his right senses being happy to see somebody like that? 'Poor Barbara,'" he mimicked. "I'm more inclined to think it was 'Poor Jake' if his wife was anything like her."

"Oh, well, I'm sure Jake can cope if they do ferret him out."

Whether or not Jake could cope wasn't what concerned her. What did bother her was the group's assumption that Barbara would have refused to accompany her husband to an "outpost" like the Bahamas. Any other woman, as one of the men had remarked, would be thrilled to have the opportunity to share her husband's life in a paradise like this. And not only here, she told herself, her expression distant as she watched farm workers tilling the soil that seemed unbreakable in its white corallike hardness. Married to a man like Jake, it shouldn't matter where he went as long as she could be with him. Jake would make even the barren Faeroes interesting and exciting.

"Well?" Toby broke the silence between them,

and she glanced at him in surprise. Had her thoughts been so transparent?

"Well what?" she summoned lightness for her tone.

"Aren't you curious about where we're going now?" He gave her a sharp sideways look. "You're not still thinking about...what happened on the beach this morning, are you?"

"No," she assured honestly. If it had been another man—somebody like Carl Madsen—who had made that assault on her sleeping senses, she wouldn't now be sitting beside him in the jeep looking forward to the remainder of the day in his company. Toby was different. He had accepted her rejection without resentment, making it clear that he still wanted to be with her. In the same way as she would have felt toward the brother she had never had, she had an affectionate fondness for him. "I thought the day was a magic carpet to be unrolled only a little at a time," she teased, and saw him grin.

"I didn't say I would tell you. It just struck me how different you are from most women; they'd have pestered me to death by now worrying about whether they're wearing the right thing for where we're going, and all that."

Denise feigned alarm. "And am I? Wearing the right thing?"

His eyes left the road again, and he gave her slacks and top a cursory inspection. "I think you'll be okay," he admitted grudgingly. "They have a prejudice against females in shorts or mini-skirts.''

"Oh, do they?'' she bridled. "I thought this was the new age for women, that they can wear what they please when they please without approval from a bunch of males! They are males, I presume?''

"Mmm,'' he said noncommittally, "but I'm not going to say one more word about them. There are a couple of other places I want to show you before that, anyway.''

They were following the coast road and lapsed into silence again as the jeep sped on at the pace Toby evidently found comfortable, though Denise spared a prayer of thankfulness that the road was sparsely traveled. Her eyes drifted to their right where tantalizing glimpses of turquoise ocean came and went between the scrublike trees. She would like to swim again, but Toby seemed intent on reaching wherever it was he was taking her. Besides, after the morning fiasco, it might be more politic to pass by the romantic lure of hard white beaches isolated from the rest of the world. Not that she expected a repeat, but

It was disappointing when the road branched to their left and there was no more ocean, just a dormant-looking body of water that Denise leaned forward to see. "What's that?'' she asked. "Is it connected to the ocean?''

"It's called Miller's Sound, so yes, I guess it is.''

"And who was Miller?"

"That I can't tell you, but with a name like that he must have been a buccaneer. Can't you just hear him? 'Avast, you swabs, and lay hold on this miserable pond, for Miller means to leave his mark here!' "

"Idiot," Denise laughed, letting her spine relax again on the seat back. "If his intention was to leave his mark, I imagine he'd choose a more compelling spot than this desolate stretch of water."

It was good to be with Toby, she reflected pensively, and wondered how she had survived her early years without this kind of lighthearted repartee with her peers. Her life had been blessed with every material comfort imaginable, but what did that mean compared to this easy rapport with someone not of her own sex? It made her feel young, lively in a way she had never thought possible.

The remainder of the afternoon followed the same carefree pattern. In Nassau there was a breathless hand-in-hand run up the sixty-six steps of the Queen's Staircase that led in turn to the ancient Fort Fincastle, an oddly shaped fortress designed to protect this eastern arm of Nassau Harbour, but which had never fired a cannon in anger. At the top of the Water Tower, on the island's highest point, a panoramic view of the harbor and of Nassau itself was unfolded.

"It looks much bigger than I had thought," she marveled, turning the glinting green of her eyes excitedly on Toby's phlegmatic profile that bore the stamp of a man well used to touristic raptures and faintly bored with them. "You're a cynic," she scolded, letting her eyes go back to the tropical view outspread for their pleasure. "You must have brought dozens of girls to exactly this spot, and you're jaded by their reaction to it."

"I'd never be jaded by any reaction of yours," Toby said quietly, his eyes fixed now on her profile, etched clearly against the sharp blue of the sky.

"Toby—" she began uncomfortably, and his hand covered hers in a quick, reassuring squeeze.

"It's okay, Denise, I'm not about to throw myself off Nassau's highest point, but.... Just let me be human for a few minutes and envy like hell the man who's going to take the place I'd like to have had in your life."

Her lashes lowered, obscuring the clouded green of her eyes for a moment before they flickered and gazed out again at the view. "There won't be any man in my life, Toby," she said unsteadily, "but if there ever were, he'd have to be very much like you." She gave him a quick smile and forced a brightness she was far from feeling. "Now, I don't see anything drastic happening to that girl over there in shorts, so this can't be the place where the male of the species objects to a show of female leg!"

His hand fastened warmly on her elbow as he went with her to the elevator that had brought them up. "No, this isn't the place, but there's still somewhere else I'd like you to see before we go there."

The somewhere else was idyllic in Denise's view. Jumbey Village, in the over-the-hill area favored by Captain Mike, held fascination for its newcomer's eyes. Taking its name from the Jumbey tree prevalent in the Bahamas, the reconstructed old Bahamian village enchanted her. Painstakingly built stone barns vied with the thatched huts of a bygone age, and she marveled like any tourist at the rock ovens used for centuries for food preparation. And at the center of the settlement were displays of paintings, wood carvings and exquisitely designed shell jewelry and ornaments. One of these, a vibrantly pink queen conch shell lighted mysteriously from within by a small bulb, caught Denise's eye, and she bought it from the smiling vendor, refusing Toby's offer of making it a gift from him.

"No, you've already given me the best gift of all," she said firmly. "I don't think I've ever enjoyed a day so much, and I want to buy this as a souvenir of it."

He desisted without further pressing, seeming to look on her statement as a cementing of the friendship growing between them despite the bad start to the day. Somewhere at the back of Denise's mind loomed the lonely days ahead in San Diego when this memento, gleaming its message of a day when she had been most vividly alive, would speak to her in the silence of her stateside home.

Glancing at his watch, Toby began to chivy her. "Time we went. I want you to see this last event of our day together. I know you're going to love it."

And she did love it. The flamingos in Ardastra Gardens, stern guardians of female virtue in their supposed condemnation of any clothing ending above knee level, delighted her and sent her eyes in laughing question to Toby's.

"And I thought you were talking about an exclusive male club," she chided lightly. "How can birds object to the length of a woman's skirt?"

"Beats me." He shrugged, the grin curving his mouth echoed in the amused sparkle of his eyes, "But that's the rule. Whether it reflects the trainer's tastes or the flamingos', women showing a more than average amount of leg are given the cold shoulder around here."

Secure in the enveloping length of her white slacks, Denise watched the undulating gracefulness of the flamingos' slenderly arched necks and laughed with amused indulgence as they followed their instructor in faultless symmetry when he intoned the key words initiating their coordinated steps. Later, when individual groups of tourists had their picture taken beside the pale coral birds, she briefly regretted the lack of a camera to record her encounter with the remarkably intelligent bevy of birds surrounding them. There would be other days, other times, she consoled herself, when

events like this would be recorded on film.
Wouldn't there?

That wistful question was debatable, she decided, climbing once more into the jeep beside
Toby. It was wishful thinking to dream of coming
here again; not with Toby, for all his attraction as
a companion. It was Jake who filled her mind as
they pursued their island journey, Jake's hard-
hewn features she remembered as they walked the
secluded paradise of Love Beach. Was this love?
This aching sense of regret that it was Toby's
sturdy stride that matched hers and not Jake's
long-legged leanness? If it was, then it was an
emotion she had never experienced before.

She took off her sandals and contented herself
with wading through the warm shore waters, her
feet washed by the white frothing roll of incredibly
clean water. If this was love, how foolish to feel
that way about Jake! Or any man, she reminded
herself dismally. A dream of erotic pleasure,
where she gave gladly and freely, was one thing.
Being the woman of her dreams in the cold light of
day was something entirely different.

When Toby turned back at last, she followed
him. This time she walked on the hard-packed
white sand, the silence between them quietly com-
panionable. A companion—that's all she could
ever be to a man. Even a man as nice as Toby
would expect, demand, more of her. It was bleak
consolation to know that one day another woman
would walk by Toby's side, one who would link

her fingers with his, her future with his. An unreasonable jealousy surged and filled her. How could the gods have been so unjust?

That they could was brought home forcibly when the jeep was once more nestled in its resting place in front of the station clubhouse.

"We've lots of time before dinner—" Toby handed her gallantly one more time from the utility vehicle "—so why don't we have a drink before making for the shower?"

"Sounds good to me." She returned his smile, forcing it slightly, and added as they linked arms to walk to the clubhouse, "But not one of Perry's Goombay Specials, if you don't mind. A medium sherry's fine for me."

"Okay." His smile broadened to a grin when he looked teasingly at her. "I must say, after a day in your company I don't need anything more stimulating than a cool glass of beer."

They were still arm-in-arm when they entered the lounge, Toby's eyes still trained admiringly on her lilting smile, so that he missed the frosty stares emanating from the far corner. Denise muttered under her breath.

"What did you say?"

"It's them," she hissed, pulling her arm from his and putting up her hand to smooth the tousled silver of her hair. "The people in the café. They're here with Jake."

"So?" Toby's gaze went around the room and fastened on the glowering group. "Oh, those ones." His voice changed, then he went on dismissingly, "It's not important. Jake would be the first one to appreciate the joke, especially where that woman's concerned."

But there was nothing of humor in Jake's steely gray eyes when he and the group of visitors passed close to where she and Toby were relaxing over their drinks. He spoke exclusively to Denise.

"Did you enjoy your day?"

"Very much," she returned coolly, her fingers suddenly sensitive to the hard-cut crystal in her hand.

The brittle voice of the dark woman intervened. "I could have answered that for her. She and her...friend here were all over each other in that miserable café we stopped at before getting here. In fact they were so absorbed they apparently forgot where they came from." Toby flinched narrowly when she turned her wrathful eyes on him as he got to his feet. "Isn't that what you told us, that you'd never heard of this ocean research station?"

"It was a joke, of course," he returned stiffly. "Nothing to make a federal case of. I apologize if my sense of humor ran away with my tongue."

"I'd say it was more a case of the beer you were swilling running away with it," she threw back tartly before turning to Jake. "I'm surprised you don't have a stricter code of conduct for the employees of your stations, Jake. I presume they *are* employed here?"

Denise's eyes flew to Jake's impassive face as he made brief introductions. What was he thinking behind the blandly polite gray eyes? The woman, Sharon Watson, gave her a sharp-eyed scrutiny that took in every part of Denise from the tip of her windblown hair to the toeless sandals at her feet.

"*You're* a scientist?" she marveled insultingly, adding to Jake with a throatily snide laugh, "I can see I'll have to alter my previous conceptions of scientists as dome-headed elderly gentlemen."

"Many thanks," Jake responded dryly.

"Oh, not *you*, of course! How stupid of me. It's just that I think of you more as Barbara's husband than a serious man of science."

"She never took my work seriously, either." He looked pointedly into her eyes. "Maybe that's why I'm her ex-husband."

Unabashed, Sharon pressed on, "That's something she regrets very much, you know, Jake. She's never really been happy with—"

Her husband, Harry, intervened with embarrassed haste. "We have to go now, Sharon, if we want to make that dinner engagement."

With nods from the other couple and none at all from Sharon, the group moved off to the door, and Toby sank down again in the comfortably armchair. "Jeez," he breathed gustily, "it's women like that who put men off marriage. How in the hell does he stand it?"

"Harry?" Denise, too, resumed her seat, her

body strung up and tense in an unusual way. "Who knows why anybody does anything? Maybe she has hidden qualities not visible to the human eye."

He laughed, then sobered thoughtfully. "I wonder if there's any truth in the rumor that Jake and his ex might get together again?"

"Where did you hear that?" she asked, more sharply than she had intended.

"Here and there." He shrugged. "We're like an exclusive club in our game—nobody keeps secrets for too long. Paul's known Jake for years, and he thinks—"

"I'm really not into pointless gossip," Denise cut him short. Draining the last of her sherry, she stood up again. "I'm heading for the shower now—see you later at dinner?"

She had gone before Toby had time to do more than nod a startled acquiescence. Her timing was off, however, because the Watson car was just disappearing through the tropical growth edging the drive, and Jake was turning in the direction of the staff bungalows. In the moments before he sighted her hesitant figure on the steps of the clubhouse, she saw with a pang that his normally thrown-back shoulders had an uncharacteristic droop about them; a despondence that must, she conjectured, have been brought about by his encounter with the departing visitors. Had Sharon, his ex-wife's friend, stirred memories too painful to cope reasonably with, dormant hopes that the woman he cared most for really did regret their parting?

The mixed feelings churning inside her remained unresolved when his head swiveled around toward her, his steps halting abruptly. The quick leap of anger in his eyes made her shrink back inside herself, though she sensed the main force of his ire was directed away from her.

"So," he said harshly as she went down the steps to join him, "you enjoyed your day with Toby, did you?"

"Shouldn't I have?" she countered the belligerent tone, her steps falling into a natural rhythm with his as they went along the sandy path between the cottages. "You make it sound as if it's a crime."

"Maybe it is." He slanted her a look, turbulence still boiling in the darkened gray of his eyes. "You're too much woman for Toby to handle, or hadn't you guessed?"

"I wasn't aware that Toby or any other man had the problem of 'handling' me, as you so charmingly put it!" she snapped, drawing in a swift, irritated breath when her toe struck a half-submerged root. She paused, eyes blazing their green fire into Jake's. "Are you so jaded in your outlook that you can't imagine a man and woman could enjoy a day in each other's company without sex rearing its ugly head?"

"Ugly?" he questioned softly, making a slow appraisal of the delicate but definite curves of her slender body. "What man could spend a day in surroundings like these with a beautiful woman without feeling those urges you call ugly? Even an inexperienced boy like Toby—"

"He's not inexperienced!" she blurted out with an impulsive defensiveness she regretted the next moment. With those few words, if she read Jake's expression right, she had given him all the ammunition he needed in the battle brewing between them.

"No?" The gray eyes flicked coldly over her face. "So Sharon was right; you two were feeling no pain after leaving the café at noon. What happened then, Denise?" They were standing so close their bodies were almost touching, but still his long, bronzed hand fastened like a vise on her wrist. "Did you find a nice secluded beach and drunkenly make love under the palms?"

Denise wrenched her wrist from his grasp and took a step or two back on the path before flailing him with her eyes. "You're ridiculous, not to mention disgusting! Who the hell do you think you are to question what I do on my free days, anyway? I'm answerable to you when I'm on the job, but my private life is my own, so why don't you just get off my back? Or won't your oversize male ego let you do that, Jake?" she mocked recklessly. "What does it matter to you if Toby and I spent the entire day making passionate lo—"

The remainder of her sentence disappeared in a

gasp as a Jake she scarcely recognized moved, dragging her with shocking impact against the smooth hardness of his supremely fit body. Her startled eyes caught barely a glimpse of the firm line of his lips parting to descend swiftly, crushingly, on hers. Too surprised to struggle, her hands went in an automatic gesture to lie flat on the taut stretch of shirt on his chest, registering abstractedly the powerful beat of his heart against her palm. Her own mouth yielded numbly to the abrasive assault his lips made on it, her mind swirling away in a sea of pure sensation. Some vague part of her recognized that in his way he was punishing her—but for what?

The question drifted from her consciousness as more urgent sensations pulsed their way through her. The soft melt of her thighs into the steady thrust of his evoked the memory of her half dream that morning with Toby on the rock. The same sweet longing divided the defensive closure of her lips, parting them to his hot male seeking. His tongue stabbed provocatively once, twice, and then she felt herself being abruptly, shockingly, put from him.

Stupidly, she stared after his long-limbed figure as he strode rapidly away from her along the sandy path that led to his house. The scent of him, the heady mixture of new sweat combined with the faint breath of the bourbon he favored lingered with her long after he had disappeared, without a backward glance, into the vine-draped bungalow set close to the edge of the track.

Then stumbling, scuffing the powdery white sand behind her, she sought the sanctuary of her own cottage, closing the door and leaning back against it as if the hounds of hell bayed at the other side. Striving for calmness, she took deep breaths and monitored the rapid pace of her heart-beat, willing it to slow and grow steady again.

What was happening to her? A man had kissed her in the way a man kissed a woman he found sexually attractive. Was that so terrible? It happened every day; she had seen the same primitive longing in the eyes of men she barely knew. It meant nothing. Those men went home happily to their wives or girl friends, the recipients of their nobler urges. The betraying looks in their eyes for a woman they lusted briefly for had no significance. Neither was there deep meaning in the fact that Jake had kissed her in a violent passion.

She pushed herself away from the door and went unsteadily into the bedroom, dropping her clothes in a disordered heap beside the bed before going naked into the shower. Under the sharp sting of the spray, she recovered some of the cool detachment that had been her defense for longer than she remembered.

A man like Jake must have inspired unrealistic hopes in the breasts of many women since his break-up with his wife. Hopes doomed to oblivion almost before they were born, because the beautiful Barbara, whatever faults she possessed, still had first call on his heart. The physical act of making love might relieve his basic biologic urges, but only one woman held the core of him. Barbara.

The soap she had lathered on her body ran from her in broad rivulets as she stepped back into the spray's orbit. Was she about to behave like some teenage groupie just because a man like Jake had favored her with his kiss? The deep hunger she had sensed in him hadn't been for her alone. Any woman would have done at that moment.

Why should she care? She rubbed her body briskly with a towel, then reached for the terry robe hanging behind the bathroom door. In a world that conformed to traditional or even modern mores, she was a misfit. A woman without love in a world oriented in one main direction.

A woman, she told herself acridly as she dressed for the evening meal moments later, who filled the spaces in her life with other things. Like work. She was fortunate that her work in marine science absorbed her intellect, taking up the slack left in other areas.

Throwing a shoulder-warming stole over her arm to protect her from the cool air when she returned from the clubhouse, she slung her open-toed sandals over her fingers before stepping out onto the fine-grained sand at the foot of her cottage steps.

The women in Jake's life whom she had castigated for their unrealistic hopes dimmed to insignificance in the light of her own preposterous yearnings. They were normal, capable of satisfying the strong physical urges of men. However poor they might be, they were infinitely richer than she could ever hope for.

CHAPTER SEVEN

ABSORBED IN HER WORK, Denise settled into a routine of sorts during the next few weeks: an early morning swim in the shallow reef-enclosed bay, followed by breakfast at the clubhouse and a morning in the lab.

"The foundation isn't crazy about setting up duplicate facilities here," Jake had told her, when the supplies that Max Pearson had been able to obtain had arrived from the mainland and still fell far short of her listed requirements. "But you can do quite a lot of basic research with what you have now, even though a certain amount of the more involved tests still have to go to Miami."

She had seen surprisingly little of him since that night on the path, whether by accident or his design she was unsure. When there were no dives in the offing he, as well as the other male members of the team, spent most of their working hours in the office complex adjacent to the clubhouse. And Jake, like Carl, seldom joined the impromptu beach parties centered around the Stein bungalow, or the weekend forays to the nearby luxury hotel where Toby comically despaired of ever turning her into a golfer, while she regularly belittled his tennis game.

The friendship that had been cemented that day of their island tour grew stronger, and there was only a faint sense of betrayal when, on occasion, Toby succumbed to the attractions of a vacationing beauty and left Denise to make a threesome with Paul and Marie. Between them there was a tacit understanding that Denise still mourned the husband she had lost two years before, and she saw no point in disillusioning them on that score. Sam, in death, was providing more protection than he ever had in life. Even Jake accepted that fact, although there were times when his eyes bored like steel rods into her when he encountered the camaraderie existing between herself and Toby.

She had seen Jake only once at the hotel. It was a Saturday evening, and she had been shocked by her own reaction to seeing him with a sophisticated, elegantly attractive woman who obviously found him equally desirable. Her eyes had strayed back again and again to where they danced hip to hip, and it had needed little exertion of her imagination to know that by morning they would know each other as intimately as male and female could. The unfamiliar claws of jealousy contracted somewhere in her chest and cut off her breath. While Denise danced with a holiday visitor to the islands, her eyes had met Jake's briefly and her lips gave a cool smile of recognition, but her heart had been a stone in her breast as her well-set partner turned her away, murmuring words she didn't hear.

Now, on this sun-kissed morning—unbelievably December—she took her usual route across the sand for her morning swim. Jake's daughter and the Steins' son, David, had arrived together the previous evening, realizing Marie's joyous anticipation of her family's reunion.

Wading into the cool clear water, Denise wondered what a child by her and Sam would have looked like. Fair, no doubt, because of their fairness, chubbily rounded limbs like Sam's, a blue green mixture of eye color.... Striking out when the water reached her thighs, she forcibly dismissed the question of what a child born of herself and Jake would be like. He already had a child with the woman he loved, so it was irrelevant.

The small girl regarding her curiously from the beach as Denise stood up and waded to shore had to be Jake's daughter, from the dark brown hair that crinkled as if used to plaits, though now it reached loosely to her shoulders, to the light gray, femininely shaped eyes.

"Hi," Denise nodded neutrally, pressing both hands over her wet hair, the moisture from that mingling on her shoulders with the glistening drops of seawater. "You must be Meg. I'm Denise."

The light eyes regarded her warily, calculatingly. "Hi," she said cautiously. "Is the water warm?"

Denise put her head to one side, considering. "It depends on whether you usually swim in a heated pool. If so, then it's cold. If not—" she shrugged "—it's unbelievably warm after the first chill wears off."

One slender foot tested the frothing wave that ran unhurriedly onto the hard wet sand and drew back with a jerk. "It's really cold," the young yet crabbily mature voice complained.

"Then don't go in." Denise shrugged, faintly irritated by the child's overly confident self-possession. "It gets warmer in a couple of hours."

The girl appraised her from head to toe with one comprehensive sweep of her gray eyes. "Do you work for my father?"

"I work with the team, yes."

"Are you the secretary?"

Denise returned the haughty look coolly. "No, Christina does the secretarial work for the team. I'm a marine biologist. I study plant and animal life in the ocean."

"Daddy's never had a *woman* working for him before," the scathing retort came.

"Really? That's strange; there are a lot of women in oceanography these days."

Denise had turned and faced out to sea, drawing a diagram with her toes in the wet sand and watching the depressions fill in with the colorless clear water. She didn't see Jake's approach until he called out, "Hi. I see you two have met."

She felt Meg's eyes on her as she swung around and faced Jake, browned and virile looking in white swim shorts.

"Yes."

He gave her a quick, appraising glance, then looked thoughtfully at Meg. "Denise is—"

"I know," his daughter interrupted, then smiled ingratiatingly. "I'll race you out to those rocks."

"Not on your life. Halfway."

"Okay," she agreed without demur, and ran, splashing, into the water, showing no signs of her earlier disdain for its coldness. Giving Denise a quick grin, Jake followed her, and soon they were stroking steadily toward the invisible point culminating their race, Jake staying slightly to the rear of his daughter.

Denise watched for a while, then turned to trudge across the sand to her cottage. Jake's child would, in the natural course of events, be a strong swimmer. That her personality could do with a smoothing of the rough edges must be a concern of her parents.

Under the shower, Denise wondered again what Jake's wife was like, but this time as a mother. Was Meg a reflection of her mother's arrogant self-assurance? Or was it her child's way of coping with the disintegration of their small family unit? She was ten now, so the breakup must have come when she was five—two years older than Denise herself had been at the time of her mother's departure. Old enough to remember the closeness there had once been between the three of them.

The bond of sympathy engendered by that first meeting was sorely tried in the days that followed. Accompanied by Jake and the polite David, who was a replica of Paul apart from possessing Marie's fiery dark eyes, on a royal tour of the station, Meg had glanced with unroyal disdain around Denise's small laboratory.

"We have a better lab than this at school," she scorned, suppressing the gleam of interest that lighted her eyes when they passed over the long row of tanks holding varicolored fish and plant life.

"Denise's lab isn't funded by doting parents," Jake interjected dryly, his eyes amused as they met Denise's. "She's managing very well with her primitive lab, though she's used to better things."

"Wow," David breathed, nose pressed to the largest tank, where a small section of the underwater world swam nervously into their hiding places in the coral Denise had provided for them. "I'd like to have a neat job like yours, collecting fish and watching them all the time."

"There's a little more to it than that, David." Denise laughed, indicating the benches where specimen particles lay in shallow trays immersed in chemical solutions, the frozen sections under the microscope. "Right now I'm determining whether the pollution carried by the Gulf Stream is affecting the plant and animal life in the Tongue of the Ocean. See here." She positioned his shoulders over the microscope. "This is a frozen section of a grouper fish. This tag tells me that it was taken from a one-hundred-foot depth on this date...." Although it was David's shoulders she held between her hands, she was more conscious of Meg's breath-holding concentration as she expounded the intricacies of her job to David. "So you see, your father and Dr. Barstow take it from there. They test the winds and currents farther out, then I take more samples, and the whole process begins again."

David looked around with a glowing face and said, "Do you think dad would mind if I went in for marine biology, Uncle Jake?"

"I doubt it," Jake returned, indulgently amused. "Why don't you talk to him about it?"

"Daddy, you said you'd take us on the ship," Meg complained. "I want to see the sub—sub-mess—"

"Submersible," David cut in loftily, then turned with a boyish grin to Denise. "Thanks a lot for showing us your fish and everything." His dark eyes brightened hopefully. "Could I collect some specimens for you?"

"As long as they're properly tagged," Denise smiled, her arm around his shoulder as the group moved to the door. "And that means depth, date, time of day."

"Sure," he said eagerly. "I'll make a note of everything."

Wondering if her limited tank capacity would hold the proliferation of fish the boy would enthusiastically bring to the lab, Denise watched the trio depart in the direction of the pier and the mother ship. Jake's grateful, and perhaps admiring, smile lingered with her even after she had turned back to the slides awaiting her attention.

But thoughts of the young girl, so vulnerable, so possessive of the father she obviously adored, obsessed Denise's mind as she bent over the microscope and scribbled notes blindly on the pad beside it. She knew there would be big problems ahead for everyone concerned, especially Jake, if he should ever decide to marry again.

JUST WHAT MEG'S PLANS WERE for her father were unfolded the following Saturday when Marie threw a beach party to welcome the two vacationing children.

Sated with swimming and water games, Denise sat with Marie under one of the weathered palm-thatched shelters dotted here and there on the rise of sand leading to the clubhouse. Meg, who seemed to have taken to the cherubic Cindy, played with her a short distance away. The male members of the party, surprisingly including Carl, who normally kept to himself, snorkeled in the thigh-deep waters of the bay.

"It's a shame she's the only one," Marie murmured to Denise. "If she'd had a younger brother or sister to care for—"

"I *will* have one soon." Meg turned on her fiercely, and Marie looked as if she wanted to bite her tongue right out of her head.

"Oh," she said perplexedly, then couldn't resist a curious, "Is your mother—"

"No," scorned Meg as Marie paused delicately. She cast a sly look, not at Marie, but at Denise. "When Barbara and daddy get married again they'll have lots of babies, and I can take care of them because I'll be their big sister."

"Honey," Marie hesitated, sympathetic in a motherly way, "your mother is married to someone else. She can't marry your daddy again."

"She can, too," the small figure insisted defiantly, the eyes that were so much like Jake's fixed with cold grayness on the concerned Marie. "When she gets her divorce from Maitland she's going to marry daddy again, and we'll be together just like we were before."

There was something shocking about such a young child's glib use of the word "divorce," and Denise felt a momentary repulsion before an intangible force made her heart stretch out to the pathetic child clinging determinedly to the dream of reenacting the blissful togetherness she recalled from her early life. A bliss that had probably never existed, at least for her parents. If her own mother hadn't died, wouldn't "divorce" have come just as easily to Denise's lips?

None of them heard Jake's approach across the soft sand until he spoke in a furiously contained tone.

"Meg, I've told you over and over again that your mother and I will never, ever, be married again. Why can't you believe that?"

Meg spun around at the first sound of her father's voice, her lower lip trembling for a moment before firming to a disciplined line. "Because mommy loves you," she blurted as if they were alone, dropping the use of her mother's name. "She told me so. And you love her, or you would have married somebody else by now."

The words were so obviously parrotted from the woman most important in her life that Denise looked sickly at Jake, knowing that he must realize the same thing. There was no joy, no triumph, in his strongly carved face, only a blazing fury in the gray eyes that were directed to his daughter.

"I've told you before, Meg, that you can't make the world what you want it to be," he said harshly, adding emphatically, "There is no way that you can bring your mother and me together again. No one's more sorry about it than I am, but that's the way it is."

Stubbornness ruled Meg's barely formed features for a moment, then with an inarticulate cry she turned and ran across the powdery sand in the direction of their cottage.

Cursing softly, Jake stared after her, dropping the fins he had been using as his jaw worked emotionally. The heel strap of one fin had ripped apart, presumably his reason for leaving the snorkeling party.

Marie rose hurriedly and scooped a protesting Cindy into her arms. "Time for your nap, poppet." Giving Denise an apologetic smile, she carried the struggling Cindy homeward.

"I guess I'd better go and talk to Meg," Jake said into the silence surrounding them after Marie's departure.

"Please—" Denise lifted a staying hand as he took a few steps in the direction Meg had taken "—let me."

"You?" He swung around to look at her with unflattering disbelief.

"I...think I know a little of what she's going through," she said hesitantly.

"How can you?" he questioned harshly, his mouth twisting in a humorless smile. "The pampered miss of San Diego high society."

Her lashes fell in a pale brown arc on her cheeks. "I'm from a broken family, too," she said with a simplicity that hid the quick surge of remembered deprivation in her formative years.

Jake looked stunned as he let himself down to a sitting position beside her. "You?" he queried again, still disbelieving.

"My mother left my father—and me—when I was three years old," she said unemotionally, seeing with half an eye the bobbing heads on the ocean not far away. "Not long after she left us she was killed, with the man she was with, in a traffic accident."

Jake muttered a soft curse under his breath and

stared unseeingly at the same bobbing heads. "I had no idea. I imagined that you'd...lived an ideal childhood."

"Is any life ideal?" she countered, rising to her feet and brushing the dry sand from her heated skin. "People marry and think it's going to be just like the storybooks tell them it should be. But it isn't, is it?"

Jake pushed himself up to a standing position before answering. "No, it isn't," he said then, his eyes a darkened gray as they glanced off hers and went down to the vulnerable curve of her mouth. "I'd be grateful for anything you could do to help. I just don't seem to be able to get through to her on the subject of her fantasies."

Denise sifted white sand through her fingers. "Is there no chance that this particular fantasy could come true?" she put carefully, and out of the corner of her eye saw his head swivel quickly.

"I'm not contemplating remarrying my ex-wife, if that's what you mean."

It had been what she meant, but she wondered as she went slowly across the sand to the Barstow cottage if she had imagined that note of quiet desperation in his voice. Was he, as Marie and Meg thought, still in love with Barbara? Did he nourish the same hopes as Meg, but hesitate to admit it because their nonfulfillment would shatter not only his life but Meg's as well?

It was her first visit to the bungalow, but its layout was similar to the Steins', and she soon found Meg stretched out on a single bed in a room at the end of the passage. The open door of the room opposite attracted her attention, and she glanced quickly at what must be the master bedroom—Jake's, presumably, although it was so pin neat that she wondered. The cool mid blue of the bedspread was folded and tucked neatly across the double bed, and curtains to match hung at the wide, shallow windows.

"Meg?" she called softly, tapping on the door before pushing it open farther. "May I come in?"

"No! Go away," the muffled voice came from the depths of a white pillow.

"I'd like to stay and talk to you for a while."

Meg raised a tearstained face from the pillow and glared at her suspiciously. "Why? Did daddy ask you to come? I wish he hadn't—I don't want *you* here." Denise winced at the emphasis but proceeded calmly to pull up the white-painted desk chair to the side of the bed.

"Your father didn't ask me to come," she said quietly. "I asked him if I might come and talk with you."

"Why should you want to?" The belligerent tone was lost in a sobbing gulp.

"Because I can remember feeling very sorry for myself, too, when I was your age and younger. My parents split up, too, when I was three years old, and not long after that my mother was killed in an accident. I used to dream about what it would have been like if she'd never left, never died. In my dreamworld my parents loved each other and me, and we were the happiest people in the world."

Meg's tears had stopped, and she stared with her gray eyes in fascination at Denise.

"I was much older than you are now when I realized that even if my mother hadn't died, they would never have come together again. They just didn't love each other enough." Her mouth curved in a wry smile. "And it took me even longer to realize that it wasn't my fault they couldn't be happy together. They both loved me, but they couldn't love each other."

"But my parents do," Meg insisted stubbornly, although there was a beginning gleam of what might be compassion in her opaque eyes.

"That's something you can't decide for them," Denise pointed out gently, stretching out a hand to circle the thin sun-reddened wrist. "You weren't the cause of them breaking up, and you won't be the cause of them coming together again. That's something that's very personal between two people, even though they're your parents and they both love you."

She was surprised and not a little overwhelmed when the small figure knelt on the bed then threw her arms around her. "I'm sorry I've been so mean to you. I really like you now; it was just that—" Meg pulled her soft-skinned face away and burst out, embarrassed, "You're so beautiful, I didn't want daddy to fall in love with you."

Denise put her hands at either side of the earnest face. "I promise you he won't do that. And even if he did, I . . . never want to marry again."

"Oh." Meg looked at her consideringly, struggling for understanding. "Your husband died, didn't he? And you loved him an awful lot, and that's why you never want to get married again."

Forcing a smile, Denise neither confirmed nor denied her love for Sam. Everyone else at the station believed her fidelity to his memory was born of an undying love they had shared. Why not Meg?

"YOU'D BETTER WATCH IT," Marie said a few days later when she stopped in at the lab, Cindy in tow. "That child's liable to get you married off to Jake if you're not careful." She looked at Denise curiously. "What did you do to switch her loyalties from her pleasure-loving mother to our dedicated scientist?"

"Don't be silly, Marie," Denise said, faintly irritated by the older woman's seeming penchant for gossipy innuendo. "She's a ten-year-old child who needs friends the same way we all do. She likes you, but that doesn't mean she wants to pair you off with her father."

"I would hope not," Marie retorted, unperturbed. "One scientist in my life is all I can handle. Still," she sighed, "Jake is—Jake." Her eyes rolled expressively and Denise laughed.

"It's a good thing Paul's not around to hear

you extol the virtues of another man. He's quite a dish himself.''

"That's odd; he was saying the same thing about you last night at dinner.'' She slanted a sly look at Denise. "Is it significant that Jake agreed with him?"

"Not in the least.'' Denise had seen the father and daughter pair take the communal path to the Steins' house the evening before. "Marie, I just hope you're not getting the idea that Jake—that he admires me in any way apart from a strictly professional viewpoint.''

Marie looked thoughtful, then stepped over to the screen door to satisfy herself that Cindy was playing happily on the sand. "It doesn't matter what we think. But really, Denise, Jake would be an infinitely more suitable companion for you than Carl.''

"Carl?''

"You did go to the hotel with him on Saturday night, didn't you?''

It was like a small town, Denise thought, crossing to bend over a tank containing the lively small fish from her first dive in the sub. True, she had gone with Carl to the hotel the previous Saturday, mainly because she had been so surprised by his invitation that she could think of no plausible excuse for refusing.

"Yes, I went with him—'' she straightened and looked almost defiantly at Marie "—and I enjoyed it.''

"Really?" Marie shrugged expressively. "He always strikes me as a pretty cold fish. Did you dance a lot?"

Denise widened her eyes in question. "No, we talked most of the time. Carl's interested in my field, too. There was nothing romantic about it," she added bluntly to the glint of disbelief in Marie's dark eyes. "Carl's interest in me is purely scientific, and that's the way I want it to be."

"I wonder if his intentions are all that pure," Marie doubted thoughtfully. "Men like Carl always make me imagine all kinds of illicit passion seething beneath their sexless exterior."

"You should be writing novels of romance and intrigue," Denise suggested dryly. "You certainly have the imagination for it."

The other woman turned resignedly to the door as a plaintive wail came from Cindy outside. "Maybe I'll do that," she called back over her shoulder, "and I'll use Carl for my first hero."

Smiling, Denise watched her scoop up the screaming child and make for the cottages farther along the beach, her small but beautifully shaped legs shown to advantage in short shorts.

Carl was certainly no storybook hero, she reflected, frowning as she turned back into the small lab. It was true that she had enjoyed the evening with him as far as the shoptalk went, but she had sensed something of what Marie had suggested on the few occasions when they danced on the crowded floor. Secretive depths of him that would be hard to unearth, supposing a person wanted to. And she didn't.

"WILL YOU COME, DENISE?" Meg pleaded as they waded from the warm waters of the curving bay. "Daddy's a great cook," she said eagerly, then honesty struggled for supremacy as she qualified, "most of the time. He's not too hot on anything that needs pastry or stuff like that, but he cooks the greatest steaks and makes fantastic salads."

"All right, Meg, you've sold me on him," laughed Denise, pulling off her diving mask from its perch on her silvery hair and slipping it over one finger as she bent to take off the long rubber fins encasing her feet.

Meg did the same, and with "I'd better go tell him," she rushed across the sand in the direction of the bungalow she shared with her father.

Meg's limbs had browned quickly in the hot sun where she spent hours each day, either swimming with David's lofty twelve-year-old supervision, or playing with Cindy on the beach or in the enclosed garden behind the Steins' bungalow.

But there was a far greater change in her personality in this past week. Where before she had been suspicious and distrustful, she now had the happy, outgoing nature of the ten-year-old she was. A lot of it, Denise knew, was due to the relaxed atmosphere around the research station, the unlimited sun and freedom from the routines that bounded her normal life, just as any vacationer shed the everyday cares and woes of the cold northern climate when they came to the islands. But there was an added freedom in Meg's case; the shedding of suspicion of the motives of attractive women who came within her father's orbit.

Admittedly, she thought wryly as she padded up the steps to her own cottage, there was only one woman apart from herself who came within Jake's everyday orbit, and Meg had dismissed Christina at the moment of their meeting. She was "too much," Meg confided later to Denise, and Denise knew at once what she meant. Christina was too overpoweringly female for fastidious men's tastes, and Jake would be nothing if not fastidious in his taste in women.

Which left Denise. Meg felt no threat from her now because she assumed that Denise had the romantic drama on her hands of still being in love with her dead husband. As the shower poured warmly over her head and shoulders, she reflected that Meg's newfound trust in her had done nothing to blur the edges of her attraction toward Jake. He just had to appear to make jelly of her knees, to speak to her to close her throat in an agonized dryness. Her nipples surged now to expectant points when she recalled his long brown hands caressing the white rise of her softly rounded breasts.

Such thoughts were deeply submerged under a cool exterior when she presented herself at the Barstow bungalow some time later.

"She's here, daddy," Meg called excitedly from the far side of the screened porch door, "she's here."

"Then ask her in," a distracted male voice filtered out from the depths of the house.

Beaming, looking daintily feminine in white Swiss lace, Meg swept the door aside and waved Denise in.

"You look very beautiful," Denise smiled, glad that she herself had worn a dressy cream linen that left her tanned shoulders bare apart from the straight narrow straps joining the bodice to back.

"You do, too," Meg returned shyly, as if unused to paying compliments to women who might constitute a threat to her father's susceptibility. Waving vaguely to the blue upholstered furniture circling the living room, she said, "Please sit down. I'll pour you a cocktail."

"Pour one for me while you're at it, Meg," Jake said, harried looking as he appeared from the kitchen. Denise noted thankfully that he was minus the apron many American men assumed on slightest contact with the kitchen area. "Hi," he nodded to Denise. "Glad you could come."

"Well, I did turn down an invite from Buckingham Palace from the prince," she told him with mock regret, encouraged by Meg's sudden giggle from the bar where she painstakingly poured martinis into two wide-mouthed glasses, "not to mention an Arab sheik's offer to show me how much oil he has stashed away in his fields."

"I don't care." Jake, falling in with her humor, waved away the grandeur of princes and palaces with the glass Meg handed him. "They can't offer you the thick, tender, secretly seasoned steak that I can. Those people you mentioned would kill for my marinade secrets, but only my daughter will ever possess the knowledge of the Barstow legend."

Meg, a soft excited gleam in her light gray eyes, deflated his grandiose speech with a dampening, "Oh, daddy, you got that recipe from that gourmet cookbook!"

Jake threw her a baleful look as he took the armchair at right angles to the sofa where Denise sat. It was obviously his favorite chair, placed as it was to get balanced sound from the stereo system.

"Not entirely, my dear," he sneered with all the evil of an old-time villain. "There are a few extra ingredients, such as the entrails of an impudent, disloyal daughter!"

Denise blessed her own instinctive choice of instigating a humorous note to the evening; she had never seen Jake in this mellow, family-man mood before, and it was only now that she realized how normally solemn his features were. Even his voice seemed to relax its clipped brusqueness as he kept them amusingly entertained.

From the steaks, delicately seasoned with herbs and exotic spices, to the strong brew of American coffee that rounded off the meal and the lightest of Jake's classical records providing a quiet background of music, the evening was an unqualified success. Denise, who hadn't expected to enjoy it, found that she hated to see it end when Jake at last suggested bed for Meg.

"It's time I left, too," she said, rising and collecting her purse from the coffee table.

"You don't have to go," Jake said casually. "Have another drink."

"Thanks, no. I think I've had my limit for one evening," she smiled, stepping to the door. "I've enjoyed it all so much, and I wish I could reciprocate but—" Her regretful smile embraced both of them as she shrugged.

Meg looked at her father imploringly, her feet beginning to dance excitedly. "Ask her now, daddy, *please*." Pinpoints of light gleamed in the eyes that were so like Jake's.

"As a matter of fact, there *is* a way you could reciprocate, if you'd be interested." Jake's expression sobered as he looked at Denise, brows raised questioningly.

"I'm...not sure how I can," she hesitated, glancing from one to the other, curious yet apprehensive.

"Meg would—Meg and I," he corrected, "would like you to come with us to Max Pearson's house in Nassau for the Junkanoo celebrations. You may recall that Max invited you at the same time."

"Yes, I remember, but—" her gaze went to Meg's shining eyes "—wouldn't you rather spend that part of your vacation alone with your father?''

''Not if you'd come with us. It would be a lot more fun if you were there, too, Denise,'' Meg coaxed eagerly. ''Please say you'll come.''

Denise looked at Jake and found his expression neutral, seemingly uncaring whether she accepted or not. ''I'd love to,'' she said impulsively, and Meg swooped forward to hug her around the waist.

''We'll have a wonderful time! Daddy's going to show us around Nassau and take us to an old house for dinner and take you to the cas—cas—''

''Casino?'' Denise supplied, her eyes questioning as they met Jake's above Meg's head. It was obvious from the child's excited chatter that they had discussed the Nassau visit in some detail— even before knowing that she would go with them.

''That's it.'' Meg stepped back, eyes shining. ''You can win lots of money there.''

''And lose a lot, too,'' Denise pointed out, but some of Meg's enthusiasm had already spilled over to her own veins. She had spent a few afternoons exploring Nassau on her own, but had never ventured much farther than the tourist-filled shops lining the west end of Bay Street. It would be lots of fun to wander through the historic streets in company with someone familiar with the background of the island. That Jake was an interesting guide she already knew from that first drive into Nassau.

"I'll see Denise home while you get ready for bed," Jake interrupted their mutual rapture, stepping forward to swing the door open for Denise. "I'll only be a few minutes, but I want you in bed by the time I get back."

"I will be, daddy," Meg said with such docility that Denise stared at her in amazement. Gone were the sullen, suspicious looks of a mere week before—in their place the joyful eagerness of a normal ten-year-old. All because she herself had established a point of oneness between them, a surety that she was no threat to the closeness between Meg and her father? It was an awesome thought, a responsibility Denise half resented. Meg's mother, Barbara, should be giving her daughter that kind of security, not a woman mixed up in her own emotions.

Jake ignored her objections that she could see herself home perfectly well, and he fell into step beside her, splaying lazy spurts of white sand behind his heels as they walked under the rustling fronds of the lofty royal palms.

"I want to thank you for what you've done for Meg," he said tautly, the evening's easy banter replaced by heavy seriousness. "She's a different girl now, free somehow—" he shrugged "—laughing more than she ever has before."

"Maybe that's because you're laughing now," Denise pointed out briskly, stifling the swift rise of pleasure his words stirred. She gave him a thoughtful sideways glance. "Children take their cues from their parents, I imagine."

"And who did you take your cues from?" They had halted as if by mutual consent under the gnarled barks of the trees edging the beach, facing each other in a moon's light that glinted in their eyes and smudged deep shadows under their cheekbones.

"My father, I suppose." She shrugged, sadness seeping through her as she remembered her father's austere life, the lack of love in it.

"He never married again?"

"No, he—I don't think he could ever love anyone after my mother."

"Because of you?"

"Me?" she blinked uncomprehendingly.

"How would you have felt about it if he'd wanted to marry somebody else?"

"I—well, I'd have—" she paused, her eyes fixed unseeingly on his, wondering how she would have felt if her father had taken another wife. Would she have felt shocked, betrayed, in spite of her mother's abandonment? "I guess I'd have hated her, whoever she was."

"So you can understand why I'm pleased—very pleased—that Meg has accepted you, likes you, wants your company?"

It came to her suddenly that Jake was grateful for her opening the way to Meg's acceptance of a woman he might want to marry someday. A woman who would accept gladly what he offered her.

"I can understand that, yes," she told him, the slight catch in her voice betraying the expected pain that knifed under her breast. She turned her head from him and let her eyes follow the silver path the moon made on the still water. The woman he married eventually would have to match inch for inch the dark passionate parts of his nature, the parts he concealed under a controlled surface.

His hand moved and touched her face, drawing it around until she looked at him again. The hard edge of his voice was blurred when he said softly, "If you're worried there might be a repeat of what happened between us before, don't be. I realize now what a crass idiot you must have thought me when I came on to you like that. I never used to be that insensitive, but the women I've known lately haven't had your quality of loyalty to a husband she loved very much." There was a brief gleam of white teeth. "That's as close to an apology as I can come. I just wanted to make sure you knew that when we go to Max's place there won't be anything like that between us, unless that's the way you want it to be."

Bending, he kissed her lightly on the lips, his fingers tightening briefly around her chin. Then he turned and walked back the way they had come, leaving her to travel the last few yards to her cottage alone.

But the close confines of the small rooms weren't appealing at that moment and, slipping off her sandals and leaving them on the sand, she picked her way across the beach to water's edge, letting its coolness wash over her feet as she walked slowly around the curving bay away from the cottage settlement.

Unless she wanted it that way—the words echoed and reechoed in her mind until she put her hands over her ears to shut them out. Still they persisted, until she admitted to herself that she did want it that way. Wanted to be with Jake the way a woman wanted to be with a man she loved, caressing the secret parts of her. Her body grew soft, fluid, at the thought of Jake making love to her.

Her feet sank into the moist sand as she paused and turned outward to the sea. How could she ever let Jake discover that one final secret, the knowledge that she was only half a woman, unable to respond to that deepest of all physical commitment? He would despise her, as Sam had, and she in her turn would come to hate him, as she now admitted she had come to loathe Sam. Sam's death was a guilt she would always carry with her; there was no reason to add to that guilt by including Jake in the list of her life's casualties.

CHAPTER EIGHT

"DINNER'S READY, Mrs. Jordan," the steward called after tapping on her cabin door.

"Thanks, Noah, I'll be there in just a minute."

Denise brushed lipstick lightly across her mouth, then smoothed the blue denim top over her jeans-clad hips. Not that it mattered, she reflected, giving herself a last cursory appraisal in the long, narrow cabin mirror. With only herself and Carl aboard the research vessel, apart from the crew, the finer points of makeup were unimportant. This trip was something far removed from a normal survey. Carl could make his scientific name from it, not to mention her chance of making biological history in her discovery of a plant life so far only known in the barren Sargasso Sea, south of Bermuda.

The uncharted area Carl wanted to explore was close to the largest Bahamian island, Andros. In the morning they would reach it, and Denise felt a thrill of excitement as she passed along the passage leading to the saloon. When Carl had first broached the possibility of a private research trip, she had felt uncertain.

"But Jake's not here," she had objected, frowning as she looked across the clubhouse table only she and Carl shared at dinner. "Shouldn't he be in on it?" Jake, accompanied by Meg, had left that day for Miami to check out new equipment that could possibly be used on the project.

Carl's face had tightened to a pinched sallowness. "I am second-in-command," he'd said stiffly. "When he is not here I am free to undertake my own surveys. I have done so many times when Dr. Shepherd was unable to take charge himself."

"Yes, of course, Carl," Denise had assured him quickly, "I wasn't doubting your authority, but—" She bit nervously on her lower lip. "Well, Jake's the head of the team. Wouldn't it reflect on him if you made this charting alone?"

He had leaned across the table earnestly, almost pleadingly. "Barstow has made many such discoveries; one more would mean little to him. For me. . . ." He shrugged eloquently.

Perhaps there had been something of compassion in her agreement to go with Carl, the man only she, out of all the team members, found compatible, even if not really friendly. Or maybe she had still been feeling the impact of that evening with Meg and Jake, an evening that had raised a tantalizing curtain on what might have been but could never be.

"Who's going with us?" she had asked, "Toby, of course, and—"

"No, there will just be us, and the crew, of

course. I have piloted the sub many times, and we have no need for an observer. And please—'' he had leaned forward again ''—say nothing to the others about this. They would no doubt want to come along, and I would like this to be my own baby, as you say.''

That was understandable enough, she reflected now as she took her place at the long narrow saloon table, laid for two at its far end. Carl appeared from deckside at the same time that Noah, the young steward, placed bowls of a hearty vegetable soup at each setting.

''I have instructed Henry to pull up anchor an hour before dawn,'' Carl said with satisfaction, seating his narrow, compact frame and reaching for his spoon. ''In that way we will be over the diving area by seven.''

''Does Captain Mike often take off on a spree?'' asked Denise dryly, hastening to add, ''Not that Henry isn't competent, but surely if the captain's job is to take out the ship, he should be on hand to do it.''

Carl concentrated on his soup, then looked at her abstractedly. ''What? Oh, the captain. He is probably losing himself to the world in a bar over the hill in Nassau. The man is hopelessly incompetent.''

''But interesting,'' she smiled, recalling the old seaman's tales in the clubhouse after dinner when he and she had been the only occupants of the lounge.

"You are too vulnerable, my dear." Carl still sounded preoccupied, and Denise looked at him curiously when she replaced her spoon and leaned back in her chair. Obviously the charting of an underwater cavern previously undiscovered was important to him as a scientist; perhaps he even cherished dreams of having it named after him. But there was a springy tautness about him tonight that made her wonder if she had been altogether wise in coming on such a trip alone with him.

Her fears proved groundless, however. He lost his abstraction as the soup was followed by bone-fish served with a red, peppy sauce and a dessert of fresh fruit. They sat companionably with their coffee on the deep-cushioned settees, then took a walk on the confined deck before turning into their separate cabins.

Undressing, Denise let her thoughts wander to Carl and his odd personality. He was clever, knowledgeable, even interesting in a dry, precise way; he was also devoid of humor, unpopular with his fellows. Maybe that wasn't surprising, she mused as she slid between the covers of the narrow bunk and clasped her hands behind her head on the pillow, staring at the pipes running along the ceiling and walls. His background certainly hadn't been one to promote the lighter aspects of life. Had he ever been in love with anyone? It would be hard to imagine him kissing a woman, making love to her.

Smiling wryly at the turn her thoughts had

taken, she reached up a slender arm and clicked off the light.

THE MISTY PEARL OF DAWN was pressing at the porthole when she woke, the engines throbbing rhythmically down below. Warm, sleepy under the covers, Denise turned over and slept again.

When she next opened her eyes it was to the sound of booted feet overhead, extra loud because the engines were now stilled. Puzzled, she lay frowning. Only diving boots, which the crew didn't wear, would make that much noise on a wooden deck. There was also too much of it for a solitary diver.

Throwing back the covers, she padded barefoot across the floor and drew up the straight chair to a position under the high porthole. Her eyes widened at the sight of a sleek cabin cruiser, dazzling white in the early morning sun, that lay anchored close to the research vessel. What was happening? Had they been boarded by government officials? But they wouldn't be wearing diving boots.

Denise hurried into her one-piece swimsuit and, neglecting sandals, crept along the passage and partway up the companionway to the aft deck. There she stopped, staring in amazement at the helmeted pair of divers preparing to board the submersible along with Carl and a burly, fair-haired man, dressed in shorts and shirts. Around them, the crew prepared for the launch.

Too astonished to move or cry out until the last

of the men disappeared through the conning tower, Denise then ran forward barely in time to see the sub disappear rapidly under the smooth surface of the sea.

Biting her lip, she stared down at the swirling disturbance the sub made. From the way Carl had talked to the men, she knew he couldn't have been coerced into taking them down in the expensive, government-funded equipment. Turning on her bare heel, she ran across the deck and up to where Henry had been supervising the launch from the small control house. His face remained impassive when she burst in and fired questions at him.

"Who are those men with Dr. Madsen, Henry? What are they doing? Where did they come from?"

"They're friends of his," Henry replied without expression. "They come from Andros. He's taken them down before, but I don't know what they do down there."

Friends? Men he was willing to share his great discovery with? More questions battered at Denise's mind, but Henry wouldn't know the answers. Or, if he did, would preserve the same kind of silence he had maintained after seeing Jake make love to her on deck that day.

Turning away, she went down to the saloon, but only picked at the bacon-and-egg breakfast Noah brought to her. What was Carl up to? He had been so down on the idea of Jake taking credit for his discovery, yet here he was sharing it with three strangers, although according to Henry, they were friends of Carl's. That was the strangest thought of all. Carl, who was virtually shunned by the other team members apart from Denise, evidently had qualities he hid from the science world he moved in.

Or were these men scientists from another oceanographic outfit? Men who were overshadowed, as Carl was by Jake, by eminent men in their field?

The questions went on and on in her mind until at last she shrugged them off and decided to do a little diving on her own. Not to the depths where Carl had told her about the unusual plant growth, of course. The sub would be needed for that.

It was well after noon when the sub returned and the men emerged from their deep-sea foray. Carl was more elated than she had ever seen him when he came to where she stood at the side rail.

"Ah, Denise. I am sorry that we had to start before you were around this morning. But we have had a very good day."

"How nice," Denise said frigidly, her eyes shifting to the three men he had taken down with him. "I didn't realize you had arranged to meet friends here."

"Arranged? No, they happened to see us anchor here this morning, and they are keen divers, so—" He shrugged. "It is not often they have the chance to dive as deep as the sub can take them, so they could not resist coming across when they saw us here.'' He stretched out a hand to grasp her elbow and turn her to where the two divers were now divested of their suits. ''Come and meet them. I have asked them to stay for dinner, and perhaps the night.''

''The night?'' Denise echoed, pulling back and staring disbelievingly into his pale blue eyes. ''You can't do that, Carl. This vessel is government property with a goodly share of private funding. It's not meant to accommodate private parties.''

''Who is to know?'' Carl's voice took on a harder edge. ''Jake Barstow will not find out unless you tell him.'' The pressure increased on her arm, and for a moment she felt afraid of Carl's coldly purposeful eyes. ''He would not approve of using these facilities for the furthering of biological science, even for you.''

''Even for me?'' she echoed, arching her blond head to look disdainfully at him. ''What's that supposed to mean?''

He shrugged. ''Only that Dr. Barstow has a—what do you call it? A soft spot for you.''

''That's ridiculous. Jake wouldn't want the ship and its equipment used for you and your friends, and you know it.'' Sudden knowledge filled her eyes when she added slowly, ''That's why you waited until he went to Miami, isn't it? You knew he wouldn't give his consent to a trip like this.''

''Of course not,'' Carl said smoothly, something evil crossing briefly over his deep-set eyes as they flickered down her swimsuit. ''But as I have said, he would not object to *you* collecting your specimens. He must be grateful to you for your effect on his daughter's unpleasant nature. When I watch you from my cottage window it is like seeing a family playing happily together. Is that what you want, Denise—to become his wife, the mother of his child?''

Flushing at the sneer in his voice, Denise threw back, ''I'm not interested in marrying Jake or any other man. As for Meg—''

''Hey, Carl, aren't you going to introduce us to your lady friend?'' The well-set man who had gone down in nondiving gear was sauntering toward them, his curiously mud-colored eyes going appreciatively over her slender curves. He whistled. ''You really believe in going first-class, don't you?''

Denise froze him with a look, then transferred it to Carl, who obviously had no intention of denying the implied relationship between them. ''I'll be giving Jake a full report when we get back,'' she told him icily before turning violently away and striding determinedly to the companionway. Pink flamed again in her cheeks when she heard the other man say snidely to Carl, ''Lovers' tiff? She looks the kind who needs a strong hand on her— or better still, two hands.''

She paced the small cabin in fury. Even with the porthole open, the air was still and stifling in the confined space. How could she have been so foolish as to come on this trip with Carl, believing his enticing talk of the unusual specimens she would find there? There was probably no life at all in the underwater cavern he had spoken of. All he had wanted was a cover for his own activities. Oh, God, she thought, running a slim hand through her hair, already dampened with sweat. He must have slipped a brain cog somewhere to go to these lengths just to be first to chart the underwater cavern. It would be a feather in his scientific cap, of course, but it wasn't *that* world-shattering.

Remembering Marie's conjecture that Carl had expected to be made in charge of the team after Dr. Shepherd's departure, she nodded in silent agreement. That was why he hated Jake so much. Jake, who to him had everything—fame, friends and an attraction for women, none of which Carl possessed.

She stayed in the cabin as the afternoon wore on. Even if she had wanted to leave the stifling confines, the sound of male voices growing progressively louder from the saloon would have made her endure any kind of discomfort.

She sat up quickly on her bunk when a tap came at the door. "Who is it?"

"Dinner's ready, Mrs. Jordan," Noah answered in his soft, lilting voice.

"I—I'm not hungry, Noah."

There was silence until she thought he must have left, then he called softly, "You like me to bring a tray?"

Denise's empty stomach answered for her.

"Please, Noah." The thought of starving until they reached home didn't appeal, though she was adamant that she wouldn't go into the saloon and be introduced to Carl's noisy friends. She was still stunned to know that he had friends at all, let alone the brash type she had met on deck.

Although there was no lock on the door, she went to open it herself when Noah returned. Gesturing to the clear dresser top, she watched him as he unloaded the tray onto it, the sleeves of his crisply starched white jacket creasing at the elbows.

"Are the—Dr. Madsen's friends staying for dinner?"

"They stayin' all night, ma'am." Noah straightened and looked at her with faintly sympathetic liquid eyes. "They're hard drinkers, so they won't eat much dinner."

Wishing more than ever that the cabin doors were equipped with locks, she ushered Noah out and found her appetite gone when she went back to the tray. Picking at the crunchy fried chicken, sipping at the chilled white wine, a thoughtful frown worried her brow. Carl must know that his career, at least as far as this project went, was over the minute they returned to the South Shore jetty. Yet he seemed singularly unconcerned. Why?

THE ANSWER TO THAT QUESTION came later, after Denise had ventured along to the bathroom facilities and showered quickly, slipping back to her cabin while the men still partied in the saloon.

It was cooler now that night had fallen, but her hair dried to a silver cap almost as she combed it. Clad only in the soft silk of pale green pajamas, she climbed impulsively onto the cabin chair and peered once more through the porthole. The cabin cruiser dipped up and down in leisurely fashion, night lights twinkling from bow and stern. One of the crew members must have been sent to see to that, she reflected dryly; none of Carl's friends would have been capable of negotiating a dinghy even over that small distance.

She froze as their voices came closer along the passage, rough, lewdly raucous.

"Let me know when you're through in there, Carl," slurred a voice she wasn't familiar with. "I could do with a little home comfort myself."

"Yeah, why should you have all the luck?" She recognized the voice of the man she had seen on deck. "We're all in this together, buddy, aren't we? Share and share alike?"

Carl murmured something she couldn't catch, and she let her breath out with a relieved sigh. Whatever Carl's faults, she knew him well enough to know that heavy drinking wasn't one of them. Dropping down from the chair, she looked thoughtfully from it to the door. If she wedged it under the handle. . . .

While her eyes were on it, the door opened partially, letting in the last of the whoops and drunken innuendos, then Carl was in, pressing the door closed behind him.

"What are you doing in here?" Denise demanded, finding her breath as her heart began to beat more normally again. "Would you please leave?"

His eyes met the flashing green of hers, then went slowly down her pajama-clad figure, lingering on the swift rise and fall of her breasts under the light top. Pushing himself away from the door, he came toward her with a carefully measured step, and Denise realized wildly that he was as drunk as the men he called his friends. They were just more noisy about it.

"I asked you to leave, Carl." She schooled her voice to steadiness, watching him as a lame bird might watch an approaching cat.

"So? And what will you do about it if I decide to stay?"

His hand reached up to a strand of bright hair that curved close to her cheek, and she flinched away from his touch.

"I can scream, very loudly."

His thin lips drew the line of a smile. "Do you think my companions would care, even if they heard?"

"Henry would hear." She hated the note of desperation that had crept into her voice, but her mind was still reeling from this new picture of Carl. Carl who had always been so coolly self-sufficient, so removed from the passions that motivated other men.

"Henry will say only what I tell him to say. For instance, that you and I have made this a honeymoon trip."

She drew in her breath sharply. "How could he do that? Henry—"

"Will say what I want him to say," Carl broke in smoothly, repeating his previous statement so that it was borne in on Denise that for some reason Henry's loyalties were with him. But why?

As if reading her thoughts, Carl went on, "Every man has his price, and Henry is no exception. A mortgage on a newly built home, a wife who can afford to give up her own employment to nurture the family he wants to have."

Marie's voice again sounded in her ears. "They're saving up to buy a house, so the extra money is very welcome." But Henry? The man who had kept silent about that love scene between Denise and Jake? Silent.... She looked at Carl's self-satisfied eyes and knew that Henry hadn't kept quiet, at least as far as Carl was concerned. That was why she had suspected that Carl knew more than anyone else about that day, the reason for his certainty about Jake having what he called a soft spot for her. Still preoccupied with Henry's perfidy, she hardly noticed Carl's hands at her shoulders until she was drawn to his wiry body and his mouth clamped suddenly on hers.

Shock riveted her to the floor as his lips pressed insistently on hers, forcing them apart, his tongue against her teeth searching for the softness behind them. Unable to move, breath cut from her lungs, she felt his hands slide over the silky front of her pajamas, his fingers pulling, tearing at the buttons until the top parted and gave them access to the firm swell of her breasts. The involuntary tautening of her nipples sent sick waves of horror through her; her hands came up and pulled desperately, viciously, at his pale hair until his head lifted with a jerk, his face convulsing with an icy passion that made him almost unrecognizable.

"Bitch!" he spat, his nostrils pinched to whiteness as breath rushed through them. A tight smile stretched his lips as his eyes went over the angry sparkle in hers, the wild flush of color under her tan, and he said softly, "So, you like it to be rough? This is what excites you?" His hands pressed, tightening painfully on her breasts until she gasped.

"Nothing about you excites me!" she gritted contemptuously through her teeth, willing herself not to cry out and bring his obscene friends running. Rage tossed aside caution as she hissed, "I hated my husband, but he was a prince compared to you!"

His eyes expressed shock, then his lids narrowed over the pale blue. "You *hated* your husband? How can that be, when you make a...a fetish of being an unhappy widow?" She breathed again when his hands dropped away; his voice was sober suddenly. "Why did you hate him? You were not married to him for long."

Denise stepped back to a safer distance and sank onto the chair when its edge nudged against her knees. Her fingers trembled as they refastened the buttons he had torn apart.

"That isn't your business." She schooled her voice to calmness, adding against the beginning speculation in his eyes, "We were...incompatible, that's all."

"In so short a time? In what way?"

Carl had retreated back into the man she knew—thought she had known—but now there was another kind of threat in him. His mathematical brain was now once more in gear, weighing the probabilities, estimating the correctness of his assumption.

"Why don't you mind your own business and get out of here!" She reached for the white terry robe at the foot of the bunk and struggled into it as she stood up. Tying the belt with quick hands, her eyes glinted furiously off the unmoving Carl. "You realize that Jake's going to be told about this, regardless of what you pay Henry to say?"

An unperturbed smile spread over his sallow features. "Jake...ah, yes, Jake. Is he aware of the reason for your aversion to men?"

Her hand clutched then lay still on the throat of the robe. "I...don't know what you mean."

"I think you do." Carl stepped up to her, the smile fixed on his face as he lifted to trail his fingers down her cheek. "See how you shrink from a man's touch? Was it that way with your husband, too?'' The mockery deepened in his light eyes as his voice took on a hypnotic quality. "He was brutal, hmm? Like an animal when he took your innocence, rough and greedy—"

"Stop it! Stop." She put her hands over her ears to block the hateful and too deadly accurate summation of her marriage to Sam.

He did stop, but only for a moment. Then he said softly, "And you think Jake Barstow is the one who will release you from your coldness, do you not?"

"*No!* No man can—" Horrified, she stared at him, knowing she had betrayed the one secret she wanted—needed—to keep hidden. Frigid—the world was as cold as it sounded, leaving her beached on a no-man's-land alone and unloved. Although Carl hadn't actually said it, it was palpable between them.

"We will make a deal, you and I," his quietly controlled voice went on as he stepped away and went to the door. "You will say nothing about what has happened on this trip, and I will keep quiet about your...disability." His gaze went coolly over her body's slender curves, visible even under the thick terry robe, and he drew an exaggerated sigh. "It is a great pity; I am not often drawn to a woman as much as I have been to you."

Not waiting for her agreement or otherwise, he went quietly from the cabin into the night stillness of the narrow passage. For a long time Denise stared at the door, seeing Carl's mocking features etched into the varnished panel, then she collapsed weakly onto the bunk, her head bowed as she tried to make sense of the thoughts churning in her mind.

Was Carl right in supposing that she looked on Jake as the savior of her feminine self, the part of her that Sam had trampled roughly over? It could be, she reflected bleakly, summoning with no difficulty in her mind's eye Jake's leanly contoured frame, the way his mouth formed one of his rare smiles, his long fingers brown against her breasts as they caressed that most female part of her. Was it possible to love someone—to be *in love* with someone—without desiring that final physical consummation?

Rousing herself, she slid off her robe and got under the covers, staring at the black ceiling after switching off the bedside light.

In the sense of loving someone idealistically, in the way long-dead poets had worshiped from afar, she supposed that she did love Jake. She would scale the Andes with him, brave the wilderness with him, battle the unknown depths of the ocean with him. But she couldn't sleep with him, be one with him in the most basic, physical sense.

Yet she knew, long before sleep claimed her, that Carl had won this first round of the new battle between them. How could she bear for Jake, who believed that her lack of response was because she still hungered for Sam, to find out from Carl that she was less than a functioning woman?

EXPECTING THAT THE NEXT DAY would be a repetition of the first, and disinclined to surface dive on her own, Denise spent the biggest part of the morning on deck alternately sunning and shading herself.

The sub, with Carl and his friends, had left before she had taken breakfast in the saloon. For the first time in her career, the sea held no allure for her. The samples Carl had promised she would find here, if they existed, interested her not at all. The only thing she was interested in was in getting back to the base port, closing herself off in her cottage from Carl, Jake, even Meg. She wasn't dependent on her salary from the Institution; she could take off and travel the world if she wished. Hong Kong, Jamaica, Lima—all, she realized belatedly, places bordering the ocean she loved.

Henry came to find her just after eleven-thirty, an anxious look disturbing his normal impassive calm. "That was Dr. Barstow on the radio," he told her worriedly.

Gladness surged through Denise just in knowing that Jake had been in touch with the vessel. Half rising from the deck chair, she said, "Is he still on? I'll talk to him."

"No, ma'am, he just left a message." Henry's

troubled brown eyes met the cooling green of hers, and he looked down at the deck, sensing her animosity. "He said we're to go back right now, quick."

"Why tell me? Dr. Madsen is in charge of this survey, as you know."

"Yes, but—" Denise ignored his appealing look and he went on, "Well, Dr. Barstow sounded really mad, very angry. And so will Dr. Madsen be if I tell him what the chief said."

"Then I'll tell him." Denise walked rapidly to the iron-railed stairs leading to the control room, with Henry following after a hesitant pause. "Carl?" she said moments later into a microphone, surrounded by the dials and levers that were the heart of the research vessel.

"Carl here—Denise?"

"Who else?" she said with dry crispness. "Jake has been on to us by radio, and he's ordered us back right now, so you'd better get up here on the double."

There was a crackling, then ". . . is not due back for another two days. Did you speak to him personally?"

Wishing she could reply in the affirmative and so make him squirm with uncertainty as to what she had told Jake, she nonetheless said resignedly, "No, I didn't. Your henchman, Henry, spoke to him."

"Very well. We are on our way up." Carl's accent seemed even more pronounced over the intercom between ship and sub. What had once been a rather charming emphasis on his foreignness now sent cold shivers down her spine despite the heat permeating the stilled ship.

Ignoring Henry, who hovered anxiously around her while she spoke to Carl, she went down to her cabin again, determined to stay there until the vessel reached shore. Not long after there was the sound of activated machinery, men shouting back and forth, and much later she saw from her vantage point over the cabin chair the three men clamber onto the cruiser from the dinghy.

The ship's engines began to vibrate under her feet within minutes, and she heaved a sigh of relief. Would his anger at Carl spill over to her? Even as the question came into her mind she knew that she didn't care. All she wanted was to be on firm land again, free—or as free as she ever could be now—from Carl.

Resting her head on the curve of the open porthole, letting the breeze lift the soft silver of her hair, she watched the low, dark line of Andros fall away as the vessel turned. The nightmare journey would soon be over; over, too, were the half-woven dreams she had begun to spin somewhere far back in her consciousness. She could never be Jake's woman; that much at least Carl had forced her to face realistically. Wanting, needing, even loving, weren't enough.

JAKE WAS THERE when they docked, a stern, white-faced Jake who leaped up the gangway as soon as it was lowered and brushed past a nervous Henry to confront Carl, who turned slowly from the rail to face him.

"What in *hell* do you think you're doing?" Jake demanded, his eyes furious slits as they went between Carl and Denise, who stood at the rail slightly behind Carl's tall thin figure. "Who gave you permission to take out this ship and its equipment?"

His blistering tone withered Denise, but Carl seemed unworried as he pushed farther away from the rail and said evenly, "I need no permission when you are away, I am second—"

"You are second-in-command of surveys when I am here," Jake enunciated clearly. "You do not initiate surveys when I am absent for a few days—" his eyes flickered contemptuously over Denise "—especially when there are only two members of the team involved."

"Mrs. Jordan was anxious to get some samples for her work. I happened to know of a place where there are scattered deposits of a weed known only so far in the Sargasso Sea. This could be interesting to you and the rest of the team."

Jake's eyes glinted harshly in the failing light. "Then it should have been a team effort." He turned his attention to Denise. "I presume you've brought back some specimens for analysis?"

"I—"

"Of course," Carl supplied smoothly, his voice heavy with irony as he added, "Would you like to see them? They're floating in one of the holding pens in the same water we took them from.''

"Yes," Jake nodded, watching Carl closely and evidently not liking what he saw, "I would like to see the reason for a crewed ship and expensive equipment being taken out into the ocean."

How could Carl seem so unperturbed, Denise wondered as she followed the two men across the deck. There were no specimens of weed, fish, coral or anything else in those holding tanks. Her eyes blinked, then opened wide as she gazed into the end water-filled pool. Thick fronds of a marine plant that was totally unfamiliar to her floated heavily on the surface.

She looked quickly at Carl and met his mocking gaze. He was even more diabolically clever than she had imagined. Despite the quickness of his ascent to the surface that morning, he had taken the time to pick up sizeable samples. Perhaps he had intended to take her down for a first-hand view of the underwater cavern when he and his friends had charted its dimensions and made their own scientific calculations. Walking back to the rail behind Carl and a still irate Jake, she realized that she knew nothing about those other men. Were they scientists, too? She had disliked them so much that she hadn't even bothered to know their names. Jake and Carl had halted at the head of the gangway, and she homed in on the last of their conversation.

"I'm not satisfied that one biological specimen

warrants taking out the ship and equipment,''
Jake said grittily to Carl, ignoring Denise. ''I want
a full report on your exact diving area and why
these samples couldn't have been picked up on a
regular survey.''

''Very well, if that is what you wish,'' Carl
returned stiffly, then looked at Denise. ''I am sure
Denise will convince you that it was a worthwhile
project. She is very excited about the implications
of such a find, and it could reflect very favorably
on our project as a whole.''

Jake's eyes, a stormy gray more reminiscent of
cold North Atlantic waters than the translucent
green of their surroundings, swept to hers, probing.

For a moment Denise was frozen into speech-
lessness by the force of an unfamiliar emotion that
leaped between them. She knew instinctively that
the question in his eyes was not solely concerned
with the importance of the samples. They also
asked about her relationship with Carl, about her
willingness to go out on a survey with a man no
one else on the team trusted. Words formed in her
mind, trembled on her lips, then her eyes eased
away from his piercing look. Telling Jake about
the nightmare aspects of the trip would take a
dead weight from her shoulders, placing it on his
much more capable ones. But she faltered at the
knowledge that a much bigger personal burden
would be an unbearable replacement.

Moistening her lips, she said in a low tone,

"Yes—Carl's right. I . . . I think this could turn out to be something. . . important."

Jake's eyes stayed on her for what seemed an interminable interval before he said abruptly, "All right. I'll expect a report on your analysis, too, before deciding what action to take." Wheeling, he went with his long stride down the gangway and along the jetty, becoming a misty outline as he faded into the half-light.

"I can trust you to make an appropriate report?" Carl's voice insinuated silkily behind her shoulder.

Denise whirled on him in a wild fury that startled even herself. "Any report I make has to be authentic. You should know that samples have to go to the mainland for further analysis."

Maddeningly unperturbed, Carl shrugged. "Samples that are never sent might have been lost in transit. Interest in our private survey will have died down and been forgotten by the time inquiries are made. And by that time—" he smiled with secretive satisfaction "—it will not matter anymore."

Denise pondered that last cryptic remark as she watched him pick up his travel bag from where he had placed it earlier close to the aft companionway and took his leave of the vessel, giving her a scarcely noticeable nod as he passed her.

Alone, her thoughts turned to Carl's guess that their private survey would be forgotten. Jake would never forget . . . and neither would she.

CHAPTER NINE

THE FEW REMAINING DAYS until Christmas passed in a pained haze for Denise. Jake, on the few occasions when he came in contact with her, maintained a brisk, businesslike attitude that revealed nothing of his thoughts or feelings and intensified the guilt over the ill-fated survey for two.

She ought to have told him, she decided time and time again as she worked at a lethargic rate in her lab, that Carl was not to be trusted, that his find of the underwater cavern was to be shared not by the team, but by so-called friends of dubious character. It would have helped to justify their government grant and private funding if the previously unknown cavern, with its interesting marine growth, was known to have been plumbed by the South Shore Project's equipment.

And that the marine specimens from those depths were interesting was obvious to Denise as she slid sections under the microscope, classifying them after reference to her library on marine biology as occurring only in the Sargasso Sea off Bermuda. It was an exciting find, and far-reaching in its implications. In some way the currents must have shifted, taking a new course to bring the weed samples south and around in a half arc to reach the Atlantic touching the Bahamas.

Jake should know about those currents and their implications. But Denise said nothing, her scientific training taking second place to her more personal concern of keeping hidden the lack in her female makeup—the lack Carl would not hesitate to make known if circumstances dictated.

So she swam and snorkeled with an oblivious Meg and made primitive experiments with the flora and fauna extracted from the vivid waters covering the lagoon. Carl and even Jake became shadowy background shapes to the wondrous world of the deep, a world she shared with the same childlike awe of a fascinated Meg.

"I'm going to be a biologist, just like you, when I grow up," Jake's daughter declared emphatically, surfacing with a particularly colorful specimen obtained from the depths. "Everything's so beautiful down there, isn't it?"

"Yes," Denise agreed, lifting the plastic sample bag where a motley collection of tiny fish swam distractedly about. "They're really beautiful."

Too beautiful, too free to take kindly to the confining tanks in her lab. Many of the specimens lost their brilliance and died in the artificial surrounds of their man-made Plexiglas existence. Removed from their natural environment, they faded away and died.

Denise felt something of that surrender to a

force greater than themselves when she danced with Jake on Christmas Eve in the clubhouse, where atmosphere strove for the Christmas spirit and fell short of expectations. Apart from the unseasonable climate, there was a constrictive air over the festivities, one that Meg alone seemed immune to. Denise found her eyes resting on the small face again and again, marveling at the transformation that gave Meg a childlike sparkle in her gray eyes, a blossom of color under the tan she had quickly acquired. Her happiness was complete just being within Jake's orbit, though she no longer clung to him as she had initially. Now she shared some of that deep, untapped affection with Denise, with Cindy, with the entire Stein household.

A child's trust, the winning and keeping of it, was an awesome thing, Denise reflected often. Meg's trust in her had been inspired by those few shared minutes in her bedroom, when Meg's sympathy for another person's hurts had been triggered, perhaps for the first time. A sympathy that was still, however, contingent upon Denise's cherishing the memory of a tragic love, a love so deep that no other could take its place.

Now, held loosely in Jake's arms, she knew that what she had once felt for Sam before their marriage had been just a foretaste of an emotion that could fill her mind with unrealizable dreams, her body with teeming, powerful impulses that were just as doomed to frustration. Would it have been different if she had met Jake first? Or was Sam typical of all men, the end result being the same?

"You're very deep in thought," Jake broke in, his voice brittle, cool. "Something bothering you?"

Denise looked up quickly into his eyes, also cool, then turned her head to look over his shoulder. "Only the reason why you haven't told Meg I won't be coming with you to Nassau."

His hand, resting lightly on her waist, tightened perceptibly, and his brows were lifted in a questioning arc when she glanced up at him again. "I haven't told her that because I wasn't aware myself that you wouldn't be coming."

Confused, Denise blinked. "I...I thought— you've been so...offhand since—"

"Since you took off with Madsen on a cozy survey for two?" he mocked grimly, glancing over her head as he steered her around the noisily gyrating Toby and Christina.

"It...wasn't as you make it sound," she said stiffly, her voice low. "It was purely professional."

"Was it?"

"Of course. Why else would I have gone?" She looked at him now with more assurance and saw a strange light flicker in his eyes momentarily.

"Why does a woman normally go off somewhere alone with a man? I'm not unduly vain, but I sure as hell can't understand why you went away with him like that when you've turned me off quite a few times.'' His voice changed to a savage jeer. "Does he have hidden talents under that cold-fish exterior?''

Refusing to answer that, which in any other man she would have put down to male jealousy, Denise compressed her lips and turned her head jerkily away. His ego had been hurt, no more than that of a man sure that most women fell like ripe plums into his arms. But her resentment was directed more to her own inadequacy than to Jake's revealing glimpse into a slighted ego. Why couldn't she have been the kind of woman who could give herself freely to a man who attracted her?

"How's the report coming along?'' he questioned with an odd inflection in his voice, his eyes probing when she brought hers up quickly to meet them. "Or am I right in supposing the private survey was for other reasons?''

Feeling vindicated, Denise lifted her chin, facing him squarely. "The report is in my desk; I was going to bring it to you after Christmas. I believe you'll find it very interesting—''

His gaze sharpened. "What do you mean, interesting? Have you found traces of oil?''

"No. But—''

She gave a startled gasp when he swung her off to the side and marched her to the door, her hand still firmly clasped in his. Her eyes automatically searched for Meg, knowing how she would interpret her father's possessive hold, but she was

wholly and happily occupied at keeping Cindy's
curious fingers from the lower decorations on the
big imported tree.

It wasn't until they were in the lab, next to the
wall-facing corner desk, that Jake released her
from the dry warmth of his hand and impatiently
demanded the report. Her fingers still tingled with
awareness of him, trembling as they reached into
the drawer and withdrew the neat handwritten
pages. Silently she handed them to him and retreated to the window overlooking the slightly
choppy ocean. But after only a minute or two her
head turned irresistibly back into the room as if a
magnetic field crossed the distance between them,
watching his frowning concentration as his eyes
moved rapidly over her writing. In some secret,
remote center inside her a warm liquid glow
spread slowly through her as, her expression veiled
by the brilliance of light behind her, her eyes went
with illicit gladness over his strong-jawed face, the
mouth controlled into a firmly held line that nonetheless betrayed the deep sensuality of his nature.

A hard man—not just in a physical sense, although his body had all the superbly fit assets of
an athlete—he was hard in his mind, in his thinking, in his feeling; he had the drive to take what he
wanted, whether in his career or in the love stakes.
But love wasn't a word a person would use in connection with Jake Barstow. Desire, yes; satisfaction of his physical appetites, yes. But all that was
tender in him, the deeply emotional part of him,

was reserved for his child, his daughter. And perhaps the wife he still cared for....

"Why didn't you bring this to me before?"

Denise blinked, so lost in her meditations that it took her a moment or two to assimilate her surroundings. Gradually she became aware that Jake had finished reading the report and had come to stand near, the direct light falling on him revealing as much as it obscured from Denise's features.

"I...I just finished it yesterday," she stammered, seeing again the deeply gouged lines beside his mouth, the furrowed indentations of his forehead. Making a supreme effort, she matched the coolness in his voice. "Why? There's nothing you can do at this point. All this seems to prove—" she waved at the papers still in his hand "—is that in some way the currents have shifted since they were last surveyed."

His eyes narrowed against the light. "A shift in currents could have all kinds of implications," he said in his crisp voice. "Pollutants carried to where they've never been before, changing the life-styles of thousands of fishermen who make their living from the sea, not to mention the people who buy and eat the fish."

The chain of life—how far-reaching it was. But Denise maintained stubbornly, "A day or two isn't going to make much difference at this stage."

"You've sent off samples and a report on your findings to the mainland?" Jake put tersely, his eyes hard and businesslike.

"I—well, no. Not yet," she said lamely.

"Get the samples ready for shipment," Jake interrupted shortly. "I'll take them into the airport myself." He half turned, then looked back at her curiously. "Exactly where did you find these samples?"

"I—I don't know. Somewhere near Andros."

He nodded. "Well, I've no doubt your lover will be able to give me a better idea of the location."

"My—?" Her breath gave out as she stared at him speechlessly, then anger prickled along her nerve ends as she lashed back, "Just whom did you have in mind? Carl or Henry?"

The lines beside his mouth deepened as he looked appraisingly at her. "Henry's a happily married man, as far as I know, so he has no need to lust after your fair skin. And I doubt if you'd be interested in any other member of the crew, so that leaves Carl."

"He's. . .not my lover."

"No?" He stepped closer, almost touching her with his aggressively posed body. "But something happened between you out there, didn't it? I could have cut the atmosphere between you with a knife when you got back."

"Nothing happened," she said steadily, meeting the speculative gray stare. "As far as I was concerned it was a purely scientific project."

"But not for him?" Jake surmised acutely, a faint smile tinging his lips as he went on, "Did you give him the brush-off, too? What happened, Denise? Did he act like any other red-blooded man in similar circumstances and share your virginal bunk?''

"No, he did not!" Trembling with anger, she went to step past him and found her upper arm caught in a viselike grip, her body swung around to meet the hard impact of his. "What is it to you, anyway?" Her eyes glinted greenly off his.

"Nothing," he admitted levelly, yet his hand exerted pressure on her arm to force her body closer to his so that soft rounds of her breasts pressed against his muscled chest, her thighs yielding to the implacable thrust of his. "I'm just interested in knowing what kind of man could erase Sam Jordan from your mind. Somehow I hadn't thought it would be somebody like Madsen.''

Her head jerked back in a silvery flash, her eyes lighting on mocking gray before going helplessly to the dark emphasis of thick brows, down to the firm line of his lips. The unfamiliar weakness that attacked her knees drained her suddenly, making her sag against his strong frame. Feebly she clutched at the front of his blue shirt with her free hand, feeling the measure of his heartbeat, the steady warmth of his sparse flesh.

"I've told you," she breathed faintly, knowing his nostrils must be filled with the light perfume she wore just as hers were aware of his masculine scent, "I'm...not interested in any man in that way. Carl knows a...lot about my work, about what interests me; that's why he took me on the survey with him.'' She knew she was babbling, filling in space while her senses became attuned to the incredible excitement jetting from nerve end to nerve end at her close proximity to a man she cared for, yet in some strange way feared. "Cared for" was too mild a term, she realized belatedly, her every sense open to the powerful waves emanating from him. Her fingers itched to touch the dark prolific spears of hair that erupted from the opened vee of his shirt, to linger on the bronzed column of his throat, to smooth the deep lines running from nose to mouth. To give—that was easy. To receive was something else again.

"You can't be that naive," Jake intruded into her thoughts again, his voice thick, heavy, as his head bent and his breath fanned warmly against her mouth. "Even you can't believe that any normal man is more interested in science than in a beautiful woman he has to himself."

"Jake, please—don't." Her words died, faded to oblivion in her throat as his mouth settled lightly, probingly, over hers. Everything in her fought the instinctive pressure to mold her body to his, but she was like molten wax when his hands shaped the slender curve of her hips and lifted, pressed her to the hardness in his thighs, needing no words to make known the extent of his arousal.

It scared her, that arousal; scared and, in a painful way, excited her, too. Was love, like birth, meant to be full of pain that brought a final ecstatic joy? With Sam she had never crossed that threshold of pain. Couldn't it—wouldn't it—be different with Jake?

"What happened out there between you and Carl?" he murmured now, so close that her widened eyes saw the beginning regrowth of dark beard on his lean shaven jaw, the darker motes blending with the gray in his eyes. "Did he share your cabin?"

"No!" Her exclamation was too quickly, too violently, given, and his gaze went piercing over her face.

"But he tried, didn't he?" he persisted.

The moment of magic was gone with his reminder of a voyage she would much rather forget in all its aspects. Pressing her hands against his warm shirtfront, she pushed away from him and surprisingly found herself free when he dropped his hands to his sides. She groped behind her for the window ledge and leaned back, snatching for breath in the storm of conflicting emotions that seemed to be tearing her apart.

"Certainly he tried," she cried wildly, "just as you tried and other men have tried. None of you seem to understand that I...I'm just not up for grabs to the handiest male! I've been married once, and I've no wish to repeat the experience with you or Carl or any other man."

"I don't recall mentioning marriage," Jake drawled into the heavy silence following her outburst. "I've been married, too, remember, and I have no wish to repeat the experience, either."

For different reasons, Denise reminded herself bitterly. Only his stubborn pride stood between him and the woman he loved. If Meg was to be believed, her mother was in the process of divorcing her present husband in order to remarry Jake. Even if Denise herself was a normal woman, capable of sustaining the passionate relationship a man like Jake would demand, he would never marry her.

"Daddy, where are you?" Meg's voice sounded from outside.

Jake turned quickly and picked up the report he had been perusing so avidly and was frowning over it again when Meg pushed open the door and poked her head around the corner. Her gray eyes went from her father to Denise, still standing clutching the window ledge.

"Oh, hi," she said uncertainly. "I wondered where you'd both got to."

Jake looked up with admirable distraction. "Denise had something very important to show me." He waved the papers in the air before tossing them down on the desk. "But there's nothing I can do about it over the holiday, so let's get back to the party."

"That's what I came to tell you about," Meg said excitedly as he came to put an arm around her thin shoulders and walk with her to the door. "Santa Claus is coming any minute, and I knew you and Denise would want to be there."

"How could we miss Santa Claus?" Jake agreed, lifting his brows as he looked around at Denise. "Aren't you coming to find out what he's brought for you? You've been a good girl, haven't you?"

Meg giggled. "Of course she's been good. Denise is...just perfect."

Denise pushed herself forcibly from the window and summoned up a wry smile. "Santa will probably disagree with you there, honey, but let's go find out."

A crusty Captain Mike, overheated in red flannel trimmed with fake white fur, dispensed the brightly wrapped packages under the tree. Each of the children was presented with two gifts, courtesy of the research team members, and the adults with one apiece from anonymous donors. While Marie was still exclaiming over the earth tones of a silk caftan, Denise unwrapped a gold pendant depicting a graceful woman diver.

"Daddy and I chose that for you when we went to Miami," Meg whispered excitedly beside her as she fastened the delicate clasp behind her neck and let the diver rest between her breasts. Her eyes lifted to where Jake was standing at the far side of the tree, his gaze on her broodingly direct, and inclined her head in silent acknowledgment of his gift.

"How could he know I would get this particular gift?" she questioned Meg quietly, at the same time breathing a sigh of relief that the small square package Jake was unwrapping was obviously not her own of an unimaginative, if expensive, set of handkerchiefs.

"Because he told Captain Mike he'd flay him alive if he didn't watch out for this special package," Meg whispered back delightedly. "Do you really like it, Denise?"

"It's...the most beautiful gift I've ever had," Denise replied throatily...and honestly. Her father, despite his wealth, had cherished a dislike of expensive jewelry to adorn the female form. When his young wife left him, she had taken little more than the basic wardrobe necessary for everyday living, even leaving behind his one concession to appearances, her diamond engagement ring— the ring Sam had suggested Denise wear because his finances would never run to anything that expensive and eye-catching.

Her eyes glanced off it now, sparkling in solitary state above the slim band of her wedding ring. Would Jake have given the woman he supposedly loved a ring that had cost him nothing, one that had been worn in bitterness by a woman who had come to despise her husband's frugal ways, his niggardliness with worldly goods as great as his aversion to displays of affection?

Jake crossed the lounge and stood by them, his daughter and the woman she momentarily trusted and loved. Jake and Meg were alike, Denise thought, in their binding love to a wife and mother who had discarded both in her search for a new

love, one that had been tarnished just as surely as
her love for Jake had been. Blinking away the
fanciful turn her thoughts had taken, she tuned in
belatedly to what Jake and his daughter were saying.

"...never had such a beautiful gift," Meg was
saying enthusiastically. "Isn't that right, Denise?"

"Yes...yes, it's true, I've never been given
anything quite so...beautiful before," she
assured the glowing Meg abstractedly, her eyes
glancing off the disbelieving mockery in Jake's
before going beyond them to where Toby had just
unwrapped the crisp linen handkerchiefs she had
provided for the mutual gift giving.

There was dancing again at the club after a
riotous turkey dinner, and Denise danced with
every member of the team except Jake, including
the brandy-mellowed Santa Claus. He took to the
floor with an excitedly chattering Marie, and
again with the voluptuously undulating Christina,
but Denise he ignored as if she was a purely
decorative adjunct to the proceedings in the
emerald velvet dress she had changed into at her
cottage.

"You have said nothing to Jake?" Carl asked in
his deadly calm voice as they circled sedately to the
music that was, Denise suspected, selected by the
romantically inclined Marie.

"I've said quite a lot to Jake," she returned
coolly, resting only the tips of her fingers on his
white-shirted shoulder.

"About the trip we took together?"

"That came into our conversation, yes. Why? Are you worried that I might have told him about your deep-sea discovery?"

His blue eyes hardened like pebbles on a northern beach. "I think you would not do that," he said harshly, and the sudden pressure of his hand at her back reminded her of that other scene in her cabin. "You are still planning to go with him and his daughter into Nassau later this week? So," he added after her brief nod, "you would not like him to discover certain... flaws in your makeup, hmm?"

The barely veiled threat lost some of its impact when Toby, overfilled with Christmas cheer, planted himself firmly between them.

"Hey, Denise, you promised this dance to me, remember?" His head swung with slow deliberation in Carl's direction. "Get lost, little man, can't you see you're not wanted around here?"

Carl's eyes glittered dangerously for a moment as he directed his contemptuous gaze on Toby's unnaturally red face, then he gave Denise a stiff bow and excused himself.

"You're very unkind," she murmured after Toby had whirled her around an exaggerated bend. She had no love for Carl herself, but some distant part of her reluctantly sympathized with his outcast status, perhaps because she had felt the same kind of alienation when she was young.

"Unkind? Hell, Carl wouldn't know what to do

with kindness if it was handed to him on a silver plate." Toby stared at her in owlish concentration. "He's bad news, Denise, and you're the only one who hasn't got the message yet. Take my advice—steer clear of him."

Denise would have liked nothing better than to have done just that, but Carl still held the whip hand. For Meg's sake, and only for that reason, she would fulfill her promise to accompany father and daughter to Nassau for the Junkanoo celebrations. After that she would reassess her position, plan an immediate future as far as possible removed from the South Shore Project. Dr. Seward would accept that the new environment of the Bahamas hadn't worked, that she would be happier in her home surroundings even though at Scripps she would be a very small cog in a very large machine. Whatever Carl's faults, it was because of him that she had made a discovery that might be significant.

"Denise, isn't it terrific?" Meg squealed excitedly, skipping into the room adjoining her own, which had been assigned to Denise. "There's a swimming pool as well as a private beach! Do you think the Pearsons have snorkel equipment?"

"I'm sure they have." Denise turned from the open suitcase she was in the process of unpacking and smiled at the small, eager face. Ever since they had arrived at the colonial-styled mansion where Max Pearson and his family made their home,

Meg had had this excited glow about her, an attitude so completely opposed to the king-sized suspicious chip she had carried on her shoulders after
her arrival on the island, that Denise's eyes held a
happy glow each time she looked at the child. It
seemed incredible that just the small effort on her
own part to extend friendliness, as well as Jake's
concentrated attention, could bring out the
natural liveliness that had been hidden for so long.
Probably ever since the divorce of her parents.

That thought led to another concerning Jake's
ex-wife. What kind of a mother was she to turn a
blind eye to her small daughter's unhappiness?
From items Meg had dropped unconsciously,
Denise had gathered that Barbara didn't hesitate
to leave her daughter at school if the normal weekend visit was inconvenient to her social life. It
wasn't hard to see that Meg had stored up all the
little hurts into one large ache inside her. The
miracle was that so far her character hadn't been
irrevocably warped. Incredibly, she still seemed to
harbor the notion of her parents becoming a married couple again, though she never voiced her
deep-down wish in her father's presence.

Now Denise said, wryly realizing that she
sounded like an indulgent governess, "Have you
finished unpacking yet?"

Meg whirled from the window where she had
been watching the play of sunlight on the pool,
looking so guilty that Denise added humorously,
"Have you even started to unpack yet?"

Shaking her head, Meg danced away. "I'll get it done in two seconds flat."

"I hope that doesn't mean throwing them in the closets," Denise called after her, smiling again as she turned back to her own unpacking.

Taking out a tissue-wrapped cocktail dress in stark black, she held it against herself for a moment and surveyed the effect in the full-length mirrors enclosing the bank of closets. It was her favorite—simply styled yet unmistakably elegant. The tight-fitting bodice exposed more than a hint of her softly swelling breasts, the calf-length skirt billowed out bouffant-style and the long sleeves fitted close to the arms. Was it too sophisticated for a night out on the town with Jake and his daughter? Shrugging, she hung the dress beside its less sophisticated sisters in the closet. She would make up her mind if and when the occasion arose.

"Anybody home?"

Jake had driven Max to the airport for the flight to the States where he would join his family, who had gone on before. Now Jake was back, and Denise was shaken by the erratic leap of her heart when she heard his voice. One part of her mind went a treacherous path of its own, fantasizing wildly that she and Jake and Meg were a family and that what she heard was a normal husband announcing his arrival at the beginning of a well-earned vacation. The other part of her mind propelled her feet to the door, caused her voice to call back self-possessedly, "Jake? We're up here unpacking."

Her heart gave another lurch when she watched his lithe progress up the curving staircase, two steps at a time. Her eyes reflected the infectious grin that deepened yet lightened the lines around his mouth and eyes, lifting years from him with a magical stroke.

Glancing around the upper galleried hall that looked down on the floor below, he said, "Where's Meg?"

"Right here, daddy." His daughter's sudden rush against him almost made him lose his balance and his bronzed arms went protectively around her. "Isn't this going to be super fantastic?"

"Fantastic," he agreed, his eyes lifting to Denise over his daughter's head. "What would you girls like to do tonight?"

"Can we go to that old Bahama house for dinner?" Meg craned her neck eagerly to look up into his face.

"Not tonight, honey, but I've made a reservation there for later this week. I thought we'd have a quiet dinner here tonight and take a walk along Bay Street later. There's a lot going on right now." He looked back at Denise. "What do you think, Denise?"

"Anything's fine with me," she returned gaily, the spirit of Junkanoo already seeming to infiltrate the quiet confines of the beautiful house. She added hesitantly, "Should I tell the staff we'll be here for dinner?"

"I'll do it," Jake said casually, releasing Meg and turning back to the blue-carpeted stairs.

So they dined in splendor that night, waited on by the attentive staff who normally attended the Pearson family. Jasper, the majordomo, was a tall, elderly brown-skinned man who exuded dignity yet made a special point of satisfying Meg's every whim, making Denise certain that he must be well-loved by the Pearson children.

The cook, too, could not be faulted. Delectably cool vichyssoise was followed by medallions of pork in an unusual piquant orange sauce, and a dessert of chilled French custard. Coffee was served to them afterward on the flagstoned patio opening off the dining room, but Meg disdained the strong Turkish flavor and chose a malted milk instead.

Sweet, thick tropical fragrances wafted across from the extensive gardens surrounding the house, and the gentle swish of ocean on beach made a soporific background to their hushed voices.

Even Meg sounded unnaturally subdued as she asked her father, "What are we going to do tomorrow, daddy?"

"I thought you had it all worked out to the fraction of a second?" he retorted lazily, amused, relaxed as he spread his length comfortably before him from the white wrought-iron chair he half lay on. "A carriage ride around Nassau in the morning, the afternoon at Ardastra Gardens."

"Oh, yes, I remember now." Meg turned impulsively to Denise, her eyes shining in the flickering flames of the patio lights. "You have to wear a skirt or dress, Denise. The flamingos won't perform if ladies wear shorts or bikinis."

"I know, dear," Denise said, but decided not to mention her visit to the Gardens with Toby. "I wouldn't dream of offending their moral principles."

"Wise birds," Jake commented dryly, his eyes flickering down to Denise's slender hips in a form-fitting aqua linen dress. "Some women just don't have the shape for men's clothes."

Meg's eyes followed the line of his. "Denise does," she defended indignantly, "and...mommy does."

Jake sat up abruptly and lifted the coffee cup beside him. "Your mother wears her clothes well," he said shortly. "She can teach you a lot about fashion sense; it'll be important to you one day."

"I don't care about clothes," Meg retorted passionately, her mouth pursing in the stubborn line that had been more familiar at the beginning of her visit. "I don't want to go to parties and give parties when I grow up. I just want to be with you and take care of you."

"When you grow up you'll have a husband of your own to care for," her father stated dryly, his features lighted in the brief flare from the match he applied to the cigar he had taken from a shirt pocket.

"No, I won't. I hate boys. Especially David Stein," Meg added with unusual vindictiveness.

"David?" Jake's brows lifted in surprise as he scanned his daughter's unruly expression. "What's he done to earn that kind of talk from you? I thought you liked him."

"That was ages ago," scorned Meg, "when we first got here. Now he thinks he knows everything, and I just don't like him anymore."

Jake drew an exaggerated sigh. "Well, that's the way life goes, honey, at least until you grow up a bit more. Then you'll be able to cope better with the battle of the sexes." He rose as he spoke, glancing at his watch. "We'd better go if we're to get you to bed at a reasonable hour. Denise?"

She blinked, lost in thought about the battle of the sexes he had mentioned so naturally. A battle he had lost, obviously, with his wife. Or had she been the loser?

"I'll just get a wrap." She jumped to her feet, her eyes going then to Meg's bare arms. "Want to come up with me and find yourself a sweater, Meg? It's going to be cool in a while."

Fifteen minutes later after parking the car that, like the house, came on loan from Max, they began their stroll down Bay Street, mesmerized by the teeming life that surrounded them on all sides. It was a holiday week in Nassau although, Jake told them, the biggest celebration and parade were still to come on New Year's morning.

"Can we come and watch it, daddy?" Meg skipped along between them, and Jake laughed.

"Certainly, if you can get up that early."

"I will, I will," she promised, twisting her head to look up at Denise. "You will, too, won't you, Denise?"

"I'll certainly think very deeply about it," she returned solemnly, the glinting smile in her green eyes belying her doubtful tone. "Look, Meg." Her hand tightened with instinctive protection when a fierce-looking monster-headed man jived along the street toward them, followed by a group of men and women wearing costumes constructed from multicolored crepe paper but less frightening than their leader's garb.

"Is he the devil?" Meg breathed, round-eyed with awe as the group swayed past them.

"More likely his idea of what a witch doctor looked like in darkest Africa," Jake supplied dryly, adding emphatically, "many, many years ago."

"That's where the black Bahamians came from, isn't it, daddy?" Meg shuddered and pressed closer to Jake's side. "I'd have hated to be kidnapped and taken away from my family and made into a slave."

"I don't think they cared too much for the idea, either," he commented acidly, his tone softening as he went on, "but these are things that happened to their ancestors. Their lives are different now; probably a whole lot better than if they'd been born and brought up in some districts of Africa."

"But is the Bahamas their home now?" Meg persisted, jumping over a depression in the sidewalk next to a construction site.

"If a person lives somewhere, honey, it's their home. But I guess their roots will always be in Africa, just as ours are in America. My great grandfather fought in the Civil War for the abolition of slavery."

"I know," Meg said simply, "and I'm glad he did. That makes him my great-great-grandfather, doesn't it?"

"It does."

Denise listened to their exchange with half an ear, slightly envious because her own roots in America went back only as far as the turn of the century on both sides. Her background was English, provided by the grandparents who had adventured to the Pacific coast of the United States with hope in their hearts and slender linings to their pockets. Yet now, by their efforts, their granddaughter was enviably independent financially. Maybe she had also inherited their inhibited sexual nature, she mused as her eyes took in the colorful scene around her. Her father had been their only child, a rarity in those days of prolific offspring.

They stopped for a drink where natives and tourists danced under the open air. Meg was entranced and totally oblivious to the significance of the erotically undulating figures before her eyes. Black or white, the wild throb of music sent their limbs jerking, thrusting, bending in a mind-less response. The flaring lamps surrounding their small table fitfully lighted Jake's lean features, making mystery of his deeply shaded eyes. Was he feeling, too, the pull of the rhythmic beat that forced its way into her veins and made her blood run faster?

Moments later, giving no indication one way or the other, Jake stirred and rose after glancing at their empty glasses. "Let's go," he said abruptly. "You should have been in bed hours ago, Meg."

"Oh, daddy," she wailed, "can't we stay just a little longer?"

"No," he said uncompromisingly, pulling the chair out from under her. "You'll have your fill of sight-seeing in the next few days."

Meg maintained a stubborn silence all the way back to the house, but once there she slid her arms around Jake's bent neck to kiss him good-night on one smooth shaven cheek.

"I love you, daddy," she whispered.

"And I love you," he returned, his brown hands large on her small waist. "See you tomorrow."

"Are you coming to bed now?" she asked Denise, who was poised on the bottom step of the curving staircase.

"Denise is going to have a nightcap with me," declared Jake, turning his daughter toward the stairs and propelling her to them.

"Oh." Meg looked from one to the other, her eyes reflecting quick apprehension.

"I'd really rather get to bed, Jake," Denise put in rapidly. "If we're having a full day of sight-seeing tomorrow I—"

"Nonsense, it's only—" he flicked back his cuff to look at his watch "—a little after ten. Relaxing for half an hour over a drink won't deprive you of too much beauty sleep."

Recognizing that her father's tone was the one that brooked no denial, Meg passed Denise on the stairs and said with a tight thrust of her jaw, "Will you come and say good-night to me when you've had your drink?"

"Of course, honey." Denise accepted the fait accompli and moved back into the hall. "I won't be long." The underlying promise was easier to make than to argue the point with Jake. The closeness that had grown between herself and Meg was a tenuous situation—despite Meg's recent personality change—one she would never willingly break.

And she had no real wish to break that brittle trust, she told herself as she followed Jake's uncompromising shoulders into the small sitting room at the rear of the spacious house. Being attracted to him, fancying herself in love with him, dreaming unrealistic dreams, were viable only at a distance. Being with him without the buffer of Meg's presence inhibited her with the bleakness of reality.

"What will you have, Denise?" Jake asked, not looking around as he crossed to the drinks cabinet on the far wall. "Brandy? Wine? Scotch?"

"Brandy's fine, thanks—not too much."

She chose a chintz-covered armchair facing the patio doors leading to the terrace; the sofas placed opposite each other would have spelled an intimacy she wasn't prepared to face at that moment. Careful not to touch his fingers as he handed her a small balloon glass, she let her gaze wander to the closed garden doors, seeing only her own and Jake's reflection in the blank-faced glass. The terrace lights had been extinguished, probably as soon as they had left for Bay Street.

Jake paced, glass in hand, to the windows and said without turning, "I want to thank you again for what you're doing for Meg. She's...a different child since you took her in hand."

"I didn't take her in hand. We found we had a lot in common, that's all." She took a sip of the strong, expensive brandy and added for want of something better to say, "I feel very guilty about using your friend's liquor cabinet while he's away."

Jake turned then, shaking his glass impatiently. "I'll replace whatever we use, and more." His lean body radiated a restless vitality as he paced back and took a seat on the sofa close to her chair, resting his elbows on his knees, suspending his glass between them. "You're the first woman she's taken to since— Well, just let's leave it at that.''

Denise looked at him, feeling an odd surge of sympathy filling her throat. He suddenly seemed vulnerable in a way he never had before; she even caught a glimpse of the younger man he had been once in the almost feminine sweep of dark lashes that curved out from his lids as he stared down into the inevitable bourbon in his glass. The lines etched into his skin lent a harsh note to his good-looking features, but he must have been devastating when he was a younger man. He must, too, have been very young when he married Meg's mother.

''Meg trusts me because she...she knows I'm not interested in taking you from her,'' she said gently. ''Even so, you must have noticed that she didn't want us to come in here together tonight.''

''I noticed.'' Despite the shadows from the floor lamp behind his head, his eyes were piercing when he looked up at her. ''But I've no intention of encouraging her to believe that she can dictate my life for me. If she had her way I'd be wearing blinkers whenever an attractive woman walked by.'' He smiled wryly, then sobered to intentness again. ''I'm a normal man with a normal man's appreciation for female qualities. Yours, for instance.'' He leaned back and drank from his glass without taking his eyes from her. ''You attract me very much,'' he added quietly, almost matter-of-factly. ''Whether it's because of your looks, or that you get along with Meg, or that you have a beautifully old-fashioned capacity to be faithful even in memory to a man you once loved, or a combination of all those qualities—'' he described an encompassing circle with one long-fingered hand ''—isn't important. What is important is that you're beginning to occupy more and more space in my thoughts, my time.''

"And what would you suggest as a remedy?" Denise managed sarcastically over the sudden erratic thrum of her heart that sent her pulses pounding with the same rhythm. "A quickie affair behind your daughter's back?" Later she would contemplate the supreme self-centeredness of his remarks, but now she was busy coping with her own tumultuous reactions. Should she feel flattered by his interest or insulted? Either way, the question was purely academic. A woman contemplating an affair, however quick, with a man had to be sure of her own capabilities.

"I can't offer you anything long-term, if that's what you mean," Jake said brusquely, then softened his approach. "I'm not good marriage material, Denise; I have nothing to offer a woman on a permanent basis."

"And I have nothing to offer on any basis," she said crisply, rising and setting down her glass on the side table between them. In an instant Jake had placed his own glass beside hers and was standing close, too close, to her.

"You're wrong there," he said softly, lifting his hand to trace with his fingertips the high line of her cheekbone, trailing an almost unbearable trail of sensation across her skin. "Don't you think I know from the few times I've made love to you that there's a lot of stored-up passion behind that cool exterior? And don't you know that it's bad for you to suppress those natural urges?" His fingers lowered to the trembling line of her lips, running his tips across their full outline, parting them over her small regular white teeth, probing the sensitive inner surfaces, transferring their moistness to his own skin. "We could be good together, Denise."

Good, yes, to a certain extent. She was normal enough to respond to the male touch of his hands on her female body, normal enough to know the suffocating need for something more, but she could never delude herself into transporting that need into the final fulfillment Jake would expect—had the right to expect.

"Denise?"

The question was half inquiry, half cajoling, as if Jake sought her permission yet knew that she was open to persuasion. Dear God, didn't he know that what she desired more in life was to be able to respond to him in the way of a woman? That—no, of course he couldn't know that. To him, she was a woman still in love with her dead husband, a man of such sweet memory that another man's touch was anathema to her. She sensed his surprise when she let her lips warm and grow soft under the pressure of his. Discretion

fled as she arched to his male thrust, returned the
kiss that seared and penetrated the soft defenses of
her lips to reach the tentative rise of her tongue
that met and clung intimately to the abrasively intimate probing of his.

"Denise—oh, God, Denise—" he was murmuring now, his kisses searing, biting at the tender
lobe of her ear, the open vulnerability of her neck
"—I want you so damned much."

His muttered avowal was unnecessary. More
eloquent was the urgent strength of his body, the
taut muscles of his thighs pressing demandingly on
hers.

"Jake—oh, Jake, I—"

"Denise? Daddy?"

Meg's childish voice floated between them,
separating them more cleanly than if a white-hot
poker had sliced between their closely twined
bodies. Denise jerked guiltily away, the dark
centers of her eyes contracting rapidly, closing off
the beginning rise of desire this man alone seemed
to inspire in her. It was her voice that called back,
"Yes, Meg, I'm just coming."

It was Jake who had been unable to make the
quick change in the emotionally laden atmosphere, she thought as she turned swiftly and
made for the door. The painful look shattering his
strong features followed her across the hall and up
the stairs she traversed slowly. It had seemed, for
a few fraught moments, that Jake attached more
than a passing significance in a relationship be-

tween them. And that had to be an erroneous impression on her part. Hadn't he told her minutes before that marriage wasn't in his plans for her or any other woman?

Forcing a natural, tranquil smile for Meg, who stood like a watchful sentinel behind the gallery rail, she went with the child into her room and smoothed the covers over her wiry young body.

"What were you and daddy talking about? Your face is red—was he mad with you because of me?"

The stone in her engagement ring sparkled in the bedside light as Denise gave an extra pat to the covers. "Of course not," she said lightly. "Brandy always has that effect on me."

"But what did you talk about?" Meg insisted, eyeing her curiously.

"Oh, this and that. Mainly about how kind the Pearsons are to let us have their home while they're away, and how guilty I feel about using their supplies."

Meg smiled sleepily. "You *would* think about that! You're so nice, Denise, sometimes I—" She broke off abruptly, her gray eyes obscured by the sudden drop of her dark-lashed lids. "Daddy'll take care of it."

"That's what he said." Rising from the side of the bed, Denise said, "Get some sleep now. We've a long hard day ahead of us tomorrow."

And even longer nights, she told herself as she went quietly from the room, knowing that Meg would be far into the land of sleep when Jake came to wish her good-night.

In her own room, taking off and hanging away her clothes, she thought of those nights, those days, to come. Was it madness to stay on with Jake and his daughter, knowing her own vulnerability to the fruitless dreams that had already begun to plague her and Jake's obvious attraction to the woman he thought she might be?

But it was too late now to back out of their family-type holiday. For her own sake, and perhaps for Jake's—but most of all for Meg's.

CHAPTER TEN

THE TERRACED GARDENS spilling from the galleried porch running the length of the old Bahamian mansion were filled with chattering, animated diners. On the level below theirs, Denise looked past the tropical foliage sprouting from a rock wall to where flaring patio lamps illuminated the lower dining area. Every table was occupied, and she mentally blessed Jake's foresight in reserving far ahead of time.

Her eyes lifted to where Jake sat opposite, leanly handsome in black evening dress, his features fitfully illuminated in the breeze-blown flame of the lamps. How easy it was to love him, to jealously want to freeze the covetous glances of the women who cast appreciative glances in his direction.

Jake was knowledgeable, witty, amusing, in his retelling of Bahamian history, ancient and modern. "The duke and duchess of Windsor lived here during the war years," he told them as they ascended the shelved flights of stairs to the court-yard of Government House, where a desultory changing of the guard ceremony was taking place.

"He was the man who gave up his kingdom for love. The people here even made up a song about it."

"Why did he have to give up his kingdom, daddy?" Meg asked curiously, twisting her head to look up into her father's leanly handsome face.

"Because the lady had been divorced not once, but twice. Once would have been enough for the British people at that time. They expected their royal family to be above reproach morally, and being divorced in those days was something bad to them."

Meg digested his words, then burst out as they made the descent to the roadside, "I think it's bad, too! People who get married should love each other for always, like—" she cast around with her eyes and added when they fell on Denise "—like Denise and her husband. She still loves him, although he's—"

"Meg!" Jake said sharply. "Sorry, Denise, sometimes she—"

"It's all right, Meg," Denise said stiffly, frozen with the realization that Jake's child believed implicitly in her immunity to other men. What would Meg think if she knew that Denise felt an electric glow coursing through her each time Jake's hand brushed hers innocuously, each time the gray eyes rested on her in a look meant for her alone?

"It doesn't always work out that way," Jake

said harshly now, his hand on Meg's shoulder restraining her from stepping out into the traffic that barreled down the hill to their left. "People make mistakes in marriage as in any other area of life. It doesn't make sense for two people to stay together if they don't love each other the way they thought they did in the beginning."

The conversation ended as he guided them across the road during a temporary lull in the traffic, and Meg seemed to put it to the back of her mind as they made a brief inspection of the small public library housed in an ancient stone building and afterward lunched at the same hotel Jake had taken Denise to on her first visit into Nassau.

This time there were no three-masted barks plying the waters edging the restaurant, but Meg found plenty to interest her in the visiting yachts and surfboard sailors constantly moving before them. The sight of Paradise Island across the water reminded Meg of her father's promise to take Denise to the famous casino.

That visit was scheduled for the following evening, Denise reflected now, coming back to the tropical ambience surrounding them. The stout waiter smilingly took their order for the Bahamian-style dinner of conch chowder and a varied fish platter that included red snapper, conch and bonefish. The chowder was enriched with sherry stirred in at the table, but Meg, despite her plaintive protests, was commanded by

Jake to have her soup without that added em-
bellishment.

Her unschooled palate, when Denise relented
and let her try a spoonful of her own enriched
chowder, made her declare with a grimace, "It
doesn't taste anything like mine."

"It isn't supposed to," Jake told her dryly, yet
there was amusement in his eyes as they met
Denise's across the table. "You'll appreciate it
more when you're grown up."

For what it does to the inhibitions, Denise
thought breathlessly, her green eyes reflecting
back to his in a luminous glow. Combined with
the predinner drink and the golden smoothness
of white wine Jake had ordered with their meal,
she had a curious sense of floating outside the
normal bounds of her existence. In that nether
world she saw Jake's face as it had appeared in
her dreams of late—lean, strong, forbidding in the
attraction it held for her. It was suddenly easy,
too easy, to feel again the touch of his warm, sensually shaped mouth on hers, to recall the feel of
the bronzed fingers, now holding lightly to his
glass, stroking warmly against her skin—the
round, burgeoning breasts that even now tautened
to erectness under the stark black folds of her
dress.

"Denise?" Meg asked, perplexed by the
woman's obvious preoccupation, "don't you
think so?"

"I'm sorry, Meg, I didn't catch what you said."

"I said, don't you think everybody should come to Nassau at least once?"

"It would be nice." Denise collected her scattering wits and drew her eyes from Jake's, which had seemed to hold her in a hypnotic trance, and directed them to Meg's faintly puzzled regard. "But not everybody can afford a vacation in a luxury spot like this."

"Mommy could, couldn't she?" Meg directed her attention back to Jake, whose lips had compressed into a taut line. "She said she might come down here before I go back to school."

Jake signaled the waiter to return the menus for their dessert selections, saying to Meg in a brusque aside, "I wouldn't count on it if I were you. Nassau's too far from New York for a visit."

"But Barbara's in Florida," Meg told him excitedly. "She's staying at the Burke place for Christmas. Maybe she'll come across from there."

A cold hand spread icy fingers in Denise's chest. Barbara Barstow, or whatever her name was now, just miles away across the water? Somehow the woman had seemed far less menacing from the distance of New York. Menacing? How could the woman Jake loved, the women who had borne Meg, be any kind of menace to Denise? At best Jake was interested in a quick affair with her; there could never be any question of anything more meaningful than that. Even if he had wanted a permanent relationship, how could she tie a

virile, sexually skilled man like Jake to an un-
responsive woman—a frigid woman, she told herself with cruel honesty.

"Don't count on it," Jake said dryly to the
shining-eyed Meg. "Your mother's not likely to
come within a fifty-mile radius of me, and she'd
have to do that if she came to see you."

"But she does want to see you!" Meg cried,
distressed as her eyes met the forbidding gray of
her father's. "I've tried to tell you that—"

Jake interrupted her sharply. "And I've tried to
tell you that—" He broke off when their dessert
appeared, moist fresh fruit for Jake and Denise, a
strawberry-ice-cream concoction for Meg.
"Thanks, we'll have coffee and crème de cacao
for two. Would you like something else to drink,
Meg?"

"No, thank you," she told him primly, subdued, and his mouth tightened to a harsh line as he
stared hard at her.

"I wonder who lived in this lovely old house
originally." Denise muttered an interest she was
far from feeling, although the house had the
elegant ambience of a past age. At least it had the
effect of transferring Jake's frosty stare from his
daughter to herself.

"As a matter of fact, it was Max Pearson's
family, who've been on the islands for a very long
time. After Max's parents both died, he sold it.
The new owners have made quite a thriving concern of the place," he said as he glanced around at

the filled tables. "Max wasn't too happy about what they planned for his ancestral home, but they're doing it tastefully and well."

"And successfully." Denise's eyes roamed in the direction his had taken, noting the well-dressed appearance of the diners who, in less salubrious surroundings, would be without jacket and tie in the casual way of tourists.

The rough spot in their evening was smoothed over, but in the early hours of the following morning Meg, caught in the coils of nightmare, brought Denise hurriedly to her bedside. Stark terror lighted the child's widened eyes as she stared at Denise without recognition.

"What is it, honey?" Denise gathered the frail body close and stroked the loosened bands of dark hair. "You've been dreaming, that's all."

Shudders vibrated through the child, and Denise held her closer, sending her calmness through her until Meg gave one last shudder and said, "I was dreaming that...that mommy was dead, and...daddy had killed her!"

"Hush, darling, it was only a dream," Denise soothed, resting her chin on the top of Meg's head, her hand stroking rhythmically on the smooth skin of her arm. "You know your daddy could never do something like that, even if he wanted to."

"I...I know, but...you won't leave me, Denise, will you?"

"Of course I won't."

And Denise did stay until the gray eyes, so like Jake's, closed finally in sleep. Meg's breathing became deep and regular before she lowered her to the pillows and tucked the bedclothes around her slight form.

What had made her dream something as awful as that? Maybe the talk about Barbara's possible visit to Nassau and Jake's terse rejection of the thought. Poor lamb, she thought as she stroked the dark strands of hair back from Meg's hot forehead. Divorce might be hell for the parents, but for a child it was devastating in its long-reaching effects.

Or was it entirely that? Had Meg sensed, with the prescience of the very young, that her father's interest in Denise wasn't solely as a friend his daughter had come to love and trust? Had she recognized unconsciously the futile attraction Denise felt for Jake?

Sighing, she rose from the bed and switched off the rose-tinted lamp on the adjoining table, gasping when her eyes adjusted to the moon's light filtering through the net curtains and discerned Jake's lean figure outlined against the doorway. Swiftly, she crossed to him and said softly, "She had a nightmare, but she's asleep again now."

She sensed rather than saw his nod, her eyes drawn against her will to the parting of his white pajama jacket where his tanned throat and curling dark hair were in sharp contrast.

"I...think she'll sleep peacefully now," she

said huskily, forcing her voice thickly through the obstruction in her throat. How could she let this awareness, this warmth that spread like molten gold through her, continue when Meg, his child, had just been having nightmares about, perhaps, this very possibility?

Yet she was nerveless, pliant, when Jake's long-fingered hands lifted to her shoulders, uncaring that through the pale green of her nylon nightdress every part of her femininity must be visible to him. Excitement shivered painfully across her skin when he drew her to the male warmth of his body and she felt his arousal. How long had he been standing there, watching her soothing his daughter?

The thought lost its importance when his hands cupped her cheeks, his fingers lost in the silver strands of her hair, and he bent his mouth to the suddenly trembling curve of hers. His lips pressed warmly, lightly, then brushed across her own in a rhythmic motion that spoke of his expertise in arousing a woman's response.

The kiss deepened to urgency as Jake's hands slid over her shoulders and down the silky covering on her back before spanning the taut slenderness of her waist and rising over her ribcage to cup her burgeoning breasts. The transparent nylon of her nightdress was no barrier to the thumbs he rubbed insistently over their tips, bringing them to erect awareness of his male touch. Her slender hips rose, pressed against him and she felt his shudder in her own bones.

"Come to bed with me, Denise," he whispered raggedly at her ear. "Let me make love to you. I'll make you forget Sam."

The last fiercely spoken statement, confident, aggressive, brought Denise down abruptly from the plane she had been floating on for the past minutes. Sam...Sam had known her inadequacies, knew that she would let him down at that last, crucial moment when her giving should have been of its finest with the man she loved.

"No—I...I can't, Jake.... Please don't ask me." Her whispered breath mingled with the warmth of his, and her nostrils were filled with the fleeting odors of cigar leaf, sweetly rich brandy, the overwhelming scent of his maleness. Unconsciously, she leaned farther into him, feeling the weakness threatening to crumple her knees.

"For God's sake, Denise," he exclaimed in a harsh, low voice, leaning past her to close the door on Meg's sleeping form, "don't you think I know you're as ready for me as I am for you?" His hands brushed over the telltale erectness of her nipples, the tautening of her flat stomach muscles as one hand went deliberately lower.

Gasping, Denise exerted a will she was unaware of possessing and wrenched from his loosened hold, her arms coming up involuntarily to cover breasts that were almost as exposed as if she was naked. "Don't you think your daughter's been hurt enough?" she asked coldly, putting a hundred miles between them although they were only a pace apart. "She trusts me, and that trust is precious to me. If you need a sleeping partner that badly, why don't you go out and find one? There must be a dozen or more women out there who'd jump at the chance!" She tossed her head contemptuously in the direction of the spiraling staircase and saw the dark line of his jaw clamp tensely.

"Maybe I'll do just that," he muttered, turning back to his bedroom, then looking over his shoulder contemptuously. "At least the women out there aren't afraid to admit their needs!"

"I'm sure they're not," Denise threw back, going with a silken swish of her nightgown to her own door and looking back at Jake, schooling herself not to see the potent attraction in his sleep-ruffled dark hair, the superb virility written into every line of his leanly fit body. "I just don't happen to share their penchant for quickie romances."

She stepped into her room and closed the door behind her. If Jake had made a rejoinder, she hadn't heard it. Her legs seemed made of putty as she went across to the dressing table, unthinkingly, staring without seeing her own reflected image in the broad mirror. Some malevolent fate had taken her life and twisted it into a travesty of what it might have been. She had been roused sexually out there in the passage with Jake, as he had made potently clear. But what would have happened if she had allowed him to take her to his bed? His mounting passion, her own progressive coldness? It had always been that way with Sam, the only man she had known in an intimate sense. How could she bear for Jake to look at her in the way Sam had, condemning, contemptuous, cruel? It would hurt more with Jake, because she knew now that she loved him in a way she had never loved Sam. Loved the perfection of his male body, the intelligence that activated his mind, the zany sense of humor that matched her own on occasion— loved his daughter who, in her vulnerability, had wound strings around her heart.

Her hand went to her mouth to stifle the hope-less cry that rose in her throat, and she stumbled to the ruffled bed and fell on it, muffling the sobs torn from her in the cool crispness of the pillow-case.

WHETHER OR NOT Jake had left the house to seek consolation in some woman's arms, which she half expected after her experiences with Sam, Denise couldn't fathom the following morning as they wandered through the kaleidoscope of color that was Nassau's straw market.

Hanging from struts over the heads of the sellers and spread on tables and ground were the colorful products of the native peoples. Wide-brimmed straw hats, embellished with red, purple, pink and blue decorations, jostled for space with handmade baskets contoured into myriad shapes and sporting similar decorations around their sides. The sellers were not oppressive, many of them busily occupied in weaving the lengths of straw into more goods for sale. It was a happy, carefree scene, yet Denise sensed an underlying tension between her and Jake.

He was polite to her, indulgent with Meg as she became more and more laden with gifts to take back to her school friends, but there was a remoteness about him that chilled her. Had his ego been bruised by her rejection the night before? Probably so. Men's egos were notoriously fragile where sex was concerned.

The question that had plagued her for most of the night returned to haunt her. Should she follow the old adage that honesty was the best policy? Tell him—the thought struck her so blindingly that she stopped suddenly and stared sightlessly at the straw wares piled on a long table counter. She could show him, prove to him that her desirability as a woman had set limits. Jake wasn't the kind to take her word for something like that; he was a strong, virile male with supreme confidence in his own abilities as a lover. With no reflection at all, she knew that he would regard her frigidity as a challenge to his expertise, in the same way lesser men had thought they could break through the barrier of her coldness.

"You like that bag, missy?" A plump arm came to lift the beach bag Denise had been staring at so intently.

"I—" Denise blinked and looked into the

beaming face, and said automatically, "How much is it?"

She wasn't in the mood for bargaining, and presently she walked away with the bag over her arm, the woman looking after her thoughtfully and with a touch of compassion.

"Oh, Denise, that's a beautiful bag," Meg cried, when she at last caught up with her and Jake as they investigated the rows of dresses, smock tops and yet more straw goods inside the hanger-like building adjoining the stalls.

Denise glanced down at it and saw it clearly for the first time. It *was* quite pretty, with daisies and grapelike bunches woven in a hyacinth blue single color, more tasteful than the more gaudy wares surrounding them.

"Yes, I like it a lot," she answered Meg, mentally telling herself that she would give the bag to Ellen, the housekeeper, on her return to San Diego.

Jake had been making purchases of his own, and as he turned from the delighted vendor he held two hastily wrapped boxes.

"One for you—" he handed a package to a dancing-eyed Meg "—and one for you." He made a mocking half bow as he held the other out to Denise. "I hear most women are little girls at heart."

Her surprised eyes met his, which appeared to have taken on a deeper hue from the vivid blue of the short-sleeved shirt he was wearing. Was there an intended snideness in his smilingly spoken words?

"You shouldn't have bought something for me," she murmured, annoyed by the flush that heated her throat and cheeks.

"Can we open them now, daddy?" Meg asked excitedly, her fingers already on the opening edges of the paper bag.

"Contain yourself for a while longer," Jake told her dryly, "at least until we're having lunch. Which, by the way—" he glanced at the watch on his dark-haired wrist "—we should be thinking about right now. There's a cruise ship in, so everywhere's going to be crowded later on."

But the place he took them to was quiet, secluded, close to Bay Street but sheltered from its noisy traffic by the buildings surrounding the square patio where they ate their meal. Huge umbrellas sheltered the tables from the penetrating rays of the noon sun, and potted palms seemed to attract the nearby ocean breeze, their fronds rustling dryly as they swayed lazily to its motion. Bright splashes of color were provided by smaller tubs filled with red blossoms, and Denise looked around her with pleasure as they sat down in the white wrought-iron chairs.

"How did you discover such a lovely place, Jake?" she asked, turning the cool green of her eyes on his face, already frowningly bent over a stiff-backed menu.

He looked up, the frown still lingering between

his thick dark brows. "When I was here five years ago," he replied half abstractedly, glancing around as another lunch party at an adjoining table laughed uproariously, obviously having observed the cocktail hour long before its time. "It's nice here at night when the table and patio lamps are lighted."

Romantic, too, Denise thought involuntarily, sensing that this was his first daylight visit to the restaurant. Was he remembering a woman he had brought here those years ago, someone he had wined and dined and taken to his newly lonely bed after his divorce?

"Can we open our presents now, daddy?" the impatient Meg demanded, the long box-shaped package held tightly on her lap.

"Let's order first honey, and then you tear off the wrappings as soon as you like." He looked inquiringly at Denise. "Decided what you want?"

"Just soup and a salad," she said quickly without consulting the elaborate menu. "After that enormous breakfast at the house I really don't need anything at all."

A brief smile touched his firm lips. "Max's staff certainly knows how to keep vacationers stuffed and content. How about you, Meg?"

"Can I have this?" she stabbed a finger halfway down the middle page of the menu, and Jake leaned over to see what her choice was. There was a silence before he spoke, choosing his words with care, and Denise noticed that Meg's choice had come from the dinner menu.

"You might find that a little hard to handle in the middle of the day, honey," he said softly. "How about a small salad, hamburger and fries?"

"Do they have that here?" Meg asked, wide-eyed.

"Sure they do."

Jake leaned back in his chair and gave their order to the waiter who appeared unobtrusively at his elbow, while Denise felt a surging glow of pleasure at his tact in handling Meg. He was a good father, considerate and thoughtful, mindful of his small daughter's sensitivity. Yet there was a forcefulness, an overriding of scruples when he wanted a momentary sexual satisfaction from a woman.

"All right, go ahead," he said indulgently now, and Meg delved into the paper bag on her lap, exclaiming rapturously as she withdrew a doll visible through the cellophane-fronted box, a turbaned black woman whose slender arms were upraised as if to support the heavy load of plastic bananas on her head. A sleeveless cotton top gave way to the voluminous straw skirt edged with a frill of cotton and more fruit and greenery attached to the open weave of the skirt.

"It's beautiful, daddy," Meg said rapturously, her eyes wide gray orbs as they ran over the figure. "Thank you! Aren't you going to open yours, Denise?"

Smiling, knowing her own gift must be a replica of Meg's, Denise lifted the package from its resting place against the table's curved central stem and carefully peeled away the paper bag. She had been right. The doll Jake had bought for her was a replica of Meg's, except that the dusky figure carried a basket of pale yellow lemons on her head, the skirt embellished with oranges and a deep red fruit of indistinguishable identity. It was gaudy, commercial, but she loved it—from the varicolored hem trim to the false gold of ear hoops falling from misty blue turban headdress.

"Thank you, Jake," she said softly, tremulously, knowing that the doll was a gift she would always keep—a memory of the only man she had ever deeply, truly loved? That Jake's reason for giving it to her was far removed from love didn't matter at this moment—that he regarded her as no more than the child his daughter was, a woman afraid to give herself to a man other than her dead husband, was of no account. The doll was a symbol of what she had never known—a spontaneous gift from her austere father, a whimsical recognition from the husband she had ended up hating.

ENTERING THE CASINO that night with Jake by her side evaporated the happy glow that had pervaded her before leaving her room, taking a last look at the doll on her dressing table whose skirts had expanded to antebellum style after being taken from the box and coaxed by her gentle fingers.

She was conscious of Jake's automatic attraction for the women who, accompanied or not, milled under the brilliant lights of magnificent chandeliers and turned their heads in his direction, their eyes covetous, almost lustful. She was, conversely, unaware of the male eyes turned in her direction, the open admiration as they flicked quickly down over the smooth tan of her shoulders and absorbed the lines of her figure-hugging dress of champagne-colored crepe de Chine and lingered on the undisguised fullness of her breasts that were only half-concealed by the low cut of her full-length dress.

"What do you like?" Jake asked, his hand under her elbow as he prepared to direct her to one of the many tables catering to varied gambling tastes. "Blackjack, roulette, or—?"

"I don't know anything about those things," Denise interrupted hurriedly, her eyes drawn to the right side of the room where more averagely dressed people were feeding coins into gray machines ranged in rows that reached to the far side of the room. "What's that over there?"

Jake leaned forward and looked across her. "The slot machines. Do you want to try them first?"

"They look more manageable than those men in charge of the tables," she said tremulously, and he chuckled.

"The dealers—croupiers. All right, let's begin over here."

His hand was firm but unobtrusive as he steered her to a vacant machine and left her there while he went to change dollars into quarters. She watched the intent expressions on the faces of the people at either side of her, jumping when a loud bell on the row behind announced a high winner.

"Here you go," Jake said at her ear, depositing a large paper cup filled with quarters on the small ledge beside her machine. "I think there's more chance of a big win if you feed in five quarters at a time."

"But I can't gamble with *your* money," she cried in horror, twisting her sleekly coiffed silver hair to look at him with wide eyes.

"We'll settle up at the end of the evening," he returned equably, and dipped into the paper cup, presenting her with five shiny quarters. "Put these in the slot, then pull this lever at the side. Go ahead," he urged as she hesitated. "We won't go in over our heads."

"I don't agree with gambling," she pronounced belatedly as her fingers dropped the coins one by one into the slot, then moved to the knobbed stick beside the machine and pulled it down. She stared fascinated as the rows of empty circles filled with fruit combinations, none of which rang the magic bell that pronounced her a winner. Disappointed, she looked up at Jake, who was standing to the side and slightly behind her.

"Don't give up," he urged. "Beginner's luck

doesn't mean much in a place like this. Try again."

She did. Again and again and again. And a strange fever seemed to enter her blood, forcing her coin-stained fingers to lift time after time to the narrow slits, her weary arm to pull on the side stick. The small wins she made, with the rewarding flush of coins into the receiving tray in front of her, fueled the sudden, unexplainable lust that filled her.

Jake himself did not gamble, seeming to derive his pleasure from watching her animated absorption in the metal machine that challenged her until the cup of coins was gone. Silently he disappeared and materialized at her side moments later with yet another cup of coins. Abstractedly she picked them up in fives and plugged them into the machine, her losses far exceeding her gains as the cup's contents dwindled again.

"Maybe if we both try," Jake suggested, and as she inserted the last of the quarters, his hand covered hers firmly as it settled on the rounded knob of the pull stick. Feeling the heated glow that had risen to her face from the excitement of her first gambling spree, she looked around and up into his enigmatically smiling face. She couldn't be doing this, gambling with money that was not her own—although she would, of course, repay Jake's outlay—but a strange kind of fever seemed to have infected her, a state of mind that negated the automatically absorbed precept that gambling was bad.

A faint premonition lessened her shock when the magical combination of three registered and Denise, her eyes ablaze with excitement, turned impulsively into Jake's arms as coins began to spill into the tray and the triumphant bell rang stridently over her machine. She needed the hard, warm touch of his arms around her then, the feel of his black-jacketed shoulder under her cheek. It was all part of the unreal atmosphere when he looked down at her, his own cheek furrowing as he twisted his head, the reflected glow of her excitement in his eyes as he bent and kissed her incredulously parted lips.

Briefly she felt his mouth's warmth and took in the scent of him before he lifted his head again and they stared solemnly, deeply at each other until a gray-haired man playing the next machine said jokingly, "Your cup's about to runneth over there."

The words might have been prophetic under other circumstances, if only— Denise's heart lay like a stone in her breast as she pulled away from Jake and set about scooping up the coins into paper cups. It hadn't been a huge win—fifty dollars, which was about as much as she had fed into the machine—but that, too, seemed right for the state of her love life. Always the bridesmaid, never the bride—the old saying ran through her mind and was repudiated immediately. She *had* been a bride, and what a mess that had turned out to be! She felt deflated, defeated suddenly, and when Jake asked if she wanted to carry on she said, all her previous animation gone, "No, I've had more than enough."

Nothing could be truer. She had had more than enough of the constant badgering of her senses, the wanting, knowing there could be no real fulfillment for herself or the man who made love to her. Soldiers made impotent by war wounds must feel this way, too, her thoughts went on as Jake guided her through the serious-faced people who might be losing more than they could afford in the glittering promise of the casino. Did they, the soldiers, have all the normal urges—the attraction to a woman, the mounting excitement, the frustration when the moment of truth came? In that sense, she reflected wryly, she herself could be classed as one of the walking wounded.

She knew that Jake had been encouraged by her uninhibited throwing of herself into his arms. He looked puzzled and faintly hurt when she said good-night to him in the hall of the Pearson home and went immediately upstairs.

But that hadn't been the right time to prove to him her fallibility as a woman—vulnerable herself, she would have cried and become sorry for herself, and he would have pitied her, been kind to her as he would to Meg if she fell and scraped her knee. And it wasn't pity she wanted or needed from Jake Barstow.

THE DAYS LEADING UP TO the big Junkanoo celebrations, the main reason for their vacation in
Nassau, were a mixture of lighthearted sight-
seeing and hours spent as a threesome swimming,
snorkeling and playing board games during the
evenings when they stayed home at the borrowed
house.

And every day, every evening spent as a family,
committed Denise more irrevocably to a love for
Jake that transcended every other feeling.

Her plans were firmly set in her mind now. She
would resign her appointment to the project and
reassume her undemanding role as a small cog in
the big machine of the Scripps Institution. In-
sulated in the cushioned comfort of the home she
had inherited from her father, she could be
mistress of her own destiny. A bleak, unfulfilled
destiny perhaps, but no one would ever know that
she grieved, not for the husband taken from her so
tragically after one short year of marriage, but for
her lost womanhood.

True to her word, Meg was up and about and
anxiously waking the people she presently cared
most about on the morning of the new year.
Shortly after five, she woke the lightly sleeping
Denise with her tensely heavy breathing from the
side of her bed.

"What is it, Meg?" she asked, instantly alert.

"It's almost time for the parade," Meg
breathed, the excited light shining in her gray eyes
slightly dimmed by an apprehension that made

Denise wonder if Barbara, her mother, would have shown irritation at being awakened this early in the morning.

"Oh...good. I'll be with you as soon as I've showered and dressed." She saw that Meg's eyes were drawn to the bared expanse of her shoulders and rounded tops of her breasts as she struggled into a sitting position. Then, with an embarrassed smile, the child went silently from the room.

Shrugging off a slight stab of irritation—Meg must have seen her mother in a state of dishevelment many times—Denise threw back the covers and slid her legs over the side of the bed.

Whatever cobwebs remained in her sleep-filled brain were dispersed an hour later when they watched the first of the daylong parades along Bay Street. The crashing sound of steel drums, supplemented by primitive pipes and noisemakers of various kinds, resolved themselves into the deeply rhythmic harmony she had heard nights before on this same street, though it had been more constrained then.

The Bahamian natives, having waited long for this day when Nassau was theirs, cavorted behind the costumed bandsmen, their own costumes fashioned from multi-colored crepe paper so realistically monstrous that Denise felt Meg press for reassurance against her side.

Later there were floats, more colorful, more flamboyantly distinctive than any she had seen in the States. Some depicted scenes from the old

Bahamas, before the tourist influx; others were sponsored by prominent businesses in the islands. The replica of a buccaneer sailing ship, complete with dusky-skinned maidens, was followed by the austere lines of a bank building, denoting the prosperity international banking had brought to the Bahamas.

Everywhere there was noise, the joyous carefree noise of people released, however briefly, from the everyday chore of making a living. Her own disappointment was as keen as Meg's when Jake suggested, after the last float had passed into oblivion, that they return to the house Max had loaned them for just this occasion.

"Oh, daddy, can't we stay downtown?" Meg begged, her eyes enormous in her small face. "There's such a lot happening here, and there's nothing at the house."

"There's lunch," Jake returned with dry firmness, "which we'd be very lucky to find down here today. And there are comfortable beds where we can take a rest before tackling the evening celebrations."

Despite her immediate protests, Meg had dark circles beneath her eyes that looked like bruises, and Denise felt the same kind of fatigue in her own bones.

"Your father's right, Meg. I wouldn't mind a little nap myself this afternoon after getting up so early." Jokingly she added as they settled themselves in the car Jake had miraculously managed to park not far away, "And I need my beauty sleep, even if you don't."

"You're beautiful at any time, Denise," dismissed Meg brusquely. "Even when I woke you up this morning so early you looked like a movie star."

Denise's eyes involuntarily met Jake's over the child's head, her wry smile fading when she sensed the picture he was creating in his mind's eye.

"Thank you kindly, Meg," she said, her color rising as she turned back to the front, adding lightly, "but even movie stars need lots of sleep to keep their looks." *And that sounds as if I'm agreeing with her about my own looks,* she chided herself as Jake maneuvered through the side-street traffic again. But the fault of vanity seemed paltry against the much bigger flaw she nourished within her.

Meg grudgingly agreed to a nap after the delicious light lunch provided at the Pearson home, though Denise in her own room did little more than toss restlessly on the covers of her bed, when she at last stretched out and waited for the sweet oblivion of sleep.

She was too conscious of Jake's presence across the corridor, too embroiled in the uselessness of her fantasies to relax into sleep. Instead, she lay dry eyed, staring at the plaster cupids decorating the outer corners of the ceiling, the muscles of her neck taut and straining.

With any other woman living in such intimate

circumstances under the same roof, would he have come to her bedroom? Would he at this moment be parting the loose folds of her robe, caressing the naked skin under it, cupping and molding her female contours to the lean hardness of his maleness, lowering that hardness over the paler hue of her skin tone, possessing her with the wild passion he had known with so many others?

Her body ached with a useless longing that devoured her, sapped her energy, ate at the very core of her. *I love you, Jake,* she cried silently, twisting her head into the pillow, hardly noticing the tears sliding from her eyes. . . .

CHAPTER ELEVEN

THE GARISH NOISES of Junkanoo were all around them again that evening when they once more mingled with the crowds on Bay Street. Wild explosions of crazy laughter and hoots punctuated the bursts of steel-band music as swaying figures, grotesque and beautiful alike, undulated along the crowded street.

Meg, her hands firmly anchored in Jake's and Denise's on either side, appeared to be less affected by the assault on her eardrums than was Denise, who found the repetitive beat of the music somehow disturbing. Almost to the point of a nameless terror, and for a grown woman that was ridiculous, she told herself as they edged their way along the sidewalk.

Feeling Jake's eyes on her, she turned her head and saw a look that questioned, almost as if he had sensed her mood. And that, too, was ridiculous. How could he know her feelings when she couldn't pin them down herself? Then, without her knowing quite how he did it, Meg was transferred to his other side and he walked between them, his hand taking the place of Meg's in hers in a warm, strong hold.

Denise automatically looked across at Meg, expecting at the least a frown of displeasure, but the child was too absorbed in the noisy scene around them to know or care about the reason for the transfer. Besides, the clasped hands were hidden between her body and Jake's, whether or not by his design she suddenly didn't care. The fear miraculously fled, leaving in its place an opening floodgate to the joy that poured illicitly through her. She was at peace, yet strangely excited by her physical awareness of him as their thighs brushed in the enforced slowness of their walk. All at once the music's thrum became an essential part of the strange new feelings coursing through her, stirring nerve ends she hadn't known she possessed into electric impulses that tingled shiveringly from the tips of her breasts to the tops of her thighs.

Glad that there was too much clamor for speech, she wished with unusual disregard of reality that this walk could go on forever, making no demands she was powerless to fulfill.

Her wishful thinking was short-lived. At one of the tables surrounding the open-air dance floor in Rawson Square sat Paul and Marie, with David as a lonely-looking third. Conscience smote Denise at her neglect of the making of arrangements for them all to get together sometime during the celebrations. Marie and Paul gave lavishly of their kindness to everyone else, but no one else, including herself, ever seemed to think of reciprocating in kind. But Jake should have....

She became aware suddenly that Marie's bright

eyes were fixed on the hand still entwined in Jake's, and she pulled away impulsively to take the chair Paul held for her.

"We wondered if we might see you around," Paul raised his voice to say. "We've seen just about everyone else we know in Nassau." He turned to where David sat studiedly ignoring Meg, who stood at his side. "Why don't you share that chair with Meg, son, then we can all sit down."

"Aw, dad," David shifted uncomfortably, "do I have to?"

"Either that or stand like a gentleman and give Meg your chair," Paul told him evenly, and David yielded a few reluctant inches that Meg accepted with regal disdain.

Before sitting down himself, Jake looked at Marie, then Paul. "Can I get a refill on your drinks? I'm just going to get something for us."

Marie looked thoughtfully at Denise at his casual use of the "us," her eyes alive with speculation, and Denise looked at Jake, waiting for him to ask what she would like. But he went off with Paul to the temporary bar set up on trestle tables at the far side of the dance area without consulting her.

"So how is the vacation going?" Marie raised her voice, but only Denise could hear over the music. Was it her imagination, or was there a snide innuendo in Marie's tone?

Deciding that she was being oversensitive, Denise smiled back and called, "Just fine. I've really enjoyed it. Jake must have taken us to see every nook and cranny in Nassau. How about you?"

Marie shrugged ruefully. "David's more interested in sea than sights. He's been taking good care of your specimens, by the way."

Denise turned to look across the table where David and Meg sat in an uneasy truce watching the gyrating dancers and decided it was too much hassle to thank him at that moment. She would buy something for him before he went back to his school.

"How are you getting along with Jake?" his mother pursued, this time with a definite gleam in her eye.

"He's been...very kind." Denise chose the words carefully, but saw Marie frown nonetheless.

"That's one of his fatal charms," she said with a cautious glance in Meg's direction, but she was watching avidly for her father's return. "Don't get hurt, Denise. Remember what I told you about Jake."

"There's no possibility of that," Denise got in before she discerned Paul, followed by the taller Jake, coming back to the table. Hurt? She would never get over the hurt of loving Jake and being unable to show the depth of that love. It had meant nothing but relief to her when Sam had found consolation in other women's arms; it would have torn her to shreds if Jake, not Sam, had been the one to flee her frigid bed. She jumped when Jake's warm breath fanned her ear.

"You said you were saving these drinks for special occasions, didn't you? What could be more special than this night?"

Her startled eyes flew up to meet the metallic glitter in his as he straightened, her heart doing a flip-flop when she realized that he wasn't referring to the excitement of Junkanoo. He had misinterpreted her clinging to his hand in their meandering progress along Bay Street, her nonavoidance of slow, almost sensual, body contact, her uninhibited return of the occasional tightening of his hand. *Oh, Jake, my love, it can never be—not as you'd want it, not as you deserve to have it.*

She drank deeply of the Goombay Special he had brought her, realizing too late that its rum content was far higher than the one Perry had made for her at the clubhouse. That thought was followed immediately by another as the alcohol hit her bloodstream and raced around her body.

Why not tonight, she wondered recklessly. Let Jake discover the deep inadequacy that had plagued her senses since she had first laid eyes on him! Let him know what a fraud, a crippled creature she was!

Two Specials later, having contributed little or nothing to the loud-voiced conversation going on around her, she went willingly with Jake to the dance floor where, amazingly, the live Bahamian band was playing music slow enough to dance closely to, albeit with the rhythm of the islands.

The unmistakable pangs of a slow-burning desire spread and glowed somewhere deep inside her, its focus Jake's hard, lean jaw that rested on the area of her temple. Long ago and far away she had felt that same desire, but now it was stronger, insistently demanding. Its force took her body from her control and pressed it to Jake's with a fierceness that brought instant response, his breath drawing in on a hiss when her hips shifted and moved deliberately, intimately.

"Dear God," he muttered, tightening his grip around her clinging body like a drowning man snatching at driftwood. "I hope you know what you're doing, Denise." The fiery warmth of his mouth began to drop erratic kisses from her ear to the sensitive curve of her neck, nuzzling, passionate kisses that rocked her with compulsive shivers that were half excitement, half denial. "Because I'm going to make love to you tonight like you've never been made love to before. Not even by—"

Sam—he needn't have cut off the word, the name. A dry chuckle rose and died in Denise's throat. There was nothing funny about frigidity. It was a fact of her life that she had more or less accepted until her meeting with Jake. Now it was his turn to discover that horrific fact about her. What better time than when her own senses were swimming in an alcohol haze?

This night had been destined from their first meeting, she realized now, walking back to their table under the sultry night sky, Jake's arm in warm possession around her waist. The final confrontation, she told herself with drunken amusement. Not so amusing was the recognition that after tonight Jake would show—what? Disdain? Contempt? Pity?

Those thoughts were pushed firmly to the back of her mind when Marie, unobtrusively but definitely feeling the effects of the drinks that had been circulating freely around the table, gave them a dazzling smile.

"Paul's insisting that we go," she said happily, making it obvious to Denise that the excitement of Junkanoo was but a prelude to the lovemaking that would take place in the Stein home that night. The bitterness of envy rose in her throat, as quickly dying away. Normal was beautiful in her eyes; it was something Marie and Paul took for granted.

The light hammering at her temples that had suggested a headache earlier in the evening blossomed out in full force as Jake drove back to the Pearson place. Even Meg's sleepy head, resting lightly on her shoulder, felt like an impossible imposition. Yet she was aware of the expectancy Jake's long, lean body exuded, the tensed sinews in his arms as he drove through partying throngs, the contraction of his thigh muscles as he stepped alternately on the brake and accelerator.

She allowed her head to rest on the high seat back, afraid, terrified, of what he was about to demand of her—what he had the right to demand of her after tonight's performance. Shame penetrated her befogged senses when she recalled how she had deliberately incited the intensification of his male desire, let him think that she would be even more forthcoming later than night.

Soon—too soon—they were traversing the short driveway to the front door, and Jake was lifting the sleepy Meg into his arms, carrying her into the house, saying huskily over his shoulder, "I'll get Meg settled."

First, his eyes added silently, *before I take you up on what you've been promising all night.* Denise's feet seemed rooted to the crushed oval of the driveway as she watched his lithe figure mount the outside steps, disappearing into the house, leaving the door ajar for her.

She followed him slowly at last, her hand on the octagonal shape of the door handle when she suddenly pulled it to and retreated backward down the steps until her feet touched the coral again. Turning, she fled precipitately around the side of the house, panic lending facility as she found the winding beach path, flitting along it wraithlike until she burst suddenly onto the small private cove ringed with palms and shrubby vegetation.

If Jake was persistent he would find her here, where the three of them had spent hours during the past days, swimming, playing, sunning. It wasn't far from the house.

But even Jake, inflamed as his senses were, would think twice about pursuing a reluctant lover. Denise kicked off her sandals and walked barefoot to the water's edge, letting the gently hissing wavelets, sparkling with the brilliance of diamonds where the moon's light struck them, froth over her feet. Oh, God, if only her head didn't hurt so much she could think clearly what to do. Heat, like a fever, seemed to be consuming her. The water lapping her feet was cool; it would cool the rest of her inflamed body, too, if she....

Her fingers reached for the back zipper of her dress—the sea-green dress that matched the translucence of her eyes, its soft folds clinging with loving faithfulness to the soft curves of her figure. Had she chosen it to attract Jake's eyes to the promising hint of fullness beneath its low-cut neckline, its emphasis on the tiny waist that flared to womanly hips in a swirl of gossamer chiffon? Bitterness compressed her mouth into an ugly line. What had she been trying to prove? "Look at me, world, I'm just as normal as the next woman."

The dress fell in a crumpled heap at her feet, followed by the rest of her clothing, the wisps of lace and nylon fashioned to provoke the titillation of man. Their promise of sexual satisfaction was as ephemeral as her own.

Stepping from her discarded clothing, she waded into the water, feeling the first shock of coldness on her ankles, thighs, hips, before stretching her arms and allowing her legs to rise behind her as she stroked slowly through the water that had been her element since childhood. Silklike, it caressed her nakedness in a way it never had before. She had never swum in the nude before, even in the private confines of her San Diego beachfront home. If the thought had occurred to her at all, it would have been stillborn at the surety of her father's icy wrath, something she had learned early in her life not to provoke.

Now she regretted her reticence, welcoming the freedom from confinement from even the briefest of bikinis. She had never felt in such close rapport with the ocean before, and she stroked slowly much farther than she had intended when a flurry behind her warned her of another presence.

"What in hell are you doing away out here?" Jake gasped his fury when he surfaced beside her, treading water as he pulled on her arm and forced her to do the same. "Don't you know it's dangerous to go swimming this far out on your own?"

Like diving, she thought dully; never go diving without a buddy, the training precept went through her mind. The thought of Jake as a buddy tinged her reply with amusement.

"I'm perfectly capable of taking care of myself," she told him, seeing yet not wanting to see the bronzed power in his lean muscled shoulders.

"Sure," he said, sounding angry, "but that only applies until you get a cramp, and what do you do then?" He stationed himself in a guardlike position in front of her. "Let's get back to shore and we'll discuss it there."

She stared at him through water-spiked lashes,

saw the dark hair plastered to his skull, the un-compromising light in his slate-gray eyes, and turned wordlessly to stroke out for shore.

What had he thought she was about to do? Go out so far that there was no possibility of return? More sobering was her own conjecture. Had she meant to do just that subconsciously? To avoid the confrontation she knew inevitably awaited her wherever Jake was? No, that was the coward's way out.

They swam steadily side by side until first Jake, then Denise, put foot to sandy bottom and waded out to the beach that seemed warm under her feet after the coolness of the water. It was the sight of an absolutely naked Jake that made her aware of her own nudity, and she unconsciously lifted her arms to cross them over the exposed fullness of her breasts, their dark pink tips risen from the coldness of the water.

"You didn't have to go and drown yourself because of me or what I wanted from you," Jake said harshly, the lean muscles of his calves tensing as he strode from her to where his clothes lay in piled disarray. "I'm not that desperate that I need to force a woman against her will."

She watched numbly as he went with purposeful stride across her line of vision. She had seen Sam unclothed only a few times and had been some-what embarrassed, but now she looked at Jake in his bared maleness and found him beautiful. The lithe lines of his figure, with the contrasting white against the bronze where his swimming shorts had covered, were everything a woman could desire. A normal woman, that was. Her voice came out more shrilly than she had intended.

"Wait, Jake, there's...something I have to tell you."

He turned, unashamed of his nakedness, and said wearily, "You've already told me all I need to know. Okay, so I don't turn you on, you're still crazy about Sam Jordan. Just don't—" he described a useless arc with his hand and had turned away to resume his stalking when Denise's emotional cry halted his steps over the damp sand.

"*I'm not crazy about Sam!* I *hated* him...and he died hating me!"

Jake's long feet left clawlike impressions in the sand as he swiveled sharply, his eyes displaying sour incredulity. "What in hell are you talking about? You've been acting like a broken-hearted widow ever since you got here!"

Denise took a step toward him, her mouth opening soundlessly, then she rushed to where two thirsty beach towels, presumably brought down by Jake, lay, lifting one and draping its folds around her exposed figure. The pressure of blood in her veins seemed to have dropped suddenly, making her heart move in a painfully sluggish half beat. Why hadn't she gone ahead in the way she had originally planned, letting Jake find out for himself that the promises she had made were empty ones, as sterile as a eunuch's were in a harem of beautiful women?

She looked at him, tall and spare and bronzed in the moon's light. Being naked might have made another man feel vulnerable, but there was nothing vulnerable about Jake, she recognized dismally, the cold barrier sheathing her insides matching the chill of the water drops that still sparkled on her long, gold-tanned legs. He was hard, confident, unassailable. The tenderness in him was reserved exclusively for his daughter.

"Well?" he gritted impatiently, shifting so that the unreal brilliance of the moon glinted off the drops on his own skin, making them shimmer like a million diamonds shattered by a hammer blow. "I think you owe me some explanation for your come-on tactics earlier tonight before your sudden desire for a moonlight swim. Now you're telling me that you and your husband hated each other's guts. What does that prove? It has nothing to do with what went on between you and me tonight, and you know it."

Denise moistened her dry lips, tasting the fine layer of ocean salt on them, wishing she was a thousand miles away from this tropic beach.

"Our marriage," she said haltingly, "Sam's and mine, was. . . a failure. Because of me." Her knuckles whitened as she clamped her fingers on the thick towel folds at her throat. "I. . . I couldn't be the wife Sam expected. He. . . he needed someone who could... respond to him. Physically. And I... couldn't.''

The words were out. Heady relief obscured Jake's stunned expression. Her feet had a sudden desire to dance across the white sand that pushed its powdery texture between her toes. The need for pretense was over. She had exposed her deepest flaw to the man she loved helplessly, hopelessly—yet her heart amazingly still beat firmly within her breast, her limbs still held her body upright.

"What in God's name are you trying to tell me?" Jake's voice penetrated harshly into her mesmerized thoughts. "Are you saying that you're... frigid?"

Denise's eyes unconsciously begged for understanding, answering his question without words.

"Like hell you are!" he ejaculated, his limbs uprooting from their treelike stance and moving rapidly toward her, his hands rough on her shoulders as he jerked her into a position where she had no choice but to look up into the glinting gray of his eyes. "What kind of cop-out is this? Don't you think I'm experienced enough with women to know when one of them has all the normal desires? Are you telling me now that you lived with Sam without sex?"

Her gaze clashed, locked with his before Denise dropped her head, her eyes fixing instead on the dark cluster of hair under his muscular throat.

"No," she said woodenly, "I'm not saying that. Sam had... a normal man's needs, and I

wasn't able to satisfy them. That didn't stop him
from trying. In between the... the other women in
his life.''

For a long time Jake said nothing. His fingers
gouged painfully into her shoulders, and then he
swore softly and continuously in the longest string
of oaths she had ever heard, ending with a fierce
groan, ''Sweet Jesus, what did he do to you?''

''The fault was mine, not Sam's,'' Denise defended tiredly, moving back until Jake's hands fell
from her. She pulled the towel closer around her.
''I didn't realize until too late that I shouldn't
have married him—or any other man. I am...
what you said.''

The words dropped starkly into the pool of
silence spreading between them, and Denise no
longer had any desire to dance. A curious numb-
ness was filtering from her midriff to the nether
regions of her body and up to dull the images im-
printing their messages on her brain. As if she
were there, she saw the San Diego house, im-
pressive in its sprawl, and her own figure moving
through each deserted room as year after year fell
from the calendar.

Alone. Like her father, she would always be
alone. But at least he had had the comfort of a
child to secure his own immortality. She would die
a withered old woman who had long forgotten the
blood's rush of desire, flesh that melted at a man's
touch.

''Haven't you heard a word I've been saying?''

Jake's, voice intruded exasperatedly into the tangled weave of her thoughts. Her lashes fluttered dazedly as she stared into the molten silver of his eyes where a half-mocking light gleamed in their depths. "You are not frigid, Denise, in any way except in your mind." His mouth tightened to a narrow line. "It's not unbelievable that you iced out your feelings. Sam wasn't your average sensitive guy. It doesn't take much imagination to know that he would be like a bull in a china shop when he was presented with a virgin in his marriage bed."

Denise caught her breath and half turned away from him, clutching at the protective towel, thankful that the eerie brilliance of the moon made the change in her skin color indistinguishable. Of course he had to realize that she had been totally inexperienced sexually on her wedding night; he was too shrewd not to have drawn that conclusion. But she hated the feeling of having been put under the microscope of his experienced eye in order to make that deduction.

"I suppose it would have been different if you and not Sam had been the one in my bed that night?" she threw out defensively.

He returned evenly, "Could be."

"You men make me *sick*!" she exploded with a violence that obviously surprised him, lifting his dark brows in twin arcs above his shadowed eyes. "Every one of you thinks that he's the one, the only one, who ca...can—"

"Maybe that's something built into a man's psyche to protect his very shaky ego just underneath," Jake said quietly, his voice faintly tinged with amusement. "Men have a lot of hang-ups, too, where sex is concerned. It's not your prerogative."

Denise swung her head back and looked at him disbelievingly. "I can't believe *you've* ever—" She broke off in confusion, hating the husky laugh that came from his throat.

"Thanks for the compliment, but I've had my bad moments, too. Most men have." His hands reached out, and she felt them heavy on her shoulders as he drew her to him, only the rough towel separating their nakedness. After a long moment of silence, he said, "I'd still like to show how frigid you're not."

Her head snapped back, breath catching in her throat as sensations fought for supremacy inside her. A dreadful excitement battled with indignation about his calm sureness, and the latter emotion won out. "Just like that? A cold, clinical experiment?"

Again amusement crept into his voice. "It won't be cold after a while, I assure you."

"No, please, I—" A wave of weakness attacked her knees and she sank down on the sand, still holding the voluminous towel around her. What he was suggesting was a cold-blooded seduction with her consent, an expert triggering of known areas of erotic stimulation, an automatic response to his male aggression.

Her head was bent on her upraised knees when she heard the rustle of Jake's movements beside her and felt the towel being lifted from her shoulders, spread out behind her. A strangled moan was drawn from her throat when the pervasive warmth of his hands ran lightly across her shoulders and eased her back to the makeshift blanket topping the mattress of white sand.

"Jake, please, I don't *want* you to—"

"I won't do anything you don't want me to do, I promise," he soothed, and she felt the beginning of unreality when he lay back on the towel he had spread beside hers and took her into the loose fold of his arms, touching her head to nudge it into place in the hollow of his shoulder, his contacts as sexless as a brother's would have been.

"Now let's talk."

"T-talk?"

"Talk," he repeated firmly, his heartbeat firm and strong and unhurried under her ear while her own fluttered alarmingly in her breast. She was acutely aware of the long leanness of his side pressing to the curving outlines of her own body, and she held herself stiffly against the hard-packed flesh.

"Did I ever tell you about my father?" he began with an easy comfort that suggested a highly civilized social encounter rather than their shatteringly unconventional position. "He was a country doctor of the old kind—in fact, he'd just made his last house call when he keeled over and died. It was the way he would have wanted it, because he spent his whole life caring for the people in the small New England town where he set up practice soon after he qualified. The cemetery was packed with the people he had served for fifty years, a lot of them the babies he'd originally brought into the world. My younger brother, Paul, followed in his footsteps, and he took over the practice. But he's part of a team in a bright new clinic, and though he's a good doctor, I doubt if he'll get the send-off my father got when it's his turn to go. It was a lot different when dad first started...."

Denise listened, startled into attention at first, even irritated by the recital of a dead man's experiences when her own problem loomed large and filled her mind. But gradually, without her consciously realizing it, she relaxed and let her body rest lightly against Jake's as she became absorbed in the happenings of a small-town American doctor. Under Jake's skillful telling, he and his family became dearly, amusingly, familiar. She could visualize his mother's chagrin, tempered by her sense of charity, when his doctor father literally removed their Thanksgiving turkey from the oven to give to the family of a woman whose tenth child he had just delivered, a family more in need than his own.

When the soft, light strokes of Jake's hand penetrated her half-dreaming state, she was too relaxed to voice a protest, even if she had had one. She didn't. The repeated, almost casual, brush of his dry skin tracing the curves and hollows at her

as his body stiffened and rolled away from her, the hard wall of his chest heaving as he panted for breath, that they must have been the wrong words. An avowal of love would imply commitment, a commitment he had made only too clear wasn't for him.

It was then that she heard the distant sound of Meg's call.

"Daddy? Daddy, where are you?"

Meg! Why, oh, why, when every dream Denise had ever cherished was coming true, had Jake's daughter chosen that moment to wake and call him? Already he had gone from her, levering himself up from the improvised bed, pulling on the pants and shirt he had dropped in his haste to rescue her from the smooth-topped depths of the ocean.

"I'll go on up to the house," he said thickly, barely glancing at her. "You come when you're ready."

Too weak to move her limbs, Denise turned only her head to watch him go, his feet throwing up sprays of sand behind him. *I love him,* she told herself in wondering disbelief, *and he loves me.* No man could make love to a woman with such tenderness, such fire, without feeling love for her. Stretching her arms above her head in feline satisfaction, Denise contemplated the stars with a beginning smile curving the lips Jake had made tender and throbbing. She felt clean, free, rid of all the doubts that had plagued her.

The heavy weight of guilt her marriage to Sam had lain on her was gone. Not completely, perhaps, because she had been as wrong for Sam as he had been for her. He had been selfish in pandering to his own desires without regard for hers; just as she had harbored false pride in not telling him of her complete and total lack of experience. Marriage with Jake would be different, a glorious oneness not only in the marital bed but in their careers. The smile abruptly faded and she sat up hurriedly, glancing at the trees surrounding the small beach.

Marriage was as far from Jake's thoughts as Saturn was from the moon. He was probably even now soothing Meg's fears as he had many times before, telling her that he had been taking a moonlight swim—alone.

But he hadn't been alone. He had been down here on this beach making nonsense of Denise's deeply nurtured convictions. He had brought to life the female parts of her that had lain dormant for so long, too long.

Groping, she found the clothing she had discarded so carelessly a couple of hours before, and the conviction grew in her as she fastened the gossamer frivolities of panties and bra and dropped the shimmering folds of her dress around her, that she had to be at Jake's side when he confronted his daughter. Meg had to see, here and now, that Jake's love could encompass a woman not her mother, that the deep bond between father and daughter would remain intact. She would get over the loss of a mother who cared only for her own selfish interests—all Meg needed, craved, was a united family and the security that a family would provide. There was already an affection, a closeness, between Denise and Meg, a trust that had grown slowly in the weeks since Meg's arrival on the island.

Her flesh was still tingling from Jake's touch as she picked her way along the beach path to the house, her arms filled with the huge towels and the purse she had carried in Nassau earlier.

She halted suddenly as Meg's voice, shrill with her child's anger, cut like a knife through the parted patio doors into the small sitting room.

"Where's Denise?" she cried hysterically. "She's not in her room. Was she at the beach with you?"

"What Denise does is her own business," Jake returned evenly. "I know you're fond of her, but that doesn't give you the right to—"

"Is something wrong?" Denise stepped into the room, blinking as her eyes adjusted to the artificial light radiating from the side table lamps. Lamps that revealed a bleak-eyed Jake staring hard jawed at his pajama-clad daughter.

"Nothing's wrong," he said, his voice admirably level as he kept his eyes on Meg's slight figure. "Meg happened to wake up and she was concerned when she couldn't find either of us in the house."

Denise dropped the towels on a nearby chair, playing for breathing space as her brain worked overtime. Meg retained little of the innocence most young girls possessed at her age. Living with a woman of her mother's sophistication must have left its effect on her, whether or not she understood the physical relationship between adults.

"Sorry, Meg. I didn't expect you to wake up, you were so tired when we got back. I had a headache, and I thought a swim was the best way to—"

Meg's inarticulate cry of pain stemmed her words, and as the child turned and rushed from the room she turned to Jake.

"Jake?" she faltered uncertainly.

Jake checked the stride he had begun in pursuit of his daughter and turned to look at her, his eyes bitterly condemning. "Why in hell did you have to come in at that point? I could have made some excuse for you not being in your room, but—God!" His glance went scathingly over her disheveled appearance, the silver tumble of her hair, the lips swollen from his kisses. "Look at you! No wonder Meg—" He bit off the remainder of the sentence, substituting instead, "I'll see to her. You'd better get to your room."

Denise leaned weakly for support against the high back of an armchair, her senses reeling as Jake went angrily from the room. He blamed her, too! Jake, who had made nonsense of her frigidity with his passionate assault on every emotion she possessed, had behaved as a total, unapproachable stranger as he went in pursuit of the only human being for whom he lowered his own emotional guard. His daughter.

Her knuckles gripped whitely to the winged arms of the chair. It hadn't been love, a sense of caring, that had prompted the driving passion on the beach. She had been a challenge to overcome, a scientifically oriented experiment in basic human response to effective stimuli...and she had reacted like an inanimate puppet to the strings he expertly pulled!

Sick, feeling used and unclean, she stared down at the intricately designed carpet spreading before her. Had she really expected a man like Jake Barstow to fall headily, ecstatically in love with her?

She hadn't expected anything, she admitted fatalistically, except the dreaded contempt in his male eyes for her inadequacy as a woman. Instead, he had shown her that, given the right circumstances, her responses were as normal as the next woman's.

Later she might be grateful for that; right now she had to deal with the hatred that rose like bitter gall in her throat.

CHAPTER TWELVE

THE WATER WAS MORE CHOPPY than Denise had ever seen it, making the mother ship roll and pitch on her course to the diving area. But queasiness of the stomach had never been a problem for her, and it wasn't now as she leaned against the rail watching the gray blue froth of water churning in the ship's wake.

Snatches of high-pitched voices whipped back to her, and she raised her head momentarily to look toward the front of the ship where David and Meg were helping Paul secure the varied assortment of diving gear that might roll off the side and be lost in a heavy list. Absorbed in what they were doing, none of them glanced down the deck to her solitary figure, and she turned her attention back to the impersonal force of the waves slapping against the side.

Meg wouldn't have acknowledged her anyway, she reflected, remembering the child's frightening change of attitude after that fateful night at the Pearson place. Denise had expected repercussions, but nothing like the coldly implacable hatred Meg had displayed the next morning. The old defensive

barriers had been drawn down over her childish
features more firmly than when she had first arrived on the island, and Denise had been helpless
to break through the steely reserve Meg had
erected around herself.

It hadn't helped that Barbara, her mother,
hadn't shown up for a promised visit to the Project. Denise didn't know why, only that she had
never materialized on the appointed day. Her
heart ached for a disappointed Meg, who had
spurned Denise's efforts to comfort her.

Jake hadn't made matters easier either by his
aloof, if polite, coolness since that disastrous
night. It shouldn't surprise her that he sided with
his daughter in his condemnation of her. To him
the successful, if curtailed, assault on her senses
was no more than a confirmation of his own masculinity; to him she was someone to be chalked up
on his list of women vulnerable to his potent attraction. His heart still lay beside Meg's with the
woman who had rejected both of them with high-
handed arrogance.

The same kind of arrogance, Denise thought,
that Jake had meted out to her. Was it possible for
the breathless excitement of love to change so
dramatically to its opposite in such a short time?
Hatred was an emotion as unfamiliar to her as
love had been, yet she recognized it for what it
was. To see Jake, to come into the inevitable contact with him, was to relive his rejection all over
again.

"Denise?"

She turned her head and saw Toby's tousled hair above the submersible's conning tower. At least he, she reflected wryly as she pushed herself away from the rail and stepped toward the sub, was still his usual friendly self with her.

"Can I help you, Toby?"

A leering smile chased away the distracted frown worrying his brow. "You could, but you're always telling me you're not willing." He waved the piece of paper fluttering in his hand. "Would you do me a favor and take this up to Jake in the control room? Something's gone wrong with the communication system between sub and ship, and I'd like to get it fixed before we make a dive."

"Oh. All right." Denise clambered up over the stationary sub and reached out to pluck the paper from his hand. "No other message?"

"It's all there." He lunged suddenly and caught her wrist, grinning suggestively. "Unless you'd like to take the message from my mouth direct to his."

"Thanks, but no thanks." She pulled easily from his grasp and climbed backward to the deck again. "Is it something drastic?" she asked from that safer distance.

"Nothing that our revered chief can't put right, I'm sure. He's a very competent man, our boss."

"Indeed he is," Denise agreed, escaping before Toby had the chance to speculate too much about the conviction in her reply. Competent—that described Jake exactly, from his handling of the research project to his liberation of a frigid woman.

His clear-cut tones reached her ears long before she had scaled the top steps of the companionway leading to the control room. Instinctively she paused, one foot on the top step, the other on the iron gridway leading to the ship's central focus.

"I want you to alter course to the diving area you took Dr. Madsen to a couple of weeks ago," he was ordering briskly.

It was obviously Henry he was addressing, although Captain Mike had taken command of the ship for this trip.

"I'm not sure I can remember just where Dr. Madsen wanted to go," Henry replied stoically.

"Then maybe the ship's log will jog your memory! Let's see, wasn't it around the third week in December?" There was a sound of forcefully turned pages, then Henry's much less sure voice.

"I don't remember that I...put down every location we anchored at, sir."

"So I see," came Jake's dry comment. "The ones you *have* set down here are all areas we've surveyed before. I think it would be in your best interest, Henry, to remember exactly where you went on that trip." Without raising it, there was deadly menace in his voice, and Henry evidently caught on to it.

"I...I'll try, sir."

Denise jumped when Captain Mike, grouchily sober, came up the steps behind her and said testily, "Make up your mind whether you're going up or down, girl! What are you doing up here, anyway?"

"Bringing a message for Dr. Ba—Jake." She swung around jerkily, her mind whirling with the implications of Jake's command to direct the ship to the location of the uncharted cavern.

The sea-blue eyes under a heavy overhang of gray eyebrows fell on the paper in her hand. "Give it to me; I'll see he gets it."

At another time she might have been annoyed by his autocratic manner or amused by his old sea-dog superstitions about women on the bridge, but now she handed Toby's message to him and fled back to the deserted main deck.

Her hands gripped tightly to the rail as her chaotic thoughts settled into certainty. Jake was about to discover the underwater cavern Carl had guarded so jealously for months past, hoping to carve a small niche for himself in oceanographic circles. Regardless of the fact that Carl repelled her on a personal level, wasn't he being totally human in desiring to be a first in this one area? Hadn't she herself been tempted to go on that fateful survey with Carl for much the same motive?

Her head swiveled quickly as warm flesh touched her arm. Carl, the man who had been occupying her thoughts, leaned on the rail beside her, his expressionless eyes trained quizzically on her.

"You seem deep in thought, Denise. May I ask why?"

Denise's eyes flickered over the narrow confines of his face, recalling with an inner shudder the feel of those narrow lips on hers, the animal attack he had made on her in her cabin, and she turned jerkily back to the cresting waves surrounding the ship.

"My thoughts are private," she informed him, tight-lipped. "Aren't yours?"

"I have found it politic to keep my thoughts to myself over the years," he conceded softly. "But there are few secrets between us, Denise, hmm?"

Denise stemmed the hysterical laugh that threatened to choke her. What irony! The hold Carl thought he had over her no longer existed—it had been broken that night on the Pearsons' beach. There was no reason in the world why she shouldn't tell Jake about his second-in-command's find. But what did any of it matter anymore? Jake, Meg, Carl would all fade into history when she was once more back in the safe, if less exciting, background she knew. Why shouldn't Carl have his brief moment of glory? He had suffered horrors in his home country that most people brought up in the milk and honey of the United States couldn't comprehend. And Jake had more than enough accolades for his work in scientific research.

"You were wrong about me," she said flatly, her eyes fixed on the restless waves not far below them. "I was wrong about me, too." She shook her head disbelievingly. "All this time, and I thought—"

Carl's fingers curved around her wrist and twisted in painful pressure. "What are you saying?" he asked harshly. "That you have been with some man and found you were not...cold to him?"

Denise brushed her fingers through her wind-blown hair and gave him a mocking side glance. "That's exactly what I'm saying, Carl. Wonderful, isn't it?"

Carl appeared not to think so, for his fingers tightened their already crushing pressure on her delicate wrist bones. "Who was this man? Jake Barstow? It must have been; he is the only man you have been with. What did you tell him about our trip last month?"

"Nothing," Denise blazed the contempt she felt at this moment for Carl and every other man in her life. "I didn't have to. Jake's already quizzing Henry as to where he took us that day. So your precious find is just going to be another feather in *his* cap!"

The warning no sooner erupted from her lips than she regretted it. Working under Jake's direction, her loyalty should have been solely to him as head of the team. Every professional instinct in her rose up in agonized guilt, and nothing in

Carl's penetratingly alert gaze sought to relieve it.

"I am grateful to you for warning me of this," he said remotely in a voice that indicated his pre-occupation elsewhere. "If you will excuse me, I have some things to attend to."

Released from his crablike hold on her wrist, Denise stared numbly after his thin body's prog-ress across the deck, his sleekly brushed fair hair her last glimpse of him as he went below to the cabin area.

About to turn back to the rail, her eyes were drawn upward by a faint movement on the bridge deck. Her heart leaped painfully in her breast when her eyes met the gray scourge of Jake's. Their gazes locked and held for interminable moments until Jake turned brusquely back into the enclosed bridge.

On legs that seemed to have turned to rubber, Denise made her way to the privacy of her cabin below decks. Jake had seen, and misinterpreted Carl's close hold on her wrist. As if she had access to his innermost thoughts, she knew that Jake was going over in his mind the events of that night on the beach, her sad story of frigidity, and believing not one word of it.

Throwing herself onto the neatly made bunk, Denise stared through the round porthole to the vivid patch of blue sky beyond it. What did it mat-ter what Jake thought, she told herself fiercely. He had used her as he might utilize the instruments

that proved his scientific point. He had touched
the right buttons for the appropriate response,
and her reaction had been predictable.

The slow warmth of tears bathed her eyes and
filled the faint hollows under them. Why did she
have to love him so much?

PERHAPS BECAUSE OF THE PRESENCE of the children, who had been promised this treat of going
on a real ocean survey before returning to their
schools in the States, the conversation at dinner
was more general than the normal shoptalk indulged in by the scientists. Although at times it
wasn't far removed from the purpose of the ship's
foray into distant waters.

"Can I go down in the sub with you, dad?"
David asked eagerly, his glowing eyes, so like
Marie's, turning briefly to Denise. "I can get you
lots of specimens, Denise, so you wouldn't have to
bother about going down yourself."

"We'll have to see, David," she smiled con-
strainedly, glancing into Jake's blandly indifferent
expression. "It depends on what we're hoping to
find in the area."

She sensed Carl slip into the seat beside her and
speculated again on the reason for his lateness.
She had seen him leave his cabin some time earlier,
dressed as he was now in gray slacks and pale blue
shirt. What had he been doing?

"Maybe Carl can be more specific on that
point," Jake said in a lazy drawl. "We're headed

now for an area you're familiar with, so maybe you can give us some idea of what we can expect. Apart from weeds from the Sargasso Sea.'' His eyes rested briefly on Denise's, flickering with a mocking glow that disappeared when he looked questioningly back to Carl.

"There is very little, apart from the seaweed, to interest a scientific team," Carl returned smoothly, spreading his napkin across his lap and lifting the spoon designated for the soup course. "However, it is your prerogative to take the ship wherever you command." The spoon dipped, and Carl concentrated on the soup's beefy thickness, seemingly oblivious to the battery of eyes on his head.

He had class, Denise had to admit, not showing by so much as a hair out of place that he had suffered a crippling blow to his scientific pride. It didn't matter that his discovery would have been greeted as small change in the oceanographic world; to him it had been important, and now others would lay claim to being first to uncover a curious configuration of the ocean depths.

She was glad when the meal ended and the participants scattered to various pursuits. Meg, who had consistently ignored her throughout the deliciously cooked meal, cajoled Jake into a game of backgammon, her cold stare defying Denise to remember the laughing, relaxed times at the Pearson home when they had played endless three-way tournaments. Paul and David secreted themselves at one end of the long table, engrossed in the chessboard between them, and Toby noisily competed with Captain Mike at the other end in a fast-moving cribbage game. Carl had disappeared as soon as the meal ended, declining the strong-brewed coffee the other relished.

An outsider from the absorbed concentration in the games going on around her, Denise sat at one corner of a sofa and swallowed her coffee in spaced sips, pretending interest in the scientific magazine she had picked from the earworn pile beside her. Halfway through an article on the massive mountain ranges occupying the world's ocean beds, far higher than any peaks to be found above water, she flipped the magazine shut and got to her feet.

"Well, I think I'll call it a day," she announced quietly to an oblivious room, hearing abstracted good-nights as she went to the aft passageway leading to the cabins. Only Jake, his eyes opaquely neutral, looked up and really saw her over the backgammon board.

Her cabin seemed stuffy when she reached it, and she stood on the chair to manipulate the stiff openings on the porthole, then leaned there with her elbows on the sweating bulkheads as she looked out at the converse coolness of moonlight on water. A romantic atmosphere that thousands of people flew miles to capture for a brief two-week vacation. Honeymooners reaching for the moon's blessing at the start of their lives together, older couples seeking a renewal of the time that had bound them willingly to each other years before.

Denise rested her cheek on her hand, her teeth leaving an imprint of their even bite on the knuckles of her fingers. She didn't fall into either of those categories, although the lovemaking she had shared with Jake on the beach had been far more of a honeymoon than the horrific minutes spent with a selfish husband.

Sighing, Denise pulled away from the porthole, leaving it open as she descended from the chair. Sam was dead now, long past caring for bodily pleasures.

But she wasn't. The thought hammered into her brain as she lay between crisp white sheets, watching the fitful shadows the moon reflected off the water and onto her ceiling. She was more, much more, than Sam had suspected. She was a woman, with all a woman's yearning that now set up a nameless ache within her. Sweeping depths of desire that taunted, teased and craved the fulfillment Jake had promised briefly. Too briefly.

Sleep came and went in fitful starts as the night wore on, a night punctuated by the sounds of the others going to their cabins. The ship moved restlessly at anchor, the weathered boards protesting what might have been ghostly footsteps pacing the deck. Huddled under the covers, Denise wondered if the returned souls of ancient mariners made any kind of noise, let alone the rhythmic creaks above her head now that sent shivers down her spine.

Fanciful nonsense, she told herself, burrowing her head deeper into the fresh-smelling pillow. No self-respecting ghost would take on the job of haunting a fully modern research ship, not even with the ship's safety being guarded on the deck above by only one crew member.

She slept deeply, and it was later, long after dawn's pink fingers had lazily painted the eastern sky, that she woke from a vivid dream of murderous, bloody warfare, shots still ringing in her ears as she sprang upright on the bunk and blinked dazedly around her. Her red travel clock ticked inexorably on the dresser, its black hands pointing to nearly eight o'clock.

There was a spurious air of silence about the ship, unusual at this time of the morning, when the subdued clatter of dishes would normally be coming from the saloon in preparation for breakfast. Not even a distant snatch of a crewman's song broke the becalmed stillness.

Sliding from the narrow bunk, Denise crossed barefoot to the chair under the open porthole and clambered up, feeling the cool moistness of morning air rush into her throat as she drew a deep gasp.

The sleek white lines of a cabin cruiser rocked gently just yards away. The same cruiser, she was sure, that Carl's friends from Andros had used to reach the vessel on that last trip!

Frowning, she reached a foot behind her and descended, sinking onto the hard chair as her thoughts whirled dizzily in her head. What were they doing here? How had they known the ship was back in the area?

Maybe they had a vantage point on Andros where they could watch out for it, and had presumed Carl was in charge and would allow them to use the diving equipment again. A mirthless smile touched her mouth. They wouldn't have bothered to come if they'd heard Jake's diving orders the night before.

"Paul and I, along with Toby, will make up the first team to go down. Depending on what we find down there—" his steely gaze had been directed to Carl at that point "—we'll schedule further trips for later in the day."

"You promised David and me that we could go down, daddy," Meg had reminded him pleadingly, but for once Jake had seemed impervious to his daughter's appeal and said brusquely that she and David could take a trip in shallower waters where there was more to see.

Telling herself that she wouldn't find out what was going on sitting there in her cabin, Denise threw off her nightdress and pulled on white shorts and tank top, running the brush through hair tangled from sleep before opening the cabin door cautiously and peeping out into the deserted passageway. Instinct told her to proceed along the narrow corridor with equal caution, her bare feet soundless on the uncarpeted boards that led to the aft companionway.

Halfway up the steps, she heard Carl's voice and froze, crouching down out of view of the deck and pulling in her breath in disbelieving gasps as she listened.

"You were right, Dr. Barstow." His voice came clearly through the windless air. "I would not have gone to so much trouble to extract weeds for Mrs. Jordan's benefit. For six months now I have known the location of this wreck and how well-preserved it is under the overhang of the cavern. And not only the three-hundred-year-old ship has been preserved," he went on, gloating, "but a fortune in gold and jewels that the unfortunate galleon was carrying."

Denise sank onto the steps, feeling herself still in the grip of the nightmare that had plagued her sleep. Was that really Carl speaking so confidently about his discovery of, not an uncharted cavern, but a treasure-laden ship that had foundered here hundreds of years ago and had lain undisturbed until he and his cohorts had plumbed the depths with sophisticated equipment and realized the potential personal gain?

What an idiot she had been not to know that Carl had been using her for a cover! Jake had been more astute than she, guessing that the survey for two had more meaning than merely charting an unknown cavern or the collection of samples for Denise's laboratory.

"Part of that fortune, if it exists," Jake's voice came in tautly, "belongs to the Bahamian government. If it's as rich as you say it is, there would still have been plenty for you."

"Why should they have it?" Carl questioned arrogantly. "They have done nothing to discover it for themselves, although they have known about it for years. My friends and I have done everything."

"With the aid of government equipment," Jake cut in with dry accuracy. "I hope you have a failsafe escape route, Madsen, because I mean to track you down and—"

"You are very foolish, doctor." Jake was cut off in his turn, Carl's voice rising to a higher pitch. "Dr. Stein has already realized the foolishness of resistance. But would it be me you were seeking, or the beautiful Mrs. Jordan?"

Denise started up from the steps involuntarily. Surely Jake wouldn't believe that *she* was involved with the treasure hunters?

"How do you think I knew about the change of course in time to radio my friends on Andros?" Carl sneered venomously. "Denise herself told me about it yesterday, minutes after you had given the order to change direction. Why do you think she did that?"

Why, indeed? Denise shivered despite the humid heat rising around her. To Jake it would seem as if she had been in collusion with Carl all along, that she was in on his nefarious scheme to defraud the Bahamian government and make off with the proceeds of a fortune that might amount to millions of dollars.

She subsided farther against the steps, her brain working with feverish activity. She could rise up now and align herself on the side of the research team, denying any connection with Carl and so keep her integrity unsoiled. But how much good would that do in the long run? From what Carl had said, it was obvious that Paul had already been injured—for all she knew, he could be lying dead on the deck a few yards distant. The shots she had thought were part of her dream had obviously been all too real!

On the other hand she could—her head lifted when she recognized the voice of Carl's beefy friend issuing orders to a recalcitrant crewman. Perhaps she could stall for time while seeming to side with Carl. It would make Jake hate her even more, but wasn't the end result more important than a temporary truce with gangsters?

Because that's what Carl and his friends were, she told herself as she stood upright and forced herself up the remaining steps to the deck. Gangsters who would stop at nothing, even murder, if their plans were thwarted. The day before, Carl had obviously segregated himself from the other members of the team because of her warning of Jake's intention. Did Carl really think she had known of his scheme and approved of it?

Drawing in a steadying breath, she sauntered

across the rough boards, knowing she would find the answer to that question within moments.

"What's going on up here, Carl?" she asked brittlely.

She could almost hear the snap of his neck muscles as his head jerked around, his pale eyes reflecting alarm at first, then, as they went down over the revealed length of her slender legs and came back up to the mocking challenge in her eyes, he relaxed visibly.

"It is unfortunate that these methods must be employed." He indicated the circle of men, black and white, who held lethal-looking guns in their hands, guns that were trained on the scattered line of team members whose attention was now riveted on Denise.

Forcing contempt, her eyes went mockingly from an open-mouthed Toby to a defiant Meg encircled by her father's arms. The scornful light gray of Meg's eyes, reflecting her conviction that nothing Denise did could ever surprise her, contrasted with the speculative darkening in her father's silver orbs.

Denise let her gaze flick lightly over Paul, who clasped his hand to a bloody wound in his upper right arm, her heart skipping erratically when her eyes met David's briefly, taking in his body's slight support of his father's leaning figure. Captain Mike, looking as if he had eaten nails for breakfast, stared tight-mouthed at the far horizon as if in that way he could ignore the mutiny taking place around him.

"What are you planning to do with them?" She nodded her head contemptuously toward the vastly outnumbered group.

"That remains to be seen later," Carl dismissed curtly. "Our main concern at the moment is to retrieve the treasure and get it to safety. After that, I do not care what happens to them. Whether they live or die means nothing to me. They will not be able to trace me in the place where I have arranged to go." A shudder ran over Denise's spine when he turned lewdly expressive eyes on her. "My life could be made more comfortably if I could take my own woman with me."

Fighting down the nausea battling its way to her throat, Denise forced her fingertips to the prominent bones of his shoulder area, schooling her voice to a low-octave huskiness as she said meaningfully, "I have an idea that a man who has the guts to grab for what he wants is just the man who can turn me on."

For a moment, as he stared piercingly into her eyes, she doubted her prowess as an actress, but then Carl's hand came up to span her waist and draw her lightly clad figure to his spare body.

"We will see how far I can turn you on tonight," he said arrogantly, his hand reaching up under the short top to stroke clammily against her skin. "If I find that you are free of the...inhibitions you displayed the last time I made love to

you, I will offer you a life many women would
envy. A beautiful home in a beautiful climate,
beautiful clothes, beautiful jewelry.''

Beautiful imprisonment, Denise added silently as he turned his attention to the team
once more, scarcely seeming to notice when
she pulled away from his hold and stood at his
side, color flaming in her cheeks. Jake had heard
his reference to lovemaking—that much was obvious from the steely contempt in his eyes as he
and the others followed Carl's demand that they
go below.

How could one look say so much, she questioned with an inner tremor? She could see Jake's
thoughts as clearly as if they were written
across the tanned stretch of his brow. Did she try
that trick of pretending frigidity with every man
who came within her orbit? A coldness any red-
blooded man would leap to remedy?

Jake, Paul, Toby and David were to occupy the
largest four-berth cabin, while Meg remained in
her own single between that and Denise's on the
port side. Captain Mike was to occupy his own
quarters behind the bridge, while Carl's cohorts
were assigned the starboard cabins they had used
on the last trip.

''Is it going to take long to bring up the...the
cargo?'' Denise asked Carl innocuously as she
watched the preparations for the first dive. His
arm stretched possessively on the rail behind her
while two of his friends, clad in diving suits,

lowered themselves into the conning tower of the sub.

"Are you concerned that there will not be enough for all of us to split?" He smiled down into her face, although there were signs of strain around his eyes as the oval-shaped submersible was levered into the water, sinking in a froth of churning green water. "Rest assured, my dear, that there will be plenty for all of us. There is so much treasure down there that it will take many dives today and a few tomorrow before everything has been retrieved."

"You trust them?" she injected doubt into the question, watching the last of the swirls as the sub disappeared from their view.

"Of course. The guards up there—" he indicated the upper control room with a sideways flip of his head "—are watching them just as closely as they guard the prisoners."

"So you're the big boss behind it all?" Denise injected what must have been a suitable note of admiration, because Carl visibly preened.

"Of course. Can you imagine one of these other men having the ability to organize and plan such a project?" His pale blue eyes lifted to the distant meeting of sea and sky. "They are peasants; they think on the scale of small men until someone opens their eyes to the possibility of satisfying their greed. They know nothing of the needs of a man stripped of his nationality, his homeland, forced to eat the humble pie of a more fortunate country. Now I, Carl Madsen, will have the only power the world respects—money! More money than most of them would earn in ten lifetimes.''

Denise resisted the temptation to gaze incredulously into what must be fanatical eyes. The possession of wealth, no stranger to her own life, had a meaning to Carl far beyond her own understanding. Wealth couldn't buy happiness, or her father would have been the happiest man alive; it couldn't buy the love of a man for a woman, the love of a woman for a man. Yet Carl believed that with sufficient money he would be a king in his exiled world.

CHAPTER THIRTEEN

THE DAY DRAGGED INTERMINABLY for Denise, the only points of interest being the occasional rise of the sub to the surface, the harvesting of loot from the collection basket at its front.

Loot that glittered and gleamed and reflected the sunshine it had not seen for centuries—golden goblets encrusted with emeralds and rubies, the duller gold of coins exposed to light when the lids of small trunks were thrown open, intricately shaped necklaces and bracelets studded with priceless gems. All were gasped over and stared at with greedy, lascivious eyes.

Only Denise felt a respectful sense of awe as Carl and his cohorts pawed avidly through the wealth of other times. Was it treasure extracted by Philip of Spain in hopes of winning Elizabeth, the Virgin Queen? Where had the ship been headed? How long ago had she been struck down and left to lie chastely in a freakish underwater cavern, to be discovered by men interested solely in its monetary value and not its beauty?

Almost choking on the food, Denise forced some morsels of the dinner—which seemed some-

how less tastefully prepared than usual—behind
lips that smiled falsely to the men who drank with
more satisfaction than they ate. In the gradually
increasing noise surrounding her, her brain ran in
circles in its efforts to come up with a plausible
way to foil Carl and his despicable friends. It was
obvious that alone she had no chance of over-
powering them, drunk though they would be as
the evening wore on. There were still the guards
they had brought on board, men who would
probably not drink with their meal, who would remain alert to any escape attempt. They seemed to
be everywhere, guarding the cabin passage at its
far end, menacing as they stood over the regular
crew while they fearfully went about their duties.

In the saloon, brandy took precedence over the
strong coffee a subdued Noah served. Jim, the
most portly of Carl's partners, succumbed early to
its effects and reeled off in the direction of his
cabin. On one of the tables, Denise noticed, he'd
left behind the glistening black pistol that had
been stuck into the waistband of his trousers all
evening, until he had irritably drawn it out and
tossed it behind him.

Denise's eyes strayed to it again and again, fearful that one of the other men would note its
presence, wondering how she could put it to use in
her attempt to liberate Jake and the other men
held in the cabin. Distaste lent wings to her resolve
when Carl rose and drew her toward the deep-
cushioned settees cornering the saloon, his hand

possessively familiar on the firm flesh of her upper arm.

"Now," he enunciated with the clarity of a man who had drunk, but not too much, "I want to know if you will be a suitable companion for me in my paradise." His hand ran roughly, familiarly, over the smooth line of her neck to the rounded mound of her breast under the crisp cotton of her sundress, his touch sure in the knowledge of its supremacy.

"I...I don't like an audience when I'm with... one special man," Denise murmured, seductively she hoped, to the mouth that hovered, prepared to kiss her own. She marveled briefly at the speed with which they were left alone when Carl thickly issued the instruction.

That he had every intention of proving her suitability to become the woman of his dreams was made starkly evident as soon as his cohorts had departed unsteadily to their cell-like cabins. His hand, unsatisfied by the feel of her breast through the protective cotton overlay, pushed down between her dress and skin, tracing the rise of her flesh to its tip, which rose traitorously to his male touch.

"Why did you let me think you were an iceberg, a woman without passion?" he muttered distractedly at her ear, nibbling with dry lips across the high line of her cheekbone, descending from there to her mouth, claiming her lips with revolting assurance.

"Carl, I—" She gasped when he at last lifted his head, one arm circling her shoulders and pulling her to the thin, hard outline of his chest, the other stroking the length of her body and pushing up alone her thigh under the crumpled hem of her skirt. "I...I have to go to my cabin for a few minutes, you understand?"

Without waiting for his assent, she pulled from him and stumbled to the table, gripping its white cloth as she went around it and halted beside the small table where the wicked gleam of the black gun glittered like a magnet. Her hand went out and down, touching the cold metal, her fingers coiling around its long handle as she turned back to where Carl still sat on the upholstered settee.

"I won't be long."

"I will wait for you to come." Carl stared back at her unblinking, as if he knew every move her nerveless hand was making as it picked up the revolver and held it to the folds of her dress against her thigh. "Wait!" he commanded suddenly, rising jerkily from the cushioned depths of the settee.

Trembling, Denise faced him with dread in her eyes. He knew. Knew about the gun pressing its metallic coldness to her thigh, her half-formed plan to release Jake and the other men to combat the fully armed contingent. A contingent, Denise realized, that would make nonsense of the one gun she now had in her possession—but for how long?

"Perhaps you should come to my cabin." His

eyes narrowed as he spoke, stepping forward to lean against the table. "There we would be sure of privacy."

Relief flooded over Denise, and she closed her eyes as its warm waves flowed through her tense limbs. "Why don't we stay here?" she got out, amazed at how commandingly cool her voice sounded. "The cabins aren't exactly...sound-proof, are they?"

To her surprise, he gave a dry chuckle. "No, perhaps you are right." His pale eyes flickered back to the comfortably upholstered settee behind him. "It will be better here, as you say. But—" his head swiveled back and he regarded her narrowly "no tricks, Denise. My patience is running thin. I will wait no longer than five minutes."

"Make it ten," she strove for lightness, "and I promise you won't be disappointed. How can I have any tricks up my sleeve when I can't even lock the door?" Her voice dropped to huskiness. "This is...special for me, too, Carl. I want everything to be just right."

"I can almost feel pity for your clod of a husband," he said softly, his eyes palely caressing the pink fullness of her lips, the lean lines of her figure. "He obviously did not discover that the key to your heart could only be turned by a man of power, one whose wealth makes your own insignificant. And I am wealthy now, Denise. You will lack for nothing in South America; clothes, jewels—everything will be yours there."

"I know that, Carl." Holding the gun close to her side, Denise edged toward the doorway. "That's why I . . . I want tonight to be special."

"Ten minutes—no more."

Evidently finding no trace of falsity in her smile, Carl turned back to the settee, shrugging off the light blue shirt, his hands already reaching for the belt around his waist when Denise fled precipitously from the saloon.

The guard at the far end of the passage turned and stared, but seemed unaware that the cabin Denise slipped into was not her own, but Meg's.

"What do you want?" the childish treble demanded, fear from the day's traumatic happenings underlining Meg's voice. Denise put a finger to her lips.

"Ssh." She brought out the gun from the folds of her dress, and Meg stared in fascinated horror at its lethal barrel. Not even Denise's treachery, her expression said, had prepared her for this. Her eyes lifted blankly when Denise whispered urgently, "Meg, I'm going to ask you to do something that could be very dangerous, but might save your father's life, as well as David's and the other men's."

"Why would you want to help us?" Meg questioned suspiciously, her gaze returning to the blackly shining pistol Denise now held loosely in her hand.

Wincing at how deeply the child regarded her as an outsider, Denise said in a whisper, "I don't have time to go into it all now, Meg, but please do what I ask. I have to write a note, do you have—?'' Her eye fell on the book Meg had been reading, and she leaned forward to snatch it up from the dresser, hearing Meg's indrawn breath as she tore out the title page. The urgency suddenly seemed to get through to her then, and Meg took a pencil from the dresser drawer.

Feverishly Denise wrote on the blank space of the page, her writing almost indecipherable as she outlined the position of the guards, particularly the solitary one guarding the cabins.

''Here.'' She folded the sheet quickly and thrust it into the breast pocket of Meg's shirt. ''Take this, and...this,'' she held out the gun, and Meg backed away in horror. ''It's all right, the safety catch is on so it won't go off. Now, do you think you can get through that porthole if I help you and take the gun and the note along to the next cabin where the men are? Here, I'll get this chair and you can stand on it—Meg, *hurry*!'' she said sharply to the terrified girl, whose confusion showed in her widened gray eyes.

Then, like a small robot, Meg reached out her hand to the gun and turned silently to the chair, mounting it while Denise hastily undid the porthole fastenings. It was only when she felt Denise's hands on her waist that she turned from the porthole and spoke.

''Are you doing this because you love daddy?''

Denise's heart skipped a beat and then another

as her eyes met Meg's calmly questioning gaze. What was the point in prevaricating now?

"Yes. I love him very much. And I love you, too."

Meg turned wordlessly back to the porthole, and Denise hoisted the light body up by the waist, whispering last-minute instructions. "Keep your head down when you get out there, and be as quiet as you can."

With an added push on the jeans-covered legs, Meg was out through the porthole and crouching on the deck, giving one last sideways glance at Denise in the cabin's cozy glow before scrambling away along the narrow strip of deck.

Carl was outside the door when Denise opened it seconds later, his eyes soberly suspicious as they went behind her into the room.

"I...I came to check on Meg." Denise closed the door firmly behind her, injecting cold scorn into her voice as she went on, leading the way back to the saloon. "Noah told me the spoiled brat sent back her dinner tray untouched, so I thought it was time I told her a thing or two. She said she wouldn't eat unless she could be with her father. She's so besotted with him it's sick!"

Carl's hand reached out and swung her around to face him, his expression unreadable in the low lights coming from the wall sconces in the saloon.

"Is that why you have given up on him? Because his daughter always comes first with him?" His fingers gouged painfully into her flesh, and

Denise suppressed the wince her face was beginning to form.

She shrugged nonchalantly, then managed to pull free from his grasp and circle the table in the seating area. She had to get Carl away from the passage entrance, and the only way she could do that was by enticing him to the pleasures he patently expected.

- "Who wants a clinging child around all the time. Besides that—" she faced Carl, her voice husky as her fingers lifted to the bared expanse of his chest "—Jake knew I was interested in you from the start. He was crazy with jealousy because somehow, after that trip you and I took together, I could never work up any enthusiasm about him."

She noted with relief that Carl had replaced the lower half of his clothing before coming to look for her. He stood erectly before her, his arms at his sides and his expression unreadable, though he did nothing to stop the exploration of her fingers over the hairless contours of his chest.

"You could not work up enthusiasm for any man at that time," he pointed out evenly, though the harsh edge had gone from his voice and his blue eyes were misting slightly, as if he wasn't entirely unmoved by her obvious attempts to seduce him.

"That was only because you took me by surprise," Denise protested throatily, resisting the temptation to snatch her hands away from the thin, clammy flesh they rested on. "I was upset because you hadn't taken me into your confidence about what you were doing, though I knew you were on to something big. Besides that," she hesitated, and gave her best imitation of a pout, "you weren't very kind about my abilities in the love department."

"Bitch!" he spat with such quiet intensity that she flinched, fear surfacing momentarily in her green eyes. His hand reached like rapiers behind her and pulled her with a jerk to the loathsome intimacy of his body. "You think by offering yourself to me you will escape the fate of the others. How foolish you are, Denise," he mocked softly, "to think that I would not know that you are like all the others of your kind. The Jake Barstows of this world are the ones who make hearts flutter, the ones who merely have to lift a finger to have a woman at their feet."

Panic threaded through her veins at the crazed note in his voice, but when her head drooped on the long stem of her neck he jerked it upright, his warm breath searing her skin as he went on fiercely, "I never had any intention of taking you with me." His fingers tightened painfully on her chin, forcing her eyes to a direct contact with his. "Did you take me for such a fool that I didn't know that your craving is for Jake Barstow as much as his is for you?" His lips stretched into a thin smile. "I wonder how he will feel about taking my leavings for a change?"

The obvious intent in his eyes as they raked the paled contours of her face was revoltingly lewd. Denise closed her eyes, fighting a wave of nausea.

Carl gave her no time to indulge in futile guessing as to how soon Jake and the other men would come to reprieve her. Her mind reeled and grew numb when Carl's mouth descended crushingly on hers, and his tongue pushed obscenely against her teeth, thrusting into the warm moistness there while his hands went with deliberate intent to her hips to press them to the frank arousal in his thighs. She felt herself borne backward to the yielding softness of the settee, her body pinned there under Carl's weight as his mouth savaged hers, and his hands tore impatiently at the buttons of her shirt.

Where was Jake? The longing for freedom was like a scream inside her head, but it came out as a muffled groan when Carl lifted his head to gaze down at the depredation his hands had wrought on her shirt. His lank fair hair brushed her chin as his mouth dropped to the quivering upthrusts of her bared breasts, finding their rose-tipped peaks and drawing his tongue repeatedly over them until she gave a strangled cry of fear and loathing.

"Jake!" She screamed frantically, all the time struggling with weakening effect against the solid weight splayed above her. Had Meg taken fright and come back to her own cabin instead of the one the men occupied? Had the guards heard her and come along to investigate?

Her own denying sobs rasped in her ears as Carl's dry-skinned hand ran down her side and rose again under the rumpled hem of her skirt and reached intimately up along her thigh. Strength suddenly left her. He was about to rape her, and there was nothing she could do about it, any more than she had been able to stop the legal rape Sam had inflicted on her from their first night together.

The weight was lifted so suddenly, so completely, from her that she stared and blinked without comprehension, the full rise of her breasts exposed, as Carl seemed to lift in the air and hang suspended for endless seconds. Then he crumpled onto the long center table, only to be picked up and smashed down again, this time to the floor.

"For God's sake, Jake," a voice sounding like Paul's pleaded, "don't kill the bastard. Leave him for the police."

Then suddenly Jake was looming over her, sitting beside her, pulling close the parted front of her shirt, fastening the buttons with fingers that trembled. His dark brown hair fell in damp strands across his forehead.

"Are you all right, Denise?" His eyes were a misty gray she hadn't seen before as they ran over her face and hair.

"Yes, I—I'm fine," she whispered, helpless against the weak tears filling her eyes and spilling over to her cheeks. "Jake, the others," she started up, her eyes going to the ceiling in panic.

"We'll get them," he assured her with husky certainty, rising yet seeming reluctant to let his hands leave the soft honey-toned skin of her cheeks.

"Meg?" she asked faintly.

"She's where you suggested in your note that we keep her, in the cabin until the action's over." Straightening, his voice was thrillingly husky as he said, "Stay right there till I get back."

She wanted to reach up her arms and hold him back from the danger lurking above, knowing as the unfamiliar protective instinct made itself known that Jake, like any man set on war, would go no matter what deterrents she put in his way.

Drained, more in an emotional than a physical way, Denise sank back against the downy support of the cushions, her eyes falling to the spot where Carl had lain after Jake hit him. Paul had dragged his long thin body from the room while Jake had sat beside her, but she still felt the imprint of that body in its intimate embrace, the touch of Carl's mouth on her skin. She longed suddenly for the cool cleansing effect of salt water on her flesh.

If she had been a fanciful woman, she might have imagined that Jake, as he had fastened her blouse over her exposed breasts with fingers that trembled in anger, really cared about her, even... loved her.

But gratitude spawned a kind of affection, and

wasn't that what had prompted his tender caring? Gratitude because she had smuggled a gun to him, saved all of them from possible death at Carl's hands. And gratitude was far from what she needed to satisfy the craving for him that had been there since that night on the beach. The half-life she had lived with Sam had been no preparation for what she was yearning now, whether Jake was physically present or not. She wanted to feel again the sensitive tips of his fingers, his lips, his body, strip away every doubt and make his possession sure and right, as if the two separate halves of them became one blazing preordained whole.

Her lips twisted in self-mockery. That kind of romanticism wouldn't—couldn't—enter a scientist's thinking. Maybe Jake was right after all in taking his pleasures where he found them, with no strings attached once the brief flame had burned out. Did those other women he had had passing affairs with feel this way, too, when he went from their lives? Yet he had the capacity for deep, loyal commitment to one woman. Barbara.

A faint rustling from the far side of the saloon penetrated her drifting thoughts, and Denise started up on one elbow, her eyes magnified to dread alertness. Relief expelled itself in a long breath when Meg's small figure rounded the table and came toward her.

"Oh, Meg," she breathed, "I thought—"

"I couldn't wait there any longer," Meg explained, her whisper fearful as she darted a glance

up to the steps leading to the upper deck, "especially after David left."

"David went up there?" Denise sat up with a
jerk, swinging her legs off the sofa and staring
hard at Meg, alarmed.

"He wasn't supposed to, but he wanted to
help."

Help! What could a twelve-year-old boy do to
combat fully grown men who wouldn't hesitate to
use the guns they wielded? For that matter, what
were any of the men doing up top? Everything was
quiet above, as quiet as if the escape had never
taken place. No scuffles, no gunshots. What was
happening? Were Jake and the other men waiting
in the dark shadows to make their pounce at the
right moment?

Denise drew Meg's slight body down to the
sofa beside her and put an arm around her thin
shoulders, feeling the child's trembling against her
side.

"He'll be all right," she soothed, as much
to reassure herself as Meg. "They'll all be
okay."

As if her words were a signal, there was a sudden burst of activity above and her heart leaped
into her mouth. Over the scuffle of feet on the
deck came shouts of command, but not a shot was
fired.

Huddled together on the settee, Denise and Meg
clung to one another, their widened eyes express-
ing the deep fear that shook them.

HAD IT BEEN ONLY A LITTLE OVER AN HOUR since Jake and the others had come below to the saloon, their prisoners exchanged for the crew members kept confined in their quarters below decks?

Denise let her eyes wander along the long table that a beaming Noah had laid with cold cuts and salads, hot rolls and steaming coffee, bright ruby wine for celebration? Paul, pale from the blood loss he had suffered from the surface wound in his arm; a serious, strangely sober Toby; a glowing-eyed David; a Meg miraculously perky after the ordeal; Captain Mike restored to ruddy dignity at the head of the table opposite Jake.

Sitting immediately to his right, Denise left out only Jake's face from her scrutiny. She had been strung-up to the point of screaming when at last he had preceded the party of victors below. Standing tall in the entrance, the elation of victory still bright in his eyes, his gaze had flicked quickly from Meg's relieved face to Denise's, which must have reflected a similar relief. The glimpse of un-controlled emotion that kept her eyes glued to his and made her conscious of the heavy beat of her heart was over before she had time to assess its meaning.

Telling herself now that she had imagined that momentary communication, Denise forced a smile and lifted her glass when Toby pontificated, "I propose a toast to the heroine of the hour—Meg."

Squirming with delighted embarrassment, Meg's cheeks deepened to red as the company toasted her. Then, curling her fingers around the stem of the small glass Jake had allowed her, she said, looking admiringly across the table at Denise, "And I would like to toast Denise—she's really the one who did it. If she hadn't acted as if she liked those horrible men and got the gun from them, they would have killed everybody." She gave a dramatic shudder, and there were smiles as everyone lifted his glass and murmured, "Denise."

Jake added with a dry smile as he lowered his glass, "I doubt if they'd have gone that far, Meg. They were interested in treasure, not murder."

"What's going to happen to it now, daddy?"

"I'm not sure," he admitted, looking down at the wine he had barely sipped. "The Bahamian government is entitled to part of it, but it's anybody's guess what will happen to the rest." He looked up and grinned wryly around the table. "Maybe a hunk of it will go into oceanographic research. One thing's for sure—" his jaw clamped on a hard line "—Carl Madsen and his friends won't sniff a scent of it."

"What will happen to them, Jake?" Denise asked as if he were the oracle. "Carl...hasn't had an easy life, and I...I wouldn't want to think of him stuck in some jail for years to come."

Jake's eyes flickered appraisingly over her, his thoughts clearly apparent. "I've no idea what's going to happen to them," he said offhandedly, "and to be honest, I don't care too much."

"Is Madsen the reason you came down here?" Paul directed quietly to Jake, who nodded grimly.

"Dr. Shepherd suspected something was going on when Madsen kept taking out the research equipment and returning without much valid information about tides and currents and so on. He talked to my chief, who suggested I come down here for a few months to keep a closer eye on things." His eyes seemed cool as they settled on Denise.

"The survey trip he took with you was, of course, a cover for more intensive exploration of the underwater cavern. Henry had filled his mind with fantasies of sunken treasure ships in this area, folklore that had been handed down from generation to generation. Only in this case," he ended heavily, "it happened to be true."

Henry's face, as well as his gentle-mannered wife's, rose in Denise's mind's eye. "What about Henry? What's going to happen to him?"

"Nothing very much, I hope. He realized some time ago that he didn't want to be involved with Madsen and company, but he didn't know how to get out of it without losing his job. One word from Madsen about his unreliability, he thought, and he was out. As a matter of fact, he was a lot of help tonight in rounding up the Andros men, so his previous cooperation with Madsen may be taken more lightly than it might have been."

"I'm glad," Denise said simply, not realizing that only the two of them were talking now until

David's raised voice filtered to their half of the table.

"But Meg's a girl, and she got to help," he complained, his budding masculinity evidently affronted by that state of affairs.

"Whether Meg's a girl or boy doesn't enter into it," Paul retorted heatedly. "I told you to stay put and take care of her, and you deliberately disobeyed me."

"Aw, dad," David flushed sheepishly, "anybody who was brave enough to do what Meg did didn't need me to take care of her. I—I wanted to do something, too."

"And you did," Jake inserted smoothly. "It took a lot of guts to hold an armed man with just a piece of pipe until the rest of us got there."

David in his turn squirmed his embarrassed pleasure as the team added to Jake's lauding, and Meg leaned forward in her seat to regard him solemnly, thoughtfully.

"Well, it's time you youngsters were in bed," Jake curtailed the fraught moment. "Say goodnight, Meg, and don't worry about anything. Nothing more is going to happen tonight."

Her hug around his neck was tightly clinging, then Meg pulled her head back and said so that only Jake and Denise heard, "I'm very glad you're my daddy."

"And I'm very glad you're my daughter," Jake responded promptly, dispelling the emotional moment with a pat on her rear end. "Now get to bed."

The lump forming in Denise's throat dispersed suddenly when Meg turned to her and hugged her warmly, whispering for her ear alone, "Boys aren't really all that bad, are they?"

Denise gave her a misty smile. "They're nice to have around," she said huskily.

"I think I'm going to follow their example," Paul volunteered after Meg had skipped away to the cabin area, David following with studied masculine nonchalance.

Seeing how Paul had nudged David's chair under the table with his knee reminded Denise of his injury.

"Paul, I don't know a thing about binding gunshot wounds, but I'd be glad to—"

"No problem," he smiled, ruffling Toby's hair as he passed by. "This guy may have his faults, but as a binder of wounds, he has no equal. See you in the morning."

One by one the team members left, Captain Mike last of all, unsteady on his feet as he climbed the steps to his quarters on the upper deck.

Denise looked quickly at Jake in the silence and saw that he was lost in whatever thoughts were going through his mind, his fingers sliding abstractedly on the stem of his glass as he stared down at the wine's ruby surface.

Wondering if he would even notice her going, Denise pushed back her chair with an unconscious sigh. "Well, I think I'll say good-night, too. It's been quite a day one way or the other."

"Don't go yet, Denise," Jake said quietly, surprising her. His eyes met hers with the power of an electric jolt, and she sank weakly back into the chair, blinking as he placed his hand loosely over hers on the table. "We should...talk."

Talk? What was there to talk about that hadn't already been said? His gratitude for what she had done to free them? That word again! She had acted as anyone else would have in similar circumstances. And he would no doubt have been just as grateful.

She rose again, pulling her hand easily from beneath his. "I've had all the toasting and gratitude I need for tonight, Jake," she snapped, betraying the slow-burning anger building inside her.

He looked up, genuine surprise in his gray eyes. "It wasn't my intention to offer gratitude, though you must know I feel it. It took guts to come out on that deck this morning and persuade Madsen you were on his side." His tone shaded to grimness. "Even to going as far as you did tonight to give us time to get out."

Leaning back in his chair as if the energy had drained from him, he surprised the deep color flooding from her throat to her cheeks as the vivid memory of how she and Carl must have looked flashed before her eyes. Carl's hands on her exposed breasts, her skirt edged far up on her thighs.

Jake got to his feet, pushing the chair away violently, giving a muffled exclamation as he reached for her and pulled her by the arms until she stared into his blazing eyes.

"I could have killed him when I saw what he was doing to you," he grated savagely through his teeth. "I would have killed him if he'd—"

"You almost did anyway." She trembled, half afraid, half excited by the depth of his anger on her behalf. "I still haven't been able to work out why you were that mad. Paul was—"

"Why the hell do you think?" he exploded, shaking her limp shoulders as if she were being deliberately obtuse. "Because I love you, dammit, why else? And God help me—" his voice dropped to a lower level "—I wouldn't let myself admit it until I saw that animal pawing you!" His head snapped back and his eyes glittered dangerously as he barked over her shoulder, "Not now, Noah! Go to bed and clean up in the morning!"

"Yes, sir," the steward said with embarrassed haste, and Denise took the opportunity to detach herself from Jake's loosened hold on her. She couldn't think when she was close to him like that. Everything was suddenly moving too fast for her to assimilate, and she badly needed space to re-arrange the whirling jumble of impressions her brain was trying desperately to cope with.

"Denise?"

"No, don't touch me, Jake. There's a...a lot of things I don't understand. Give me some time." She knew the trembling of her arms, her body, must be clearly visible to him, but she bent her head away as she clutched the nearest chair back. Of all the stupid times to cry, this must be the most!

"Why not?" he demanded, ignoring her plea as he whirled her around into the sinewy hardness of his arms, his jaws savagely set as his eyes ravaged her face.

"Because—oh, hell!" She dashed a hand across her face, smearing the tears in a wider arc. A glitter lighted the emerald depths of her eyes as they clashed with his. "Because you don't love *me!* Right now you're grateful to me, and...and Meg seems to like me again, but that's as far as it goes, Jake! You're not in love with me, you're still—"

"Still what?" he insisted with deadly quietness when her words were cut off by a heaving gulp of misery.

"Barbara," she whispered. "You still love her."

"You mean my ex-wife?" His voice was cold, yet his arms still held her prisoner against him, so close that she felt his muscles tense at mention of his wife's name. "Don't you think that if what you say is true she wouldn't be my *ex* anything?"

The deep thrum of his heart against her breast was steady, unagitated, and Denise spared a fleeting thought about whether she might have been mistaken all this time. But....

"It takes two to make a marriage," she said dully, "only one to break it."

"And you think Barbara was the one who broke it?"

Denise's brow knitted with concentration as she tried to recall just what Marie had told her at the beginning. Something about the fight over Meg, that Barbara had fought for custody to spite Jake, that Jake was still madly in love with her.

"Marie—" she began, after moistening her dry lips.

"I should have known Marie was behind your thinking," he interrupted, contempt making a thin line of his mouth. "If anybody can be guaranteed to get the details wrong, it's Marie!" Waving Denise into the chair she had recently vacated, he swung away and paced around the table. "Sit down while I tell you about Barbara and me. When we married, we were very young—she was nineteen, I was twenty-two. We ran away to get married because her parents thought I was a poor boy after a fortune." His lips twisted in a wry smile. "I guess I can understand that, because at the time I was still at university with very little money of my own.

"Barbara wasn't the kind who could or would take a job to help us through a tough beginning, so—" he shrugged "—I gave in and let them provide us with an apartment and a small staff, because Barbara was completely incapable of running even a small household. We were happy for about six months, then Barbara found out she was pregnant. I think that was when she first started to hate me, because I wouldn't let her get rid of the baby—Meg.''

Denise's breath seemed trapped in her throat when he came back to sit beside her at the table. Her eyes never left his face as he went on, ''I stuck it out for Meg's sake, but finally I realized the situation wasn't doing any of us any good, and that it would never improve, so I... initiated the divorce. I wanted Meg to be with me, because I didn't think her mother was one hell of a good example for a young girl, with Barbara's boyfriends in and out of the place at all hours, but the courts decreed otherwise. I agreed to Meg's being sent to boarding school because I figured that would do her less damage than living constantly with her mother.''

Tentatively, Denise reached out with her hand and touched his, wishing she could smooth away the harsh lines beside his mouth with her fingertips. His muffled exclamation and twist of his wrist to clasp her palm to his own came at the same time as he looked at her with eyes stripped of all but raw, naked emotion. An emotion, she realized with a palpable shock, that she herself had roused in him.

''Barbara hasn't meant anything to me for years now,'' he said huskily, his hand fierce in its grip on her finely drawn bones. ''I wanted it to work if only for Meg's sake, but whatever we had in the beginning just... disappeared and never came back. There have been other women, you know

that, but none I wanted to mess up my life with
again. Until you came.''

''Oh, Jake,'' she whispered, raising her free
hand to the hard leanness of his jaw, feeling the
rough growth of dark beard before allowing her
fingers to fulfill their yearning to smooth the
harsh lines at his mouth. ''I love you, Jake,'' she
breathed softly, moaning a little when he turned
his mouth into her palm and kissed it with lingering deliberation.

''You said that once before.'' He looked up into
her eyes, his voice unsteady. ''And fool that I was,
it scared the hell out of me then.''

''Not now?''

''No.''

''Why?''

His hand eased up to her wrist and circled it,
keeping her palm against his cheek as he answered
her.

''From the first time I saw you, looking so
beautiful and so damned unapproachable on that
plane, I knew there was something different about
you. I didn't just want to get you into bed, I wanted
to know you, really know you. I had this urge to
find out what lay behind the turn-off in your
beautiful green eyes, to break through whatever
was putting the ice into them and make you become
the person I sensed you were underneath it all.''

''Did you really want to get me into bed on the
plane?'' she asked, excitedly incredulous, and he
smiled.

"Not on the plane, no. There were too many people around for that. I just thought that if you were an entertainer of some kind, I could fight off all your star-struck fans and—" his smile widened to wickedness "—get on with the task of getting to know you better."

A flickering vision of a white beach bathed in moonlight passed across her mind, and there was a catch in her voice when she said, "You did get to know me better. I...I wasn't very satisfactory was I?"

She saw the way his face convulsed into agonized lines, and then he rose and took her with him, lifted her into his arms and sank into the cushioned padding of an armchair, as if sensing her distaste for the settee where Carl had "made love" to her earlier.

Made love—there was no comparison between what Carl had done and what Jake was doing now. His mouth kissed her eyes closed and traced the high lines of her cheekbones with the gentle fervor of a monk embracing an icon of his faith. But there was nothing remotely monklike in his sensual possession of her mouth, the warm sweep of his hand over the high curve of her breast after he had disposed of the buttons on her shirt. His tongue, growing bold with plundering passion, was rough against her own.

Withholding nothing, her response burst like a dam inside her, flowing uninhibitedly to breasts that swelled to fill his hand. An excitement shuddered through his lean body. His mouth lifted and dropped urgently to the soft swell of her flesh, crossing the tanned line to bury itself in the smooth whiteness before gentling a pink erect nipple between his teeth.

She wanted him to go on, on forever, never letting her leave that world where every movement of their bodies drowned them in sensations that pulsed, surged, pained and set up a craving for more.

It was Jake who began their descent into the less rarefied atmosphere of the saloon, the proximity of Meg and the sleeping team, the reality of what was happening between them.

"I think that answers your question," Jake said unevenly, his fingers fastening slowly the line of buttons on her blouse. Denise was fiercely glad that she had showered and changed before their meal. She couldn't have borne it if those were the same buttons Carl had torn at.

"Not entirely," she smiled lazily, tracing the line of his mouth with a fingertip.

"You'll never know how sorry I am about that," he said with pained grimness, "but we'll have to wait until we're married and have the legal right to do this where any one of a dozen people can't walk in at any time."

"Is that a proposal?"

"You'd better believe it. Do you know what hell it is to stop myself from throwing you down on that couch and making a night of it?"

Denise expelled her breath in a long sigh. "You don't have to marry me just for that, you know."

"I'm not marrying you just for that, in the same way I hope you're marrying me for something more than that." Jake frowned, easing her off his lap and getting stiffly to his feet.

"Will Meg mind?" she asked, worried.

Jake pulled her to him again and fitted his arms comfortably, possessively around her. "Why should she mind? She's getting a far better mother than the one she's known for years now."

Both of them seemed to be taking it for granted that Meg would be a part of their lives together.

"What about Barbara?" Denise probed. "She won't give Meg up just like that."

Jake gave her a bleak smile. "There you're wrong. When we called her in Florida she had already left with her next candidate for her marriage bed. She's selling the apartment, and they'll be traveling most of the time, so even if she has any objection to losing Meg, which I doubt, we won't have much of a fight to get her. We'll settle down somewhere and make a home for her . . . and for the brothers and sisters she'll have later on." He changed to a teasing note, "You do want children, don't you? That's one of the many things I don't know about you yet."

"Yes," she said simply, adding, "on one condition."

"And that is?"

"That we raise them in San Diego in the house where I grew up."

A cold mask fell over his features, chilling her. "I wouldn't have thought that place holds many happy memories for you. There was your father, who I'd say wasn't the best parent in the world. And Sam Jordan."

"That's just why, don't you see? None of the old ghosts will hang around with Meg, and... our children to live and laugh in it, and *you* only have to step inside the door to make it our home."

His hand pressed her head back and their lips met in a slow, languid kiss of commitment, wordless but nonetheless real. And under the solemn surface of Denise's thoughts, wild ecstasy surged and ebbed within her.

She was loved, and she loved, in a way she had never thought could be. The sweet quality of seduction Jake had used on her unawakened emotions permeated her whole being. Physical passion would be important, exultantly so, but it was only one part of the whole sphere of love. All the days of their lives lay ahead, days of living with the family of their making, nights when they would be in their private world for two. Who could want more than that?

"WILL YOU WRITE TO ME every day?" Meg split the question between her father and Denise, raising her voice again at the bustling noise of Nassau airport, where crowds awaiting the New York flight milled around the departure area.

"Well, maybe not every day." Denise laughed, wrinkling her nose at the formally dressed Meg, neat and unfamiliar in plaid wool skirt and dark blazer jacket. "Twice a week," she promised, angling her head up toward Jake. "One from your father and one from me."

"You won't forget to pick me up at the end of next month?"

"Just so we don't, we'll make a note of it on the calendar," Jake put in dryly, adding a warning, "but it all depends on your mother's agreement to us taking you out of the school."

Denise felt her midsection contract. What Jake hadn't mentioned was that Barbara might not be willing to let Meg go on a permanent basis at all, even if she no longer had the desire to spite Jake.

"Your flight's being called now," he said matter-of-factly, bending to pick up Meg's small flight bag. "You're sure you have everything you need?"

"Of course I have, daddy," she scorned. "It's just a short flight."

She went to hug Marie and Paul, waiting close by with David, then clung unashamedly to Denise. "I love you," she whispered, "and I'm very glad you married daddy."

"I love you, too," was all Denise could get past the lump blocking her throat.

When Jake came back from the departure door

after Meg and David had gone through, she wasn't sure if the tears blurring her vision were giving his eyes that watery look, or if they were Jake's own tears. She said nothing, however, as he nodded wordlessly to a similarly affected Marie and Paul, and took Denise's arm, leading her quickly out to where the car waited.

Silence prevailed between them as Jake drove swiftly, determinedly, into Nassau, where they had arranged to have lunch at the hotel restaurant overlooking the harbor. Denise glanced at his set face once or twice, but made no effort to intrude into her husband's private grief for the daughter he had just sent off to her lonely school life.

Husband! She cast a disbelieving look at his well-molded features, the long capable hands resting tautly on the wheel, and marveled at the reality of the ties that now bound them.

Legal ties so far. Their hastened marriage had taken place only the day before, so that Meg's ardent wish to be present was possible. Impossible had been the true freedom of a honeymoon first night, conscious as they had been of Meg in the next room, frazzled from packing and repacking her clothes for the next day's journey.

"Will you mind waiting?" Jake had asked huskily, each word a caress as they lay together in the double bed of his cottage. His mouth had been a temptingly warm fan at her ear as he whispered, "I want to hear you when I make love to you, hear you telling me that I'm pleasing you." With only a pang of regret for that lost night of togetherness, Denise agreed, knowing that for this special time in their marriage she wanted that privacy, too. A privacy they would have tonight and all the other nights until Jake's assignment finished here in the Bahamas.

As the lush, green vegetation flashed past, Denise looked ahead to the time when she and Jake and Meg would be together as a family. The Sri Lanka project lay in between, but Meg would be well taken care of by Marie in the sprawling old beach house in San Diego until Denise, Jake and Paul returned from the Indian Ocean project.

Marie had been ecstatically grateful for Denise's offer of the California house while Paul worked with Jake off Sri Lanka, delighted to make a home for Meg until Jake and Denise came back to plant their own roots there.

"I'm sorry." Jake ruefully broke the silence between them only when they were seated at a window-side table in the restaurant, a lively scene of yachts and cruise ships from Miami providing a colorful backdrop. His hand reached out to twine with hers on the dark blue cloth. "You haven't been treated much like a bride, have you?"

"At this minute," she said unsteadily, blending her green gaze with the gray of his, "I'm the happiest bride there ever was. And I have the feeling—" she smiled tremulously, turning her hand so that their palms met in intimate closeness "—that thirty years from now I'm still going to feel this way."

What readers say about
HARLEQUIN SUPERROMANCE

"I couldn't put it down!"
M.M.,* North Baltimore, Ohio

"The new SUPERROMANCE
was just that— 'Super.'"
J.F.B., Grand Prairie, Texas

"Just great— I can't wait
until the next one."
R.M., Melbourne, Florida

"I am anxiously awaiting
the next SUPERROMANCE."
A.C., Parlin, New Jersey

* Names available on request

DISCOVER...

HARLEQUIN SUPERROMANCE

Contemporary Love Stories

From the publisher that understands how you feel about love.

Almost 400 pages of outstanding romance reading in every book!

HARLEQUIN
SUPERROMANCE

Contemporary Love Stories

Longer, exciting, sensual and dramatic!

Here is a golden opportunity to order any or all of the first four great HARLEQUIN SUPERROMANCES

HARLEQUIN SUPERROMANCE #1
END OF INNOCENCE
Abra Taylor

They called him El Sol, golden-haired star of the bullring. Liona was proud and happy to be his fiancée...until a tragic accident threw her to the mercies of El Sol's forbidding brother, a man who despised Liona almost as much as he wanted her.

HARLEQUIN SUPERROMANCE #2
LOVE'S EMERALD FLAME
Willa Lambert

The steaming jungle of Peru was the stage for their love. Diana Green, a spirited and beautiful young journalist, who became a willing pawn in a dangerous game...and Sloane Hendriks, a lonely desperate man driven by a secret he would reveal to no one.

HARLEQUIN SUPERROMANCE #3
THE MUSIC OF PASSION
Lynda Ward

The handsome Kurt von Kleist's startling physical resemblance to her late husband both attracted and repelled Megan—because her cruel and selfish husband had left in her a legacy of fear and distrust of men. How was she now to bear staying in Kurt's Austrian home? Wouldn't Kurt inflict even more damage on Megan's heart?

HARLEQUIN SUPERROMANCE #4
LOVE BEYOND DESIRE
Rachel Palmer

Robin Hamilton, a lovely New Yorker working in Mexico, suddenly found herself enmeshed in a bitter quarrel between two brothers—one a headstrong novelist and the other a brooding archaeologist. The tension reached breaking point when Robin recognized her passionate, impossible love for one of them....

COMPLETE AND MAIL THE COUPON ON THE FOLLOWING PAGE TODAY!

HARLEQUIN SUPERROMANCE

Contemporary Love Stories

Harlequin Reader Service

In U.S.A.
MPO Box 707
Niagara Falls, NY 14302

In Canada
649 Ontario St.
Stratford, Ont. N5A 6W2

Please send me the following HARLEQUIN SUPERROMANCES. I am enclosing my check or money order for $2.50 for each copy ordered, plus 59¢ to cover postage and handling.

- [ ] #1   END OF INNOCENCE
- [ ] #2   LOVE'S EMERALD FLAME
- [ ] #3   THE MUSIC OF PASSION
- [ ] #4   LOVE BEYOND DESIRE

Number of copies checked @ $2.50 each = _____

N.Y. and Ariz. residents add appropriate sales tax $_____

Postage and handling $_____.59

TOTAL $_____

I enclose_____.

(Please send check or money order. We cannot be responsible for cash sent through the mail.)

Prices subject to change without notice.

NAME_____

(Please Print)

ADDRESS_____

CITY_____

STATE/PROV._____

ZIP/POSTAL CODE_____
